Critics Herald *Troy*:

"A sexy, sweeping tale, filled with drama, sassy humor, and vividly imagined domestic details." —*Booklist*

"A welcome surprise to anyone who struggled or snoozed through *The Iliad*. Adèle Geras . . . brings the ancient city of Troy and its residents to blazing life. . . . A memorable read." —*Chicago Tribune*

"Engrossing. . . . Delivers the sack of Troy as an ambitious, cinematic affair."
—*The New York Times Book Review*

★"With exceptional grace and enormous energy, Geras recreates the saga of the Trojan War from a feminist perspective. . . . Mythology buffs will savor the author's ability to embellish stories of old without diminishing their original flavor; the uninitiated will find this a captivating introduction to one of the pivotal events of classic Greek literature."
—*Publishers Weekly* (starred review)

"An impressive retelling of Homer's classic tale. . . . Intelligent and captivating." —*VOYA*

★"Successfully wrought. . . . Geras handles both her chosen perspective and her subject's grand themes with aplomb." —*The Horn Book* (starred review)

"Troy has it all: love, hate, sex, death, intrigue, babies, battles, monsters, gods, and animals. And the brilliant thing is that Geras lets us sample the sweetest and darkest corners. That's why this book is so wonderful: it lets the reader roam. So I think I'll have to pass my copy on after all, and buy a new one to lend to friends of all ages, confident that they too will think it one of the best books they've read."

—Gaye Hicyilmaz,
The Times Educational Supplement

The screaming crowd that had been watching the battle since it started fell silent all at once. Hector and Achilles were there, close enough for all to see, close enough for their panting and their groans to carry up to those who were watching. No one breathed. The sun burned down on the men struggling under the walls. Marpessa tried to turn her eyes away. It was too close, too painful even for her, but suddenly she saw a woman standing on the sand, and a chill ran through her. This was the Goddess Pallas Athene, dressed in garments of shimmering bronze. Even from this distance, Marpessa could see her clear gray eyes turned on Hector, and she shivered. Achilles' spear had fallen out of his hands, and the crowd on the wall began to shout, "Kill, kill him, Hector! He's yours! Kill him!"

TROY

Adèle Geras

TROY

HARCOURT, INC.
San Diego   New York   London

www.HarcourtBooks.com

This work was first published in the UK
by Scholastic Ltd, 2000
First U.S. edition 2001
First Harcourt paperbacks edition 2002

The Library of Congress has cataloged the hardcover edition
as follows:
Geras, Adèle.
Troy/Adèle Geras.
p.   cm.
Summary: Told from the point of view of the women of
Troy, portrays the last weeks of the Trojan War, when
women are sick of tending the wounded, men are tired of
fighting, and bored gods and goddesses find ways to stir
things up.
1. Trojan War—Juvenile fiction.   [1. Trojan War—Fiction.
2. Troy (Extinct city)—Fiction.   3. Mythology, Greek—
Fiction.]
I. Title.
PZ7.G29354Tr   2001
[Fic]—dc21   00-57262
ISBN 0-15-216492-8
ISBN 0-15-204570-8 pb

Type set in Trump Mediaeval
Designed by Kaelin Chappell

A   C   E   G   H   F   D   B

Printed in the United States of America

This book is dedicated to the memory of

REGINA GLICK

with affection and gratitude

ACKNOWLEDGMENTS

I would like to thank Anne Jackson for all her help. She lent me videos, tapes, and most importantly, Richmond Lattimore's translation of Homer's *Iliad*, and Malcolm M. Willcock's excellent commentary on the text.

Thanks also to Matthew Clark, who took time out from studying for his A-levels to advise me about such things as names, and the passage of time and the seasons.

And I am, as always, grateful to Norm, Sophie, and Jenny.

TROY

THE BLOOD ROOM

"They'll be here later on," said Charitomene. "You may be sure of it. It'll be a fierce battle today, and we must be ready for the wounded, poor creatures. Put that pallet over there, Xanthe, where it's cooler."

Xanthe did as she was told. Please, dear Gods on Olympus, who see everything we mortals do, she thought, help me now. Please . . . keep Boros away. Please . . . let it be other men who bring us these bodies. She shivered. Since the day when he'd first approached her, his words (*What's a frisky little filly like you doing all alone here? I've seen you before, haven't I? Aren't you the one who helps with the sick? Don't you recognize me? I cart the bodies off the battlefield. I'm surprised your parents let you out so near sunset. Don't they know there are nasty men around? Oh, very nasty, really. You wouldn't want to bump into them, my flower. But don't worry . . . I'll see them off, anyone who dares to try it with you . . . They'll never tangle with me. I'm known, see. One blow from this fist . . .*) went around and around in her head, and with them a vision of his face, with its thin, lipless mouth and his eyes the color of phlegm, set too closely together in his enormous head. She tried very hard not to think of him, and most of the time she succeeded.

She had told Andromache that she didn't want to be sent down to the market any longer, and if Andromache thought she was being silly, she said nothing about it. Maybe, Xanthe thought, I'll never see him again. Maybe it wouldn't be him today, bringing them another broken person. Maybe it would be someone she had never seen before. She prepared the pallets, and the water, and the bowls of oil used for cleaning the worst wounds, and when all was ready she left the Blood Room and went to sit on the low wall just outside, breathing in the warm air. She listened, but there was no noise of battle from the Plain. It hadn't begun yet, but she knew that it would.

Xanthe hated the war. Every day the huge wooden gate they called the Skaian Gate, which faced the Plain and the sea beyond the Plain, opened wide, and the chariots poured through, filled with armed soldiers. Lord Hector always led them out. Behind the chariots came the foot soldiers. The Greeks came, too, in chariots and on foot, from the tents that they had put up on the beach, and then both armies began to hack and stab one another and many died. It was horrible, and I must, Xanthe said to herself, stop thinking about it. I must find something else to fill my mind. It was then that she noticed the eagle. She recognized it at once, from images of eagles on pottery and tiles, but nothing had prepared her for its shining magnificence. It was much bigger than any bird she had seen before, and its feathers shimmered bronze in the sunlight.

"You're looking right at me, eagle," Xanthe said quietly, in case her voice frightened the bird away.

"You are truly beautiful, and your eyes are like liquid gold."

It tilted its head and spread out its wings, as though it was displaying itself for Xanthe's benefit.

She said, "Have you come from the mountains? How wonderful to be able to fly over the city on those bronze wings! I wish I wasn't stuck here on the ground. I wish I could fly with you!"

The eagle stared at Xanthe. It was so close to her that she could have stretched out an arm and touched it, but something, some dread, held her back. That curved beak looked fearsome.

"Xanthe!" Charitomene was calling.

"Farewell!" Xanthe said, and as she spoke, the bird rose straight into the air and hovered so near her that she felt the draft from its moving wings. It hung in the air, and then it was gone, soaring higher and higher over the city. Xanthe watched it until it was nothing more than a speck in the distance, then she turned to go back into the Blood Room.

OVER THE CITY

The eagle circled over Troy, and in the city, everyone who looked up and saw it stood openmouthed, and not one of them recognized the Father of the Gods, Zeus himself. I am used to it, he thought. He disguised himself often. Usually, it was true, in order to get a little closer to a human woman who had taken his fancy. That girl down there was a pretty thing, but too young for his taste. He'd become a white bull for Europa; and for Leda (yes, the mother of Helen of Troy herself, though many forgot that Helen was his daughter) he had been a swan: white and powerful, with a dangerous black beak and yellow eyes. And now he was an eagle, flying over Troy and looking at the war, which had gone on for many years. Too many years, Zeus thought. It is time the whole thing was over. When he caught sight of the Greeks camped on the shore, beside their ships, he found it hard to believe that they'd spent nearly ten years away from their firesides. The fate of the city had been decided long ago, of course. Zeus realized this, but still, he *did* find himself impatient with how very long the whole thing was taking. When this mood came upon him, it was his custom to come down from Olympus. It made him feel better, for a little time at least.

The city was beautiful: built on a hill, with walls so thick that at the top they made a place wide enough for many people to walk on, and the Trojans gathered there every day to watch the fighting. There were broad stone steps leading down from the walls, just near the gate they called the Skaian Gate, the one that faced toward the ocean, where every night Phoebus Apollo drowned the fiery chariot of the sun and disappeared in a flame-colored blaze. The streets of Troy were well made, and they led up to a fine citadel. That was where the temples were, and Priam's Palace. By human standards, this was a magnificent building. It had within its walls a banquet hall, a bathhouse, vast kitchens, more bedrooms than there are fingers on two hands, storage chambers, stables, courtyards, walled gardens, and all most elegantly arranged. Hovering over it, Zeus had often thought he would not mind at all living in such a palace himself. And even by my standards, he said to himself, Priam has fathered an enormous number of children. He has fifty sons, or so they say, although in these matters there's always some doubt. The Father of the Gods, for his part, had long ago stopped believing what women chose to tell him. In any case, Hector and Paris *were* royal princes, and they and their brothers lived in their own smaller residences next to their father's Palace. He thought: The gates of the city are strong. They have withstood years of siege, and still they stand firm. The rivers Skamander and Simois water the land around, and the fields near the city used to yield corn and crops, until the Greeks tightened their hold, just recently. For the first few years of the war, no one starved, but now there is hunger in Troy.

The eagle was moving swiftly now across the Plain, borne up by the strong winds that swept over it ceaselessly. Soon, soon, the battle would begin. He must find a place where he could watch everything. He thought: My wife, Hera, and Pallas Athene, my daughter, are down here all the time. They interfere in the conflict whenever it suits them and keep the weapons of war turned away from the humans they're protecting. They go about in the city without disguises and reveal themselves to any mortal who takes their fancy. Hera hangs around with Agamemnon and Odysseus and their comrades instead of looking after me, as a good wife should. Aphrodite practically lives with Paris and Helen. Some say the war is being fought over Helen, but it's not as simple as that. Wars are never about just one thing. Money comes into it, and trade comes into it. That's my experience. And Ares, God of War, is kept busy. Very busy indeed. No sooner is one skirmish over than another begins. It's not going to be easy for the Fates, making sure that everyone who's set to die does die, but they'll triumph in the end. They always do. The war will just go on and on until the time comes for it to be over.

The eagle settled itself on a boulder at the edge of the Plain and watched with folded wings as the two armies raced toward one another. A noise like thunder filled the air, and dust rose from the ground in clouds.

ON THE PLAIN

Alastor stood on the Plain and wondered whether his mother might not have been right, after all. He had never imagined it would be anything like this. He knew it would be noisy. He knew it would be hot and dusty and that the metal armor would hurt and chafe his skin and be heavy on his back, but he could never, not in his wildest fancies, have understood the terror. The fear that filled him made him nearly sick, and he was ashamed, too, so that tears sprang into his eyes from time to time, and if no one else had been there to see him, he would have turned and fled, and run back to the gates, back to the city, back to safety, and coolness, and somewhere where he didn't have to hold his dead father's sword, which was too heavy for him. He should still be playing with his wooden toy sword and fighting pretend battles with his friends.

Why do you have to go? his mother had moaned. *Isn't it enough that your father and your brother are dead? Haven't I lost enough?*

It had never occurred to Alastor that he might die. He imagined himself plunging daggers into Greeks, but when it came to it, it was harder than it looked. All the talk of carving them limb from limb died on his lips the moment he ran onto the Plain behind the others. A chariot would have been safer, but he was put in the rear of the army by Lord Hector himself. How calm he had seemed! Could it be that people got used to this?

Alastor sighed and was just summoning up the courage to run into the fray again when he saw something that froze him into stillness. Standing right next to him, towering over him, was a warrior he had never seen before, even though he'd been watching the battles from the walls since he was a small boy. This man was enormous and armored in black from head to foot. His helmet had a crest of crimson horsehair rising from it, which waved in the hot wind that blew down from the mountains. Also, on a day of intense heat, the warrior was wearing a black cloak that fell from his shoulders to his ankles and billowed up behind him like a storm cloud.

"Don't be frightened," said a voice like knives being scraped across stone. "It's not your day to die."

"How do you know? Who are you?" Alastor shouted out over the noise of men yelling in rage, screaming with pain, and howling out their anguish.

"I am Ares, God of War," said the warrior, and Alastor took a step toward him, thinking to speak to him, to ask him . . . but he'd gone. Vanished. Where could he be? Alastor looked around to find him again, and then suddenly a Greek soldier was rushing toward him. This man had an arm raised above his head, and something was in it. I can't see what it is, Alastor thought. A spear? A sword? And I can't see his face . . . Where's his face? His nose is covered in silver, and his helmet is burning, and there are flames all around

8

his body . . . That must be the sun, and I know I must move. I must move my hand. Move it now.

Alastor felt as though time had stilled and noise had stopped. He watched his own hand with the sword it was carrying traveling toward the Greek, toward his body. And he was suddenly a statue and saw a silver knife flying through the white air, and the knife found his flesh and stuck in it. No pain. There's no pain, he thought, and he pulled on the knife, and it came away wet with something red. Is that my blood? Alastor wondered. It must be my blood. And then his hand moved again, and the sword, his father's sword that was much too heavy to carry, pushed itself . . . I didn't push it. I couldn't push anything. It pushed itself into the Greek's body, and he fell, and all around him the sand grew dark with blood. Whose blood is it? Mine or his? Alastor saw the sky whirling around him, and then he, too, was lying on the ground. He closed his eyes. I'm not dead, he thought. I can hear them talking. Someone is speaking.

" 'Nother poor sod for the Blood Room," said the voice, and Alastor felt himself lifted and carried. I'm not dead, was his last thought. I'm in agony, so I can't be dead. Then the darkness came.

THE BLOOD ROOM

"Here they are, Xanthe," said Charitomene. "Let them pass."

Two men stood at the door of the Blood Room, and one of them was Boros. Both he and his companion were sweating and covered in dust. They were carrying someone by the arms and legs, and the one who wasn't Boros winked at Xanthe.

"Here's a nice juicy specimen for you, my blossom," he said, leering at her. "No important bits cut off or damaged at all, if you get my meaning." Xanthe looked back at him unblinking, so he went on explaining: "Wedding tackle all present and correct."

"Put him down here," she said coldly, and turned away as they approached her. I'm not your blossom, ox brain, she thought. Not yours or anyone's.

"You should feel sorry for us, Xanthe," said Boros. "Some of the poor buggers we have to deal with look just like porcupines, they've had that many spears chucked at them."

"Thank you," said Xanthe, because, whatever she thought of these men, Charitomene had taught her to be polite. "Lay him down over there, please."

They put the body down without much care, and Xanthe winced. Boros turned to her, wiping his filthy, bloodstained hands on the front of his short robe. He leaned so close to her that she could smell his breath.

"A word with you, my pretty." Xanthe looked down at the ground and said nothing, so Boros continued. "I've been asking about you. Did you notice that I called you by your name? I've found out that you're in the service of the Lady Andromache, and also that you have no parents and no brothers."

Xanthe nodded. What was all this about? She wanted to ask, but Boros might think a question showed that she had some interest in him.

"Also," said Boros, "I've asked around, and it seems no one has asked you to marry them. No one's even shown an interest."

"I don't want to get married," Xanthe said, suddenly terrified.

"Tasty little thing like you? Rubbish! Need a proper man, you do, to look after you. Otherwise, who knows what might happen? I said it before, didn't I? Plenty of nasty men around. Anyway," he went on, "I'm going to see Lady Andromache and tell her I'm willing to marry you."

"But I'm not willing to marry you," Xanthe cried before she could stop herself.

"We'll see," said Boros. "Lots of girls say no when they mean yes. I've been around, and I know what I'm talking about, believe me. What's the matter with me anyway?"

Xanthe was on the point of telling him, when his companion called him from the door, "Boros, get a move on. The dead'll be rotting in the sun if we stay here much longer."

The two men left the Blood Room, and Xanthe,

trembling, turned to the body in front of her, grateful that Charitomene was a little deaf.

"Poor things," the old woman said. "They've a thankless task down there on the Plain among the dead and wounded, picking up bits of bodies and corpses . . . Only the Gods know how they keep on doing it day after day without going mad."

Xanthe hardly heard her. Never, she thought. Never never never. Lady Andromache would not be so cruel . . . I'll tell her what I feel when I look at him, and she'll never make me marry such a creature. I would die. I'd go down and see Mother Poison. Everyone knows her little house under the walls. They say she's a sorceress. Everyone crosses to the other side of the roadway when she walks in the city. Still, they go to her for help, and there's nothing, they say, that she can't cure. But she also mixes potions that can snuff the life out of a body in less time than it takes to say farewell. And I'd go and find her. I wouldn't be afraid. I'd die before I'd touch such a man. I'll never let him touch me. No one can force me.

Xanthe knelt down beside the body that lay writhing on the pallet in front of her, and as always the sight of someone in pain banished all other thoughts from her mind. "Hush," she murmured. "Be still, little dove, little bird." She had to say something. Iason, who had been her friend since he was a tiny boy playing in the sand with her and her sister, and who was now a stablehand in the royal stables, had told her long ago something that Hector himself had said: You could tame wild horses by whispering to them and blowing softly into their nostrils. Always, always, the same words came into her mouth unbidden, even if

12

she was bathing the sunburned and hardened limbs of a grown man. Pain turned the strongest warrior into a baby. She had seen it happen often: Some called on their wives or even on the Gods themselves, but most men cried for the mother who had suckled them. And Xanthe felt herself a mother and wanted for each body that came before her nothing but ease and restful sleep. She smoothed and stroked and crooned and wept and held men in her arms whose brows were aflame with fever, and whose eyes looked at her and saw nothing. This one, she noticed, as she cut away the bloodstained tunic from his shoulder, was young. His cheeks were as smooth as her own, and the skin on the arm that hung down on the floor was golden and velvety and reminded Xanthe of apricots. She sat back on her heels and looked at his face. His dark hair was matted with blood, his nose was straight, and his mouth was beautiful, like the carved mouth of a statue in the Temple of Athene.

"Shh, my lovely, my little one," she whispered, and she wrung a cloth out in cool water and laid it across the young man's forehead. His eyes flew open, and Xanthe gazed into them, and then turned to the door where she thought she saw . . .

"Charitomene, did you see him?" she asked.

"Who?" asked Charitomene. "There's no one been in here since those men left."

"A boy. A little boy just came into the room."

"All the little boys are with their nurses. It's almost sunset. Perhaps you were daydreaming."

Xanthe said nothing. She looked at the child standing in the black shadows near one corner of the room. He was holding a quiverful of arrows in his hand and

13

smiling at her. She knew him at once. It was Eros, the son of Chaos, the bringer of Love, who hid in Aphrodite's skirts.

"Say nothing, Xanthe," he lisped. "The old woman will not believe you. She cannot see me. That's how I have arranged it." He giggled, like any ordinary small boy.

"She'll hear me speaking to you," Xanthe answered.

"I've closed her eyes and ears," Eros said. "Soon you, too, will think you have dreamed me. Your head will be filled only with visions of Love."

"The Gods are powerful," Xanthe said. "They do with us whatever suits them."

"Stay still," the boy said. "Watch."

He took an arrow from the quiver that hung at his back, and shot it from a bow that seemed to Xanthe made of blue light. The arrow hung in the room like a silver thread, and dissolved before her eyes. She looked down, half expecting to see a translucent feathered shaft still quivering in her breast, but there was no sign of a weapon. Still, she could feel she had been wounded. Her heart was throbbing and swelling and breaking open under her ribs like a ripe fig in the sun. She searched the corners of the room again for Eros, but he had vanished. Was this it? Was this what they spoke of when they spoke of Love?

She glanced down, and the young man's eyes were open. They were a color somewhere between blue and green, like water, and she felt suddenly as though she were falling and falling. She opened her mouth to speak, but the breath had left her body, and her lips were dry.

"Where am I?" The youth spoke so quietly that Xanthe had to lean forward to hear him.

"This is the chamber set aside in King Priam's Palace for tending the sick." She did not tell him that she called it the Blood Room, because the reek of blood rose through it like a mist: the stench of iron and salt, with something sweet in it, like fruit rotting in the sun. She didn't mention, either, that this was the room where corpses were made ready for their funeral pyres and their journey to the Underworld.

"My name is Alastor," the young man said through teeth clenched against the pain. "Did you see me? Did you see me on the field? Did you see me fighting?"

"I try not to see it," Xanthe said. "I used to go down to the wall above the Skaian Gate and watch the battles, but that was when I was a little girl. I thought it was something to wonder at. The soldiers were so handsome in their helmets and shields, and the sun made the spears and swords glitter. We all called out the names of our heroes, just as though we were watching the Games."

Alastor bit his lip to stop himself crying out in agony as Xanthe probed the gash in his shoulder. She went on. "When I was nearly thirteen, I came here, to this room, to help with the wounded, and after that I couldn't watch anymore. I saw what they could do, those silver shining spears. I hate them now."

"Tell me who you are." The young man groaned as he spoke.

"My name is Xanthe," she said. "You shouldn't speak. Your wound isn't deep, but I must clean it and bind it with herbs, and the pain will be great."

"I won't feel it. Not if you speak to me. I wish,"

he muttered, "you could have seen me. I was brave. Everyone said so. Perhaps one day I'll defeat them. I'll . . ." He was panting as Xanthe poured oil into his wound. "I'll kill a thousand Greeks."

"Quiet," Xanthe hissed, suddenly angry. "How can you think of killing when your head was nearly severed from your body? Don't speak. Don't say another word." Her own words faded to silence as she heard the cries coming from outside.

"Listen, Charitomene," she said, turning to the old woman. "What is that?" She shivered. The noise was like nothing she had heard before: a keening, high shriek, like a bird pierced to the heart, or some creature whose limbs were being cut apart by knives. Xanthe put her hands over her ears just as a woman rushed into the room and threw herself down at Alastor's feet, weeping and weeping. Xanthe opened her mouth to say something, anything, but could not think of the right words. Charitomene left her seat beside the door and came to stand beside the stranger.

"Lady," she said, "from your tears I can see this is your child."

"My only child," said the woman. "My only son, and now he lies here dying."

"No," said Charitomene. "Take comfort, Lady. He's far from death, although his wound is deep and will keep him from the field for some time."

At this the woman sat up and looked about her. She wiped the tears from her face with the scarf that covered her head, and Xanthe noticed that gold discs were sewn to the hem of her skirt and that her arms were heavy with bracelets of shining precious metals. The hair that showed under her scarf was gray and thick, but her eyebrows were dark and met above her long, straight nose. Her small, red mouth was pinched and sour and looked as though it would find it hard to stretch into a smile. Clearly, Xanthe thought, Alastor favored his father.

"I thank the Gods," said the woman, "that they have spared my darling boy." She sniffed. "But why is he here? Why isn't he lying where I can look after him? Why didn't they bring him to his mother's house?"

"He will come into your care soon enough, Lady," said Charitomene. "And meanwhile, he's here in the citadel because someone—who knows, maybe even Lord Hector—gave orders that he should be brought here. We have all the proper herbs, and Xanthe has hands as soft as doves and cares for the wounded as well as any healer."

"Indeed," said the woman, and she turned her gaze to where Xanthe sat, still holding Alastor's hand. "I would thank you not to touch my son unless your healing demands it. I see no good reason, for instance, for you to cling to him now."

Xanthe let Alastor's hand fall onto the pallet. She looked at the tiles on the floor, so that she would not have to meet his mother's pale and hostile stare. Why, she thought, am I so weak? I should tell her. I should say something. A hand holding yours is a comfort when you are in pain. I'm helping your son, and if you truly loved him, you would want him to be soothed, made better. I'm a person, too. I'm not nothing, to be pushed aside by you, or anyone. Xanthe sighed. The woman bent over Alastor's body, not even noticing that her clothes were in danger of covering his mouth. I can't do anything for the moment, Xanthe thought,

17

and it isn't true that I am not nothing. I am as near to nothing as it's possible to be. Men are less than Gods, and women are less than men, and poor women are less than rich women, and girls are least of all, and poor girls are even less than that. Better to be an ox. Much better. An ox can be slaughtered for food, and its skin stretched and dried and clothes made from it to keep off the cold. Its bones can be carved into spoons and fastenings for garments, and ground to put on the crops. What use am I? If I were to vanish at this moment, who would miss me? My sister. And Iason. Polyxena, my friend. No one else for very long, not even the disgusting Boros. He'd forget all about me in days. Andromache would find another young girl to serve as a nursemaid in her house, and the baby would love her exactly as he loves me. I'm necessary to no one.

"You, girl," said Alastor's mother. "Listen to me."

Xanthe bowed her head. "Yes, Lady," she said.

"You are to care for him day and night, do you hear? Until he is quite restored."

She has decided, Xanthe thought, that I am useful after all. For the present.

"But I would be grateful," Alastor's mother continued, "if you didn't speak to him too much. I don't want him bothered with servants' chatter and gossip. He wouldn't be interested in what you have to say, believe me. And I will visit him at sunset each day, and just after the sun rises, also. I will bring what food I can. Be ready for me."

She stood up and swept out of the room without a backward glance or a word of thanks to either Xanthe or Charitomene.

"Some sheep," said Charitomene, "have better manners than many fine people—have you noticed that?"

"Shh," said Xanthe. "What if Alastor hears you? He's sleeping, but he could wake at any moment."

She went to sit again beside the young man and looked at his hand. She's gone, Xanthe thought. She will not know, and I want to touch him. Looking around fearfully, as though Alastor's mother could be hiding in the shadows, she picked up his hand and closed her fingers around it.

"Has she gone?" Alastor spoke in a voice thick with pain. "My mother?"

"Yes," said Xanthe.

"Then I can open my eyes again. I kept them closed while she was here. I didn't want to speak to her. She'd have asked me . . . questions. I don't want to answer questions. I was hiding from her."

"She's your mother. She loves you. How can you hide from her?"

"Her love is like the sun. Get sunstroke if you stand in it too long."

"I wish I had a mother who loved me like that," Xanthe said.

"Where is she? Your mother?" Alastor asked. "Tell me about her and about your father. Tell me where you live. Your voice is like cool water, like honey. Speak to me."

Xanthe blushed with pleasure at his words and began. "We were born on the mountain, my sister and I, but no one knows who our parents were. Our father was a shepherd, maybe, and our mother . . . I think perhaps she was a wood nymph, or a water spirit, because my sister is strange. She sees the Gods all the

19

time. Walking about among us, among real mortals. She almost never speaks, not like me. Her name is Marpessa. She is younger than I, but also wiser. Her hands . . . They can do anything: make clay into shapes, and paint it, and weave such pictures into cloth that you would swear the men and women in them were going to leap out of the fabric and stand beside you. Charitomene says I have healing hands, but my sister's hands are magical."

Xanthe looked down at Alastor and saw that he was asleep, and murmuring as if troubled by a fever dream. "Never mind," she said, pushing his damp hair back from his brow with one hand. "Later I'll tell you other things."

She prayed that no one else would be brought to them today and that Charitomene would not find her some other task to do. I wish, she thought, I wish I could sit here and look at him forever. She took his hand in her hand and held it tight.

"His skin's burning," she said to Charitomene. "And his eyes are closed again, but he's almost speaking in his sleep."

"It's the fever scorching him," said Charitomene. "Go on bathing his brow until he's cooler, and then we can dress the wound."

Xanthe dipped the cloth into the water once more. *Alastor*, she thought. What a beautiful name it is. It sounded like music in her head when she said it to herself. If I cannot be with Alastor, she thought, then I will be with no one. Sleep, she murmured to him in her mind. Sleep and dream, and I'll watch over you.

HELEN'S PALACE

Once, when she was such a small child that she could scarcely walk more than a dozen steps without stumbling, Marpessa had fallen into the river. She'd been peering into the stream when, all of a sudden, she wasn't on the bank any longer but on a bed of white pebbles and looking up at the sky through ripples of water. They'd pulled her out at once and dried her face and kissed her and scolded her for not staying next to her sister like a good girl, but now when Marpessa thought of that time, what she remembered was the blessed, cool, pale green, translucent silence. Since then she had tried always to surround herself with tranquillity and peace, and she almost never spoke, except (rarely, rarely) to Xanthe.

"Your silence, Pessa," Paris said, "is like a goblet of clear water. It refreshes me. My lady, who is the treasure of my heart, as you know, has more words in her mouth than there are jewels in a necklace. Some say"—he leaned toward Marpessa and winked—"that Menelaus was overjoyed to be spared her chatter when she came to Troy with me. This whole war is being fought because I've threatened to return her and her husband cannot bear to have her back."

Marpessa smiled. She'd heard this joke a thousand

times and smiled at it a thousand times, also. Helen, lying on a low couch, giggled, as she did at almost everything Paris said. The two of them reminded Marpessa of a pair of lovebirds: pretty and twittering and preening their feathers from morning till night. The giggling soon turned to touching, and then the Goddess Aphrodite appeared in the room. Marpessa was the only one who saw her, in her robes the color of the sky at dawn: palest turquoise edged with gold. She smiled at Marpessa, just as she did every time she came to visit, and put her finger to her lips as if to say: Don't speak a word, child, but watch what they do. The Goddess sat down beside Helen and stroked her gently on her bare arm, and Helen started to laugh and pull Paris toward her. Then he laughed, and after the laughter came the stroking, and the stroking made them giggle all the more, like small children out of control. Next, Helen's breath thickened, and she began to pant as though she had been running in the heat, and after that they went into the bedchamber.

"The sounds of love will begin very soon," said Aphrodite. "Isn't it strange how like the sounds of war they are? All that groaning and crying!" Marpessa nodded and said nothing. The Goddess was right. Sometimes there was a high-pitched scream, like the scream of a pig being stuck through with a long spear.

"I must go, child," Aphrodite said, gathering the misty folds of her dress around her. "Here they come now. But I'll return. You may be sure of that."

She was gone like a curl of smoke, and before long Paris and Helen came out of the bedchamber.

"Marpessa!" Paris smiled at her. He was always in

a good humor and kind to her after a visit from.
Goddess. "Bring us wine. Loving is thirsty work."

"Leave her alone," said Helen. "She's just a child.
Too young to know of such things."

"Plenty of girls her age are already well and truly
married. And you know what they say: You're never
too young to learn," said Paris, and he drew a finger
along Marpessa's arm. She shivered, not knowing
whether his touch thrilled or disgusted her.

She would ask the Goddess next time she saw her.
Only Xanthe knew that she could see the Gods. Marpessa had never told anyone else. Poor Cassandra was
thought mad for the things she said, and no one believed a word that came from her mouth, even though
she was a princess. Imagine, she'd told Xanthe, what
they would say if I said I knew what the Immortals
looked like! Marpessa had long ago decided that it was
better to tell her stories on the loom. There the shuttle pulled the thread to and fro and to and fro, and
figures grew under her hand. She'd been weaving for
years. When she was a tiny child, she'd been brought
down with Xanthe from the mountain to the city. A
hunting party had found the two girls all alone. No
one knew what had happened to their parents, and
Hecuba took pity on them. At first both girls lived
with Charitomene, who was a servant to Hector, but
after she had grown a little, Marpessa was sent to
learn weaving at Helen's side and grow up to be her
attendant at the loom. She could still remember the
first woven picture that she ever saw.

"Time drags itself along like a wounded deer,"
Helen had said to her that first day, speaking to the child
she was then as though she understood everything.

ing pictures that tell stories. This war, do you know how it began? How it really ore I came into it? Look. What can you

Marpessa shook her head and didn't answer, but she took a blue thread from the basket that lay at Helen's feet and handed it up to her, pointing at the sky.

"Oh, you clever little thing!" Helen clapped her hands and kissed the top of Marpessa's head. "Of course the sky is exactly that shade of blue."

Tears stood in her eyes, and she wiped them away with a corner of her scarf. "Forgive my tears, pretty one. You remind me of the daughter I left behind when I came to Troy. You will be the best weaver in the city, I can see that already."

Helen's prophecy had come true. Marpessa turned to the hanging she was working on, chose a scarlet thread, and remembered what had been stretched on the wooden frame that day, nearly ten years ago.

The Judgment of Paris

The background: reddish brown for earth; dark green for vine leaves, and foliage on trees; blue for the sky; gold thread for stars
    Paris's tunic: dark blue
    Hera's robe: purple
    Athene's robe: white
    Aphrodite's robe: scarlet
    The apple: half pale pink, half pale green

At the wedding of Peleus and Thetis, the guests had eaten well, and then, as the sky darkened and the stars came out, the music began, and the dancing, and wine sparkled in every goblet. All the Gods and Goddesses had come to celebrate, except for Eris, the Goddess of Discord, for no one wants quarrels at a feast. Splendid gifts had been laid in front of the bride and groom, and then suddenly, out of a blue sky, a golden apple sailed from the air and landed on the ground. Eris had thrown it in a fit of temper, and on it was written TO THE FAIREST OF ALL. *Hera, the wife of great Zeus himself; his daughter Pallas Athene, the Goddess of Wisdom, with her owl on her shoulder; and Aphrodite, the Goddess of Love and Beauty: Each one said that the apple was hers by right.*

"Stop your noise, ladies," said Zeus, "for you will never agree. But there is a young man on Mount Ida who is known for his good judgment. Hermes will lead the Goddesses there, and we will ask Paris—that is his name—to decide who should keep the apple."

Paris was astonished to see the Goddesses standing before him, together with Zeus's messenger.

"The Father of the Gods greets you," said Hermes. "You are to award this golden apple to the Goddess who is the fairest of all, in your eyes."

"The task is impossible," said Paris. "How will I judge between three such beauties?"

He looked from one Goddess to the other, and they smiled at one another and then at Paris.

Hera spoke first: "Young man, the choice is easier than you think. Give me the apple, and your reward will be the power only I can give you."

"Do not listen," said Athene. "Close your ears to her voice and attend to me. Choose the Goddess of Wisdom, and I will give you victory over all your enemies. You will win every battle that you fight."

Aphrodite came to Paris and wound her arms around his neck, so that he could smell the fragrance of her skin. She whispered in his ear.

"Mine," she murmured. "Of course the apple is mine, because I know what you want. Give the fruit to me, and you shall have the most beautiful woman in the whole world to be your bride. Think of the joys you will share. Think of her white hands on your body."

Paris did not hesitate. He picked up the apple and gave it to Aphrodite. A flash of blue lightning tore the sky in two as Hera and Athene gathered their garments around them and left the mountainside without a backward glance.

"Perhaps," Paris said to Aphrodite, "I should have been less hasty."

"Too late," said Aphrodite, smiling. "Your fate, like the fate of your city, is sealed."

"But will it be worth it?"

"It will," said Aphrodite. "You have stepped into a story, and you must stay there till it ends. Come, sit beside me while I tell you of Helen of the White Hands, the wife of Menelaus . . ."

THE GOSSIPS

THE KITCHENS

"Greeks!" said Theano, grinding the oats in the bowl in front of her to a fine powder with a thick wooden pestle. "I spit on Greeks and all their works. Wouldn't trust one of them further than I could throw a javelin."

"They're full of tricks," said Danae.

"Devious," said Halie, who considered herself better bred than her companions, although she would never have said so to their faces. She certainly spoke better than they did, in a more refined way.

In the old days, when there was food to cook, Halie, Danae, and Theano cooked it. They'd worked in Priam's household since they were girls, first as cupbearers and wine pourers and tile sweepers, and scrubbers of dirty platters and pots. Then they passed on to preserving fruit and vegetables and transferring olives into jars and covering them with their own clear, greenish oil, and basting sides of meat as a young boy turned it on the spit over the coals, anointing the sides of ox and boar and sheep with a paste of fresh herbs gathered from the mountain and pounded with salt. Now they had all three grown old, and there was less to do in the kitchen.

"And even when there's something to cook," said Theano, "they give it to one of the young ones, don't they? All we're good for is easy tasks, like folding the washed clothes. Nothing for us to do all day but sit on this bench and talk."

So they talked and talked, from when the sun crossed the threshold to when the Goddess Artemis showed her changing silver face in the night sky. Today they were talking of the Greeks.

"Odysseus," said Halie. "He's the worst. Or the best, I suppose, if you look at it from the Greeks' point of view."

"He's never the worst," said Danae. "Better than most, I'd say. I can remember when they came here before the war, those Greeks. Honored guests they were then, which just goes to show. That Odysseus always had a kind word for us."

"Younger then, weren't we?" said Theano. "And a bloody sight less wrinkled. Even Greeks act polite when they're chatting up girls with breasts like melons."

"Speak for yourself," said Danae. "Peaches, that's what I had, even then. Never had anything you could rightly call melons."

"They're not bothered," said Halie. "Men, I mean. If there're no melons, peaches will do. Or grapes in a pinch."

The three old women wheezed with laughter.

"Anyway," Halie continued. "Odysseus was kind. He thanked me for filling his cup. I remember it like it was yesterday. And he never wanted to fight in this war. You must've heard the story. In this story, Agamemnon was even trickier than Odysseus."

Danae and Theano nodded but settled down more comfortably to hear their friend tell it once again. A story passed the time. A story took your thoughts far away from your own troubles. A story could make you laugh or cry. It could fill you with wonder. And the stories you'd heard already were the best of all, because you knew there would be no disappointment at the end. There would be no unpleasant surprises. Of course, new stories that no one had told before were truly best of all, but they were rare, and hearing one for the first time was like coming upon a scarlet flower you didn't recognize hidden in a crevice in the rocks. The old stories were good enough meanwhile.

"Right, then," said Halie. "Let me tell it. Odysseus's kingdom is that rocky little island called Ithaca. Full of mountains it is, and very few flat fields, and Odysseus lived there with his wife, Penelope, his baby son, Telemachus, and his faithful dog, Argos. One day Agamemnon and Menelaus came to the island to ask Odysseus to join them and sail with them to Troy, to fight in a war. Wanted to rescue Helen, didn't they, from the Trojan prince who'd carried her away. They found Penelope and the whole royal household in despair.

" 'Oh, Lord Agamemnon,' said Penelope. 'I can't do a thing with him. He's lost his reason! He's quite, quite mad, and you wouldn't want a madman in your army, now would you?'

" 'Where is he?' said Agamemnon, and Menelaus chipped in:

" 'Yes, we want to see him. Take us to him, I beg you.'

"Penelope led the two visiting kings to a field near the seashore. Little Telemachus was in her arms.

" 'There he is,' she said. 'There is my lord.' She pointed to where her husband, Lord of Ithaca, mind you, was walking up and down with a plow yoked to his back, like some kind of farm animal. He had a bag slung round his neck, and as true as I'm sitting here, he was taking handfuls of sea salt and throwing them onto the earth as if he were scattering seed.

" 'Give me the baby,' Agamemnon said, and he took the child from Penelope's arms before she could stop him.

" 'What're you doing?' she cried. 'Where're you taking my baby? You give him back to me!'

" 'He'll come to no harm with me, Lady,' Agamemnon said, and he laid the baby on the bare earth, right in the path of Odysseus's plow.

" 'Let's see,' said Agamemnon, 'if your husband's cracked enough to drive a furrow over his son's body.' "

"And he wasn't! Of course he wasn't," said Theano, clapping her hands. "He wasn't mad at all! He turned the plow away so's not to hurt the baby, and that was how those other Greeks knew he was only pretending to be mad all along!"

"And so," said Danae, "they forced him to go to war against us."

"If you ask me," said Halie, "they're all soft in the head—men. Ours and the Greeks'."

Her companions nodded, and they all three went on sitting in the sunshine.

THE STABLES

Polyxena thought: What is the use of having a dear friend like Xanthe when she's always in the Blood Room or with Andromache and never there to talk to? She decided, instead, to go and visit Iason in the stables. She had been down to the market and was on her way back to her grandfather's house. I wish, she said to herself, that I had any other name in the world. It is my misfortune to be given the same name as Priam's youngest daughter. I am not like a princess. She knew that some people—unkind people, in her opinion—called her "Monkey-face." Polyxena had a wide mouth and enormous eyes. Her wild black hair was caught into a knot at the back of her head. She strode about the city and the citadel just like a boy, and all the old women clicked their teeth and sucked their tongues and said that no one would ever want to marry her. Her mother was dead, but during her lifetime she had spent day after day lamenting, and all Polyxena said was: "I don't care if I never marry. I'll be a huntress like the Goddess Artemis."

"Close your lips and don't insult the Goddess," her mother would cry, and Polyxena would grin and go and find Xanthe. Now that the friends were a little older, they sometimes laughed to think that they were both nursemaids: Xanthe taking care of little Astya-nax, and Polyxena in charge of looking after her grand-father, who was always called the Singer.

"I know," Polyxena once said to Xanthe, "that he's an old man who's sat beside Priam's throne for years and years and plucked his lyre and told the ancient tales, making us all laugh and cry and wonder at his words, but he's just like a small child. He almost never sleeps, and rises before the sky is light, and guess who has to get up with him, and see that he has everything he wants? Me! Also he's much more talk-ative than a child, and walks so fast I can't keep up with him."

Polyxena spoke to Xanthe of many things, but she never mentioned her feelings for Iason, who looked after Hector's horses. The three of them had been friends since they were tiny children playing in the sand, but now everything had changed. Iason had taken to looking at Xanthe with love-struck eyes. Po-lyxena had sat in King Priam's halls long enough to recognize adoration when she saw it.

"He's besotted with you," she told her friend.

"No, I'm sure he isn't," Xanthe answered. "He's a friend, that's all. He looks at you in exactly the same way."

Polyxena said, "You live in a world of your own, Xanthe, and you wouldn't know a person in love if he was dished up to you at table with parsley in his mouth. I, on the other hand, keep my eyes open. I'm right. I always am, about such things."

She spoke lightly, not wanting Xanthe to see how much Iason meant to her. No one needed to know. It could remain a secret. Polyxena prided herself on her good sense, and the least sensible thing she could think of to do was to pine away over someone who wasn't the slightest bit interested. *And what,* she said to herself sometimes, *is it about this young man that is so desirable? He has no money, no position, and he limps. Why do you like him so much? Why* (she knew the Singer would say something like this) *don't you let me arrange a match with someone from one of the old families? I know everyone . . .*

Polyxena smiled as she went into the stables. Iason's face made her heart leap. She could not explain it. It was simply the way things were. And the way things would continue, if she did not disturb them by telling anyone her thoughts.

"Iason," she called out, stepping into the horse-smelling shade. "Are you here?"

"Polyxena, welcome," said Iason, coming out from behind a huge mare he was grooming. "Tell me all the stories."

"You think I'm some lesser kind of Singer, don't you? I don't want to tell you anything. You tell me something. Tell me the name of this horse."

When Polyxena had gone, the stable was suddenly darker and much quieter. There was always laughter when she came to see him. Most of the time, Iason thought that life would be much easier and more pleasant if people were more like animals. Ever since he was a small boy, he'd loved them, and in Hector's stables there was always a population of cats and dogs, skinny now from the lack of food in the city, and fearful of being caught and cooked for meat themselves.

He gave them shelter, without saying anything to anybody. There were plenty of people who wouldn't have approved of him taking meat from his own mouth to give the strays. The horses were different. They were almost as important as the fighting men, and somehow or other Hector found oats for them. Iason loved the horses best of all, and never had any trouble talking to them. There they were, standing in their stalls, always whinnying with pleasure when he came to them with their food, placid under the comb, and warm and comforting when he was unhappy. You could tell a horse everything, and it wouldn't judge you or condemn you or think you stupid. A horse had no opinion at all about the way you looked. It mattered not a scrap to any of Hector's stallions that Iason was skinny and shorter than many young men. They didn't care that he wasn't riding out to battle with other soldiers. It isn't my fault, he told himself over and over again, and remembered the wild boar on the mountain. When he was a small boy, Iason was the fastest runner of all, and fearless. Then one day (a long time ago now, but he still thought of it with a pain somewhere in his stomach) he'd been allowed to go out with the men, up the mountain to hunt. He'd started running through the undergrowth, like a strong swimmer breasting a green and leafy current, and then there were the yellow eyes on a level with his own, and a sharp pain in his thigh, and then the hard earth under him and above him a canopy of leaves and blinding sunlight going around and around, and the sound of shouting, and the boar roaring like something out of a nightmare as he fell bleeding next to Iason, pierced by many spears. Later, there were the days and days without moving, sweating with fever and waiting to see what would become of him. He lived. He lived, but his left leg was almost useless for anything more energetic than walking. He would be a burden to his comrades on the Plain, and that was that. Lord Hector had rescued him.

"There's more than one way to help your city," he told Iason. "Come and look after the horses. They're just as important as the men, and I know you like them. More to the point, they like you. And they know you."

That was true. Ever since his babyhood, Iason had been visiting the stables and petting the horses. Still, it was tactful of Lord Hector to put him somewhere where the swift legs and strong arms of other young men wouldn't be constantly before him. Part of him occasionally wished that he could fight, but a larger part (and, thought Iason, only the Gods and I know this) was grateful to be spared bloodshed and pain and possible death. Does that make me a coward? he wondered, and sometimes the fear that it did kept him staring into the darkness when all was quiet.

The horses know everything about me, he thought. I do what I can. Tears sprang to Iason's eyes unbidden when he thought of the fate of many of the creatures that had passed through his hands. Beautiful white mares, roans and grays and blacks, all with their own pet names when he was caring for them, but there on the battlefield once they were dead, nothing but carrion. The vultures came down and picked the flesh from those noble bones, and the skeletons were left on the Plain, unburied. No one cares, he thought. Not really. No soldier dared to grow too attached to the horses that pulled his chariot, but Iason had seen them, from where he hid himself, behind the feed barrels: They came to the stable before the battle, sometimes, and spoke to their animals as though they were human. Hector, the tamer of horses, was well known for it. He had whole conversations with them, and with Iason he discussed their welfare as though they were dealing with human beings.

He'd told Xanthe once how much he liked all animals, but when she asked him why, he hadn't the words to explain. It wasn't that he was stupid. He wasn't. It was only that the thoughts in his head did not easily travel to his lips. Xanthe . . . When they were small children, she and Polyxena had spent hours with him. Together, the three of them played leapfrog, piggyback, and knucklebones, but the pretend games were the ones he played when he was alone with Xanthe. He was Perseus and she, Andromeda, chained to the rock. He was Theseus and she was Ariadne. Orpheus and Eurydice. Perhaps she'd forgotten, because it was all so long ago, and they were older now, but Iason remembered well what he had felt as she clung to him, and it seemed to him that he had always felt the same, even when he was nothing but a little boy. Then and now, his heart beat faster when she was standing next to him. Her face came to him in dreams, and in those dreams she spoke to him as she never spoke in life, and did things he blushed to imagine her doing in reality. She was always friendly to him still, that was true; but they were both working now—he in the stables and she in Lady Andromache's house, and now in what she called the Blood Room— and sometimes days and days went by and he hardly saw her, much less had the opportunity to talk as they used to talk. He saw Polyxena much more frequently. She visited the stables nearly every day, and her laughing face always made Iason feel happier. He enjoyed her stories about what was going on in the Palace, and he felt no shyness near her. I'm fortunate, he thought, to have such a good friend, but Xanthe . . .

"I would do anything for her," he told Hector's favorite stallion, Aithon, as he poured the water into his trough. "I'm stupid, aren't I? I wouldn't find it a bit difficult dying for her, but telling her how I feel . . . That's almost impossible. My tongue lolls about in my mouth, and I don't know where to put my feet. And how am I supposed to find out what she thinks of me if I don't speak? You can't help me, can you?"

The horse, happy to be spoken to, nuzzled him and made snuffling sounds, and Iason leaned his head against the black neck and closed his eyes.

THE BLOOD ROOM

Alastor was still asleep. Xanthe stood up and turned her attention to the work that still had to be done. Tonight Andromache was taking Astyanax into the Great Hall, and she was free for a while. Somehow, whether there was food or not, some tidbit or other was always found for him, as for most babies, while their mothers grew thinner and thinner.

"That's the order in difficult times," Charitomene had explained to her once. "Men, fighting men, get fed first. Then babies, then young people, and old people last of all. Men before women there, too, naturally."

Naturally. Xanthe went from pallet to pallet, gathering together blood-soaked cloths that were lying on the ground. She made a pile of these beside the door. Later Theano or Halie would send someone down with a big basket to fetch them. She bent to whisper to each man as she passed. None of them was Alastor, but they were all in her care, and those who were a little recovered spoke to her and smiled at her and thanked her, and for a moment her heart lifted. When the Blood Room was as tidy as it could be, she looked at the shelf in the corner where healing herbs were lined up in stone jars, and checked the supply of oil. What would become of them when that ran out? It was used for so many things: to clean, to soothe, to ease pain, to dress wounds.

"You've done enough, child," said Charitomene. "Go to Paris's palace and find your sister and sit with her for a few minutes before you go home. Do you ever see her?"

"Of course I do," said Xanthe, "but you're right . . . I would like . . . There is something I must talk to her about."

Charitomene chuckled. "I wonder what that might be. Don't look so innocent. I see how you're looking at him, that Alastor. There's no future in it, you realize that."

"It's nothing to do with Alastor," Xanthe said, in what she hoped was a haughty manner. Privately she thought: Silly old woman. What do you know about Eros's arrows? I know how Alastor looked at me, as if I were a Goddess who'd stepped down from Olympus. Marpessa is the only one who will understand. Aloud she said, "I'm not going home. I'll be back as soon as I've seen Marpessa, and you can go and eat and rest. I don't mind sitting here for a while this evening, and you can come back when you're ready. I don't have to put Astyanax to bed. Andromache's taking him into the Great Hall."

"And when will you eat? I expect you think that love will fill your stomach," said Charitomene.

"Marpessa will find me something," said Xanthe, deciding to ignore Charitomene's teasing. She bent and kissed the old lady—after all, the closest she had ever had to a mother—on the top of her head.

"You go and rest now. I'll look after everything."

Marpessa was sitting in the garden under Helen's beloved pomegranate tree when she caught sight of her sister coming toward her. She stood up.

"Xanthe! Is something wrong?"

"What a greeting! Why should anything be wrong? I wanted to see you, and tell you about something that happened today, that's all. I'm out of breath."

"Sit," said Marpessa. She wondered why it was that she always felt older than her sister. Perhaps it was because she could see things, imagine things that Xanthe never considered.

"I saw Eros today," Xanthe said. "I truly did. He was in the corner of the Blood Room, and he shot an arrow into my heart."

"You were dreaming," Marpessa said.

"I wasn't," Xanthe said. "I saw him clear as clear. And if I was dreaming when I saw him, then who's to say that you're not dreaming, too, when you see things?"

Marpessa smiled. "Maybe I am. Who knows? That's why I never speak about it if I can help it, and you should be quiet, too. You've seen the way everyone avoids Cassandra as if she were diseased. People are frightened of her. They don't want to know about anything extraordinary."

"You're not listening. I had an arrow shot into my heart today. Aren't you curious to know who has filled my heart with love?"

"You're going to tell me, I'm sure."

"His name is Alastor. He's the most beautiful man in the whole world. His mother is awful. She pushed past me to get to him without even seeing me. She only talked to me when she saw what a good nurse I was."

"You'd better not hope for too much from this Alastor," said Marpessa quietly. "They have a habit of marrying their own kind, those rich mother's boys."

Xanthe stood up. "You, too! Why can't anyone be pleased for me, hopeful for me? Charitomene said exactly the same thing. I don't care. I know nothing may come of it. I'm not stupid, but strange things *can* happen. I can ask the Gods to look on me favorably, at least. I can at least *dream* about what could be, can't I?"

"I'm sorry. I didn't mean to be horrible. Forgive me."

"I forgive you; of course I forgive you. You're my little sister. I have to go back now. There's no one in charge of the Blood Room."

Marpessa stared after Xanthe as she ran down the hill. Ever since they were tiny children, she had worried about Xanthe. Everyone could be hurt, but her sister was more easily hurt than most. All her feelings had been left uncovered, and Marpessa imagined them like new summer poppies, growing in a wheatfield with nothing to protect them from the scythe.

ANDROMACHE'S GARDEN

Andromache sat under the fig tree with Astyanax at her feet. He was playing with a carved wooden horse, making it gallop through the dust and around and around the terra-cotta pots. A fig tree, a vine, two lemon trees that were always heavy with pale golden fruit in their season . . . It was a beautiful place, and here it was sometimes possible to forget that down on the Plain there was nothing but agony and death. Andromache shivered. Who was this at the gate? Who was this ugly-looking, enormous man who had come into her private garden? He was covered in dust and blood. How did he dare? She sprang to her feet. Where were the servants? Why had they not stopped him from entering? She stood up and walked toward him.

"This garden is private," she said. "If you are looking for the stables, they are up there, past the Great Hall."

"No, my Lady Andromache. I am looking for you. Please forgive me for coming here, but my business is private. My name is Boros. I am . . . Well, I used to be a fisherman, but there's not much of that going on, thanks to those bastard Greeks—please excuse my tongue, Madam—so now I help on the battlefield. I collect the casualties and bring them into the city."

"I'm sure you do that very well, and we are all most grateful, but I still don't know what I can do for you."

"I want Xanthe," said Boros.

"Xanthe?" Andromache said. "I don't understand."

"I want to marry her."

"She's too young," said Andromache, feeling disgust rising in her throat like bile. "And I need her for my son. He's devoted to her, and she looks after him."

"Not devoted to her like I'll be, Madam. I'll be very devoted to her every night, I can promise you that, if you get my meaning." Boros laughed, showing cracked and blackened teeth.

"You may go," said Andromache. "Your suit is out of the question, I'm afraid."

"I'll go," said Boros. "But you shouldn't say no just like that. Not without thinking. Sometimes saying no just like that has consequences . . . yes . . . consequences."

Andromache drew herself up to her full height, and still she did not reach the man's shoulder. "Are you threatening me?" she hissed. "I would remind you that I am the wife of Hector, first prince of Troy, and at a word from me he would skewer you with his sword as my cook skewers the lamb for a feast—do you understand? You are to leave Xanthe alone. Or you are the one who will learn what consequences are. Go now, please."

"I'm going," said the man, and made his way to the gate. As he left, he turned and called out, "Who knows how long Lord Hector is for this life, eh? They say that Achilles can't wait to get him alone. Farewell."

Andromache sat down again, breathless with terror. Never. She would never let poor little Xanthe fall into the hands of that creature. And she would say nothing to anyone about his visit. Nothing.

She sighed and wondered, not for the first time, how long it had been since she had been completely without fear. There were so many things to be afraid of these days. The war. More than anything else, she feared that. She imagined it like an open mouth, waiting to swallow living men: Chew them into bleeding corpses, and spit them onto the sands of the Plain for the vultures to pick at before they could be buried. Apart from the war, she feared for Astyanax. Other women, older women who knew such things, had told her that this fear never leaves you. Always, even in the best days, your whole body is alert for any danger that threatens your child. And if your husband is determined that your son should grow into a hero, and gives him tiny swords to play with, what then? What can I show him, Andromache thought, that is half so exciting as chariots and horses? My loom? My wools? Are my lullabies as thrilling as the stories he will hear from the men, who lie and lie and speak only of glory?

Another fear, a lesser fear, was about herself. My little brown bird . . . That was what Hector called her in tender moments, and that was, she supposed, what she was like. She was small, and thin, and sharp featured, with pale, brownish hair, which she wore braided and twisted up on top of her head. When she and Hector had married, jewels had been heaped on her, and she wore them for her husband's sake but never felt at home weighed down with gold and sparkling things. She was, though she never dared tell any-

44

one, quite relieved that most of them had been sold for grain. Everyone thought she'd been generous and selfless to give them up. You wouldn't catch Helen going unadorned.

And that was her most secret, hidden fear: Helen. Not her so much, but the effect she had on people. Was it really possible that Hector was the only man in Troy who was left cold by her? That, Andromache thought, was unlikely, but she had been watching him for years and found no evidence of anything . . . well, of anything to justify the jealousy she felt. Her heart contracted whenever she looked at Helen, and even though she knew it was fruitless to long for something you couldn't have, her beauty filled Andromache with envy. Oh, if *she* could only be so shining, so tall! If only *her* flesh were creamy pink! If only *her* eyes were blue and green at the same time, like water in a deep pool! If only *her* lips were red and moist, and as for her breasts . . . Hector said that he liked small-breasted women, but that was exactly what he *would* say. He was kind. Once, long ago, she had seen Helen in the bath and had never forgotten the swelling curves of her bosom, the pinkness of her nipples, and the perfection of the skin all over her body. Stop thinking like that, she told herself. Stop at once. You're like a silly young girl who can't have what she wants. Thank the Gods for all you *do* have, and go and find your son and kiss him. Who knows what has become of Helen's daughter?

PRIAM'S PALACE

The Singer had been called the Singer for so many years that he'd almost forgotten the name he'd been given at birth.

"Sweet Singer," King Priam called him, and "Wondrous Singer," and he'd told him things he wouldn't have dreamed of telling the bearded old bores who sat about the Great Hall giving counsel, and putting on airs because they were, in their own words, the Elders of the City. Not in my words, the Singer thought. In my words they're a company of flapping gray birds pecking and pecking at any grain falling from the king's table. And there weren't that many tasty crumbs nowadays. The Singer sighed. What sort of poet was he, what sort of story spinner or tale teller could he call himself, if his mind turned always to memories of the fragrance of a young boar roasted whole on a spit and basted with green olive oil and rosemary and thyme gathered from the mountainside?

Once, long ago, he and Priam were young men together, and walked in the shadow of the trees on the hills behind the city, and spoke of the brave deeds and beautiful women that lay hidden in the time that was to come. The Singer often compared himself to a tree. I used to be a tall, straight cypress, he'd say to anyone who would listen, and now I'm a gnarled old olive tree. It was true, too, not just a fanciful way of speaking. His limbs were twisted and his eyes resembled two black olives embedded in the shrunken piece of wood that was his face. Still, he had a full head of hair, and his beard reached nearly to his waist. Also, he could walk and walk, for which he was grateful. And he had his senses and his voice. But who foresaw this war? The oracles spoke of it, to be sure, but no one paid any attention to them. Women's stuff, the Singer thought. That was what we called all soothsayers and auguries. More fools us. Neither Priam nor I knew that one day we would be hungry old men dreaming of pastries dripping with honey and stuffed with dates and nuts and fragrant with spices carried to Troy from the East.

The Singer looked around the Great Hall. There was Polyxena, the joy of his life, and a wonderful nursemaid for an old man. And Andromache and Hector, with their child sitting on his mother's lap—little Astyanax, the joy of his grandfather's heart, and of Hecuba's. The Singer noticed that Andromache showed everything, every morsel of food put in front of her, to her little son, and if he ate it, then she went without. Was it any wonder that her cheeks were like parchment?

Where was Xanthe? The wounds must have been particularly dreadful down there in the Blood Room to make her miss the evening meal. Polyxena tried not to think about such things, and looked at her grandfather, sitting in his usual place. He was silent, which was strange. Most of the time he flattened the ears of anyone unfortunate enough to be sitting next to him. She sighed and gazed around the Great Hall, with its painted columns and its wondrous roof inlaid with woods of every kind in intricate patterns. Then she stared at the floor tiles and admired the blue birds and leaping fawns and flowers baked into the clay. That was what you did when there wasn't anything of any interest on your plate: You examined the platters and the pots, and you tried to overhear some interesting tidbit of something or other. Gossip. A story. She sighed. When her grandfather passed over to the Elysian Fields, she should be the Singer. Even though she was only a girl, she was the one who knew the songs, who could tell the tales of Gods and men in ancient times. She'd learned them from her grandfather, who told them to her over and over again, although, in his words, *You will marry and all my songs will end up being sung to a baby in your arms. Why did my daughter not give birth to sons who would have carried on this gift, which the Muses themselves gave me?* Polyxena knew there was no real answer to that. Everyone wanted sons, even if most of them ended up in that awful Blood Room. What use were girls, except to prepare food and give birth to children? Polyxena had already made up her mind that she would be different. She had seen Love, in all its strange shapes, since she was a little girl, and it seemed to her to be nothing but a kind of lunacy. That was one very good reason not to breathe a word to Iason about her own affections. Love made people behave in stupid ways. Look at this war. The Singer had told her that Priam's asking more money from the Greek chieftains for passing through the straits was one of the causes of the war, but that wasn't how the songs went. For love of Helen . . . That's what the stories said. *More romantic,* said the Singer. *It's a poet's first duty to give the public what it wants.* Polyxena sniffed. What about the truth, though? she thought, dipping a dry crust into the last of the olive oil. What about that? Paris wasn't as beautiful as he used to be. He'd put on weight from all that lying around on cushions with Helen. She smiled. Fancy being fatter after years of not eating! That was another truth. Down there in the city they were cooking anything that moved, but up here in the citadel, and in Helen's rooms especially, there was always some pastry or sweet that one ally or another had managed to smuggle past the Greek lines and into Paris's mouth. Some said that Aphrodite brought nectar and ambrosia from Olympus down to her favorites.

Helen's getting bored with him, Polyxena thought. She no longer follows every move of his with her eyes as she used to. Everyone else does, though. Men as well as women. His eyes were still the clear, pale blue of summer skies, fringed with long lashes. His nose was straight, and the famous golden hair—well, maybe it wasn't quite as bright as it used to be, but it still fell on shoulders that looked as though they had been carved out of olive wood. What did it matter that in some lights you could see the beginnings of a double chin, the suspicion of a pot belly? Paris remained beautiful enough to make most women breathless. And his appetites seemed to have grown with the years. He was always on the prowl. The young servant girls in Helen's house had told her, *You have to watch*

Paris. His hands are everywhere, and he'll push you up against a wall and kiss you, whether you fancy him or not. And more, if you'll let him. There were at least four girls in this very hall—Polyxena could see them, pouring the wine and carrying dishes from the kitchen—who'd let him go further and regretted it. One of them had given birth to a child who died, and another had pined away till there was hardly anything left of her but skin and bone. *I love him,* she'd told Polyxena. *And he said he loved me, too.* Polyxena wasn't cruel enough to speak the words she ought to have spoken: Any man will whisper that, or anything else that comes into his head, and you're a fool to believe a single one of them when Aphrodite has them tied up in her ribbons.

Tonight the talk was not of love, but of Achilles. Children in the city had been terrified of the name for a long time. *Behave yourself,* nursemaids would say, *or I'll send Achilles to get you.* And the little ones would shiver. A monster, that's what they imagined he was, but Polyxena knew better. Once, long ago, the Singer had pointed him out from the walls, and he'd seemed a fine man to her: tall and fair, and wearing armor that caught the light of the sun and glittered. Word from the Greek lines was: Tomorrow they were going to attack. Agamemnon's armies were restless. Even though the gossip was he'd quarreled with Achilles, still there were rumors of battle everywhere. Some said Hector's days were numbered. Polyxena couldn't believe it, but it seemed that Hector was eager . . . yes, eager . . . to meet Achilles on the Plain. He thinks he's going to win. Iason, who often spoke to Hector in the stables, had told her so. In spite of everything people said, in spite of all the unfavorable oracles, in spite of rumors that Pallas Athene herself walked at Achilles' side, in spite of all Cassandra's mutterings, Hector thought he would be victorious.

Andromache didn't think so. Andromache was terrified. Polyxena was sure of this, and she was also sure that this dread was the only sensible thing to feel when you were facing the possible death of a husband you loved. That Andromache loved Hector was never in doubt. He loved her, too, and if there *was* any truth in the tale that he lusted after Helen, well, he'd learned over the years not to show it. Helen's eyes, Polyxena thought, traveled to Hector's face a little too often, perhaps. Or maybe that's just me. I like to see stories being played out in front of my eyes. Maybe I see them when they aren't really there at all. I shall pinch my nostrils to keep out the smell of all those festering wounds and sores and go and talk to Xanthe about it.

THE BLOOD ROOM

"I knew you'd be here, Xanthe," said Polyxena, stepping into the Blood Room. "Have you eaten? How can you bear it?"

Xanthe smiled at her friend, who was holding her nose with two fingers and grimacing.

"This place stinks," Polyxena said. "Surely you've been here long enough? Can't you leave these bleeding bodies for a bit and come with me? You missed . . . I don't know what to call it anymore. It wasn't really a meal. Remember meals? Remember food? There wasn't much of that around. Just a handful of flour and water baked with a pinch of salt, and soup that was water that'd had a bone waved over it."

"Shh," Xanthe said, pointing to where Alastor lay beside her. "He's feverish. I must stay with him for a little while longer."

Polyxena peered down.

"Oh, I see. The luscious Alastor. Well, well, well. What a tasty-looking creature he is, isn't he? I wouldn't mind bathing the fevered brow myself, only I should warn you, it's a waste of time. He's got a mother. Phrontis. Frightful Phrontis, I call her."

"I didn't know her name. She's been here already," Xanthe said. "Why should I worry about her? She's nothing to do with me. She is rude and not very beautiful."

Polyxena settled herself on the floor and opened her mouth. Xanthe prepared for a story. Polyxena knew everyone, loved gossip, and was always ready to pass on the latest scandal. Sometimes it seemed to Xanthe that her friend managed to be in several places at once. Certainly she knew all the strange connections that linked one household to another. Xanthe wasn't always a good audience, but when it came to Alastor, she found herself wanting to know every single thing about him. How peculiar love was! Why should she need to know the color of his bedcover or what he saw when he looked out of the windows of his house?

"Aha!" Polyxena grinned. "You can't wait to hear everything. I can tell. Sometimes, when I talk, I know you're not listening. I can see your ears closing, I swear. Well, I can't say I blame you really. At least half of what comes out of my mouth probably isn't worth hearing. Maybe this isn't. Maybe I shouldn't say anything. I'll be discreet for once." She closed her lips firmly and turned away.

"No, please," Xanthe said, putting her hand on Polyxena's arm. "Please tell me. I really . . ."

"Ooh." Polyxena giggled. "You *have* been struck by the arrow, haven't you? Coo-ee, Aphrodite . . . Your baby's been doing some mischief here. Take pity on her, Lady!"

"Shh!" Xanthe said. "You're forever calling on the Gods. They'll punish you for it. But tell me. Please tell me about Alastor's mother."

"You said it yourself," said Polyxena. "Only you

were very mild, as usual. She's a monster. That's it. No more and no less. She devours little girls like you. No one is allowed anywhere near her beloved boy. She has plans for him, and they do not, I can tell you, include a motherless waif in the service of the Lady Andromache."

Charitomene came shuffling in at the doorway, and bent her head in greeting.

"Come," Xanthe said. "Charitomene's here. We can go now."

Suddenly, she wanted to be away from the Blood Room, and away from Alastor. She wanted, above all, to stop Polyxena telling her these things. And yet at the same time, she wanted to know everything about him and his family. Of course, it's none of my business, she thought. Perhaps his monstrous mother has already arranged for him to marry someone. No, I won't think that, Xanthe decided. Not till I have to.

The two girls left the Blood Room together.

"My grandfather," said Polyxena, "has stopped singing about heroes and ancient battles and the exploits of the Gods, and now thinks about nothing but his stomach."

Xanthe smiled. Polyxena was almost as talkative as her grandfather, and always said she'd inherited his gift.

"Telling stories," she said once, "is in my blood."

"Your blood," Xanthe had answered, "and our ears."

HECTOR'S PALACE

THE SLEEPING QUARTERS

Xanthe had been waiting a long time for sleep to come to her. When there had been plenty of spare oil to burn in the lamps, the feasting and singing went on almost till dawn. Now, though, everyone disappeared to their beds soon after sunset. Xanthe shifted on her thin mattress and stared at the wall. From Marpessa she'd learned that darkness was never truly dark, and that real silence was found only in death. There were sounds all around her, even though it was the middle of the night and the whole household was asleep. These had nothing to do with daylight: the howl of winds on the Plain; and even farther away the murmuring of the ocean, Poseidon whispering to himself. Tonight, Xanthe thought, is strangely quiet. For years and years, there had been other noises, borne up and up until they reached the ears of every Trojan: the shouts and cries, the clash of arms, and the roaring and yelling of soldiers drinking and waiting for the next day's battles. Often, just before dawn, different sounds would come floating on the air: blood-freezing moans, and cries that seemed barely human. Xanthe, up early to attend to Astyanax, trembled every time she heard them.

"What are those sounds?" she'd asked Marpessa once. "Could they be sacrificing something down on the beach?"

"Bad dreams," Marpessa answered quietly. "They visit the Greeks as they lie sleeping and spread their black wings in every tent."

Xanthe knew all about bad dreams. In hers, Boros was always standing in a cave, surrounded by bones, and she was about to be devoured, and her bones were going to be scattered on the ground. She woke up sweating at the exact moment when his hands closed around her waist.

And so now, whenever Xanthe heard the nightmare voices, she felt pity for the enemy soldiers, but never dared to speak of her feelings to anyone. Every good Trojan was supposed to beg the Gods every day to come down from Olympus and destroy Agamemnon, Menelaus, Odysseus, and, above all, Achilles, together with all the men who had pitched their tents on the beaches of Troy.

Xanthe wished the war would end. She wept with all the others at every Trojan death, but also found herself sometimes thinking of the wives and babies that the Greeks down there had left at home. She pictured them standing on another shore, far across the ocean, catching sight of a ship and hoping and longing, and then noticing the black sail raised on the mast, and realizing what it must mean.

Xanthe sighed. The only sounds she could hear now were snuffly snores and heavy breathing coming from the women's room next door to her tiny chamber, which was, in Andromache's words, "more like a cupboard than a real room."

Andromache had asked her to move into this tiny cubbyhole so that she could be near at hand if Astyanax woke up in the night and wanted her to comfort him until he slept again. Astyanax. *What a name for a baby,* the old women had said when he was born. A bit of a mouthful, everyone agreed, for such a scrap of a child, but there was great rejoicing that Hector had an heir.

Xanthe remembered that day, nearly two years ago, and how everyone had gathered in Priam's Great Hall to see the child.

"Another hero," Hecuba said, holding him in her arms and making kissing shapes with her lips.

"Someone to rule in Troy," Priam said, "long after we are forgotten."

The precious bundle was passed from hand to hand like a treasure, and everyone laughed to see how small Astyanax looked when his father held him.

"Why is he crying?" Hector asked his wife. "Surely he shouldn't cry when I hold him? Doesn't he recognize his own father?"

"It's nothing," Andromache said. "He's hungry, that's all. Give him to me."

And I, Xanthe thought, was the one who carried him from his father to his mother, and he stopped crying as soon as I cradled him in my arms. And even though they say that newborn babies see nothing at first, I know better. He looked at me and his baby mouth moved as if he was trying to speak to me.

"He's happy with Xanthe," Hector said. "Let her help you, Andromache, with the care of my fine son."

Andromache left the Great Hall then, and took Astyanax away to feed him. Xanthe remembered something else from that day. As she looked from face to face all around the room, everyone was smiling, except Cassandra. Her face was unnaturally white, and her lips were twisted as though she was in great pain. Tears stood in her eyes, and as Xanthe watched her they brimmed over and rolled down her thin cheeks. Everyone, everyone but Xanthe, was looking anywhere but at the mad princess. That was what people called her, but Xanthe felt sorry for her.

She lay now on her mattress and stared at the black shadows and gold light flickering on the wall. The baby was frightened of the dark, and so a torch was lit each night and set in a bronze holder to bring a little brightness into the rooms. There it was again, the sound that wasn't the sea, or the wind, or anyone snoring. Someone's crying, Xanthe thought, and trying to stifle their tears. Not the baby, then. She smiled as she stood up and pulled a cloak around her body. Certainly not Astyanax. He didn't care if he woke the whole household.

"That child," Charitomene often said, "has a voice to shake the footstool of Zeus himself on Mount Olympus."

Xanthe wished she had a gold coin for every night that she had paced up and down with Astyanax in her arms, singing to him and soothing him to sleep again.

"He's always quiet for you," Andromache once said to her with some sorrow in her voice. "He loves you, Xanthe."

"And I love him," Xanthe answered. "I love him as much as if he were my own baby."

"That will come to you soon enough." Andromache sighed. "You will want a man and a baby of your own."

"Not yet, Lady." Xanthe smiled. "I want to stay here and look after Astyanax."

"If it were not for this war . . . ," Andromache said, and laughed. "Have you noticed how much of what we say begins with those words? Well, then, if it were not for the war, we would have found you a fine bridegroom and given you a dowry, too, in return for all your good work in this house, but you know what war means, don't you? Nothing but sorrow and tears and no money to spend on anything useful, when every penny must be counted and exchanged for weapons or more men, or whatever food we can still scratch from the soil." Her voice grew bitter and hoarse, and she stopped herself and shook her head.

"Enough. My words will frighten the baby. I can sometimes feel the milk curdling in my breasts."

"I'm happy to stay here," Xanthe said, stroking Astyanax's little foot. "I don't care if I never leave this house."

Until today, Xanthe thought as she tiptoed along the gallery. That was true until today. For a moment, for not much longer than a heartbeat, she allowed herself to think of Alastor, and of Alastor and herself together, in spite of everything Polyxena had told her. She thought of a child that was their flesh and blood, hers and Alastor's, and then the idea of it was gone like a beautiful dream that slips away from your mind when you try to remember it.

Xanthe stood in the doorway of the baby's room and saw Andromache huddled in a corner, with a scarf held up to her mouth to muffle the sobs. She was trembling all over.

"Oh, my dearest Lady," Xanthe cried, and ran and crouched beside Andromache. "Why, why are you weeping? Has anything happened? Is someone ill? Tell me . . . Let me help you. Is the baby sick?"

Andromache shook her head.

"No, no," she said, and then, "Forgive me, Xanthe. I'm flooded with all these tears . . ." She laughed without any joy and said, "I sound as if I'm speaking underwater, don't I? I'm so sorry. But wait. I'll dry my eyes, and soon I'll be strong again, you'll see. There. That's better. I'll try not to cry again. And please, Xanthe"—Andromache's eyes widened and there was terror in them—"don't say a word to anyone. You must promise. Not anyone. Especially don't breathe a word of this to my husband."

"Is he sleeping?"

Andromache shook her head. "He is walking about. I know where he goes, but . . ." Tears filled her eyes again. "Oh, Gods, how much longer can it go on? I can't bear it, Xanthe. I'm so tired of being brave. How can I smile and smile and keep saying I'm not afraid? And I know—never mind how, but I know—that tomorrow will be full of blood and death. There is so much of it. How will we live?"

"Lord Hector is strong," Xanthe said. "And so brave. There isn't a soldier like him anywhere. Certainly not among the Greeks."

Xanthe didn't know how true her words were, but Iason said such things to her all the time, and everywhere Hector went, he was greeted as a hero.

"Achilles," Andromache said. "They say that

Achilles is like a mountain with a fire burning at its heart. And Hector has left his bed. He's with the horses."

Xanthe nodded. Andromache continued. "He speaks to them before battle, especially Aithon. That's the one Hector loves best of all. He strokes their necks and calls them by name and comforts them. He says they know."

"Yes," Xanthe said. "They know everything. My friend Iason, who works in the stables with Lord Hector, he says so, too."

"And Hector swears that the night before a battle, they are quiet and nervous and startle in their stalls and don't eat their feed. He can soothe them, he says. He speaks to them with his hands."

Xanthe wondered what she should say. She tried to know as little as she possibly could of the battles that went on down there below the walls. She had never told anyone, not even Marpessa, of how frightened she was of everything to do with the war. The sound of a sword blade striking a bronze breastplate, and the sight of the horses, sweating in their harnesses and pulling the chariots, pounding over the earth at a gallop—it all made her feel ill and cold. And when she saw the bloody carving-work blades and spears performed on limbs and flesh, an anger that tasted bitter on her tongue rose up from her stomach, and sometimes she had to stop what she was doing and wait for the sickness to pass.

"The Gods," she whispered to Andromache, "will protect Lord Hector."

Andromache shook her head. "I think the Gods—," she said, and then stopped. "Never mind. I shan't

61

say it, in case bad luck should follow the words out of my mouth. But I am filled with dread, Xanthe, and if Phoebus Apollo chose not to drive his fiery chariot across the sky tomorrow, why, then, perhaps I would be calmer."

Xanthe didn't answer. What could she say? The Gods, she thought, decide what's to become of us, and we submit. As if she could read what was in Xanthe's mind, Andromache said, "The Gods have our lives in their hands. But go now, child. We'll wake Astyanax if we go on talking. Go to your bed, and I will go to mine. Hector will return, and mustn't find me with red eyes."

Xanthe looked back from the doorway as she left the room and saw Andromache standing over her son's cradle, her head bowed and one of her hands bunched into a fist and pressed against her mouth.

HELEN'S PALACE

Marpessa couldn't sleep. She had spent as long as she could tidying the baskets that held the wools. She had looked at her favorite hangings: Theseus fighting the Minotaur she liked especially, remembering as she gazed at the bull-like shape in the middle of the labyrinth that the great hero had once, long ago, stolen Helen away from her family. Her mistress had been younger than Marpessa was now, and yet whenever she spoke of Theseus, it was with respect and wonder and admiration. Marpessa put out her hand to touch the woven surface, and then turned. Someone was in the room with her. She saw him at once: Paris, leaning up against a column. By the look of him, he had found supplies of wine somewhere that no one knew about. He was flushed and sweating in the warmth of the night. He said, "Not yet asleep, Marpessa? Is something troubling you?"

"Nothing, Lord Paris, thank you. But there was much to tidy after our work today."

"You can't tell me," said Paris, "that you're satisfied with all this . . . this weaving nonsense? Truly?"

"I am," Marpessa said, suddenly filled with dread. What did he mean? Was he about to send her to the kitchens or to deal with the laundry? "I enjoy it."

"I don't see you being here much longer. Some young buck will come along and ask you to marry him. Where we'll find a dowry for you is another matter."

"I don't want to marry. I don't want to leave this house. And besides, the Lady Helen has given me gifts from time to time. I am happy as I am."

Marpessa thought of her box of treasures. It was nothing that could be called a dowry, of course, but Helen had started giving her small gold coins and sometimes even precious stones when she was too young to know more than that they were pretty and caught the light. The box to keep them in, made of olive wood carved into the pattern of a vine, was also a gift, and Marpessa loved it more than any of her other possessions.

"Take care of this box, Marpessa," Helen had whispered. "It will be of use to you later, I promise."

Paris interrupted her thoughts. "Well," he said, "I'm delighted to hear it. As far as I'm concerned, you're an ornament to the household, and I'd be sorry to lose you. How about a good-night kiss? After all, I'm like a father to you, aren't I? You sat on my knee when you were tiny, do you remember that?"

Marpessa nodded, silent. Paris's words were innocent enough, on the surface, but he was hemming her in: standing with both his hands against the wall on either side of her head. The only way she could escape was by ducking under one of his arms and around his body. Could she do this in a way that wouldn't anger him? She must try. She laughed as she bent and twisted and came out safely into the space of the room.

"I'm not tiny now, though," she said. "And I'm very tired. I will bid you good night. Lady Helen is waiting for you in the bedchamber."

Paris sighed and shook himself. He stared at Marpessa, looking a little dazed.

"You're quite right. Of course she is. How could I forget the most beautiful woman in the world? I'll tell you something though, if you promise not to tell a soul. It's a burden sometimes, and that's a fact. Screwing someone a bit less beautiful is a relief sometimes. Helen has . . . very high standards. And she takes me for granted. That's what it feels like. Others are more grateful, I can tell you that."

He wandered away to the bedchamber, a little unsteady on his feet. It was the drink, Marpessa decided. The drink was talking. Paris loved Helen more than anyone had ever loved a woman. Everybody said so.

THE STABLES

"Are you sleeping, Iason?"

"No, Lord Hector." Iason scrambled to his feet. "I was brushing him. He's a little restless, but not too bad."

"I'm grateful to you, boy," Hector said. "There aren't many people I would trust with my horses, but I know they love you, as though you were one of them. And Aithon loves you almost as much as he does me."

Iason smiled. Hector was standing near the horse now, and talking to him.

"Tomorrow, my friend," he said. "When the sun rises, I will come here myself and prepare you for the chariot."

"No, Lord Hector," said Iason. "I'll do that. You will have enough to do."

Hector laughed.

"That's true, but you know how it calms me to be with the horses. They're often easier to talk to than humans. That's what I find. I can tell this creature things that I would never tell anyone, not even my beloved wife."

Amazing, Iason thought. Even a great soldier, a

great hero like Hector, sometimes didn't know what to say. That made him feel better. Maybe all those other young men who whistled at the girls and called out crude suggestions as they walked about the city . . . Maybe they, too, weren't saying what was truly in their hearts. Iason went to the stable door and looked at the sky. Dawn would soon be here.

THE BLOOD ROOM

Alastor opened his eyes and wondered for a moment if this was the kingdom of Hades. He was lying flat on his back on a thin pallet on the ground. This place was nowhere he recognized, but it smelled of men, sweating and bleeding, and there were sounds of groaning coming from somewhere. He tried to turn his head, but pain like knives heated on a blacksmith's fire and plunged into his neck stopped him, and he was left staring into the darkness about his head. He closed his eyes. Had he really seen him again: the Black Warrior, the one who had come so close to him on the battlefield? He'd been there, yes, yes he had . . . *in the corner of this very room, staring at me from under the iron helmet, his eyes as cold as death. I re-member,* Alastor thought, *exactly where I saw the Warrior before. He said his name was Ares. I was on the Plain. I've been wounded.* He frowned, because his head felt as if it were full of mist and heat and little bits of thoughts that didn't seem to fit together into any sort of sense. Was there a girl? There were cool hands and light reddish hair and a soft voice, weren't there? Someone had dressed his wound. And his mother had come and wailed and wailed in her special way that seemed to say, *Look at me, listen to me. This is how it's done. This is proper sorrow. Real sorrow. Learn from me.* No. Perhaps he was being unfair. She loved him. There was, as she told him over and over again, no one else this side of the River Styx left for her to love. Alastor wished he could have living brothers or sisters to help him with the weight—that was how he thought of it—of his mother's love. He moved one hand a little and cursed under his breath because his arm had turned to stone—that was what it felt like—and he didn't have the strength to lift it as far as his neck. His skin was on fire. He ran his tongue over dry, cracked lips. *A battle. There was a battle,* Alastor thought. *It wasn't a big, important battle . . . more of a skirmish, but still, I was one of them. One of the men. The soldiers. I was a soldier.*

Then someone laid a cool hand on his brow, and a voice said his name. Alastor struggled to open his eyes, and the voice said, "You're badly sunburned, boy. Keep your eyes closed if that's easier for you."

"I'm dreaming," Alastor murmured. "I hear my commander's voice. Lord Hector. You sound like Lord Hector."

Alastor laughed, and then stopped laughing because his whole body hurt.

"That's because I *am* Hector, son of Priam."

"But Lord Hector wouldn't . . ." Alastor couldn't find the energy to stitch the words together. Lord Hector wouldn't come *here* in the middle of the night, when he could be lying in his own soft bed beside the Lady Andromache. Certainly he would never come to this evil-smelling room to see one of the lowliest of his foot soldiers. Alastor opened and closed his mouth.

"You look like a fish," Hector chuckled. "I can

guess what you want to ask me. Why have I come here, to this room? I'll tell you." He sat down beside Alastor and wrapped a cloak around himself.

"I can't sleep. I saw you today, how you fell at the hands of that bastard Greek. He didn't last long, I promise you that. But I wanted to make sure. You're Oidos's son, aren't you? I knew your father, long ago, and so I thought . . ." Hector fell silent.

"Thanks," Alastor whispered, but whether any sound at all came out of his mouth, he didn't know.

"I'll tell you something now," Hector said. "I'll be ready in my armor before the sun rises. My whole life has been like a long walk to this day, to what will happen on this day. I know it. Achilles is waiting for me down there, and I'm waiting for him. All I've wanted, from the beginning of the war, was to meet him face-to-face. The time has come for it. For one of us . . ."

Hector stopped speaking. Alastor knew what he meant to say. They would go on fighting until one of them, either Achilles or his own dear commander, was dead. Without moving his head, he turned his eyes to look at Hector. This man, with his bare arms and uncovered head, was not the commander he knew. He looked nothing like a hero at all. He looked exactly like everyone else. Alastor thought of the heavy, burnished bronze helmet with its tall scarlet horsehair crest, and how the nosepiece hung down and divided Hector's face in two. How frail he seemed without it, and how soft the flesh of his calves looked when it wasn't bound around with shin guards of leather and brass. Hector was getting to his feet.

"Farewell, boy," he said. "Think of me."

Alastor summoned all his strength.

"Good fortune," he said, and the effort of saying it hurt so much that womanish tears sprang into his eyes. "You are Lord Hector. You're brave and fearless and all Troy longs for your victory."

"I am Hector, true enough," Hector said. "But fearless? Only a fool is without fear. Be well."

Alastor watched him make his way to the door, and then he was gone. I will sleep, Alastor thought. I will dream of him, of Hector, riding and riding behind his swift, black horses.

HECTOR'S PALACE

No one was looking at Xanthe, sitting on a low stool under the window. If Marpessa were here, she thought, she'd say that the Goddess of Dawn was coming, rising up from her bed in the mountains to the east wearing a mauve dress with a long pink train. Andromache had woken early to help Hector put on his armor, and now he was ready. He went into Astyanax's room and plucked the child out of his bed.

"What's the matter with him, Andromache? Why's he crying now?" Hector held his son at arm's length, around the waist. "All I want to do is kiss him before I leave."

"He's frightened. He doesn't recognize you in the helmet. I've told you before. Take it off before you pick him up."

Hector took the helmet off and put it on the ground. He smiled.

"You've told me over and over again. I'm sorry."

Andromache also smiled but said nothing. She knows, Xanthe thought. I know, and so of course she knows as well. They are men, and men forget things before a battle. Their heads are empty of everything but what they will do in the fight; how the sword will lie in their hands, how their enemies will flee at the sight of them. Babies and what they need are not in the same universe as what goes on in men's heads. Astyanax was calmer now. His mother held him, and Hector came close to both of them.

"A kiss for you, my darling boy," he said, and put his lips to the baby's soft cheek.

"Da da da . . ." Astyanax's hand patted Hector's nose. "Nose!"

"How clever you are! You're my big beautiful soldier."

"He's . . ." Andromache opened her mouth and then closed it. Xanthe knew what she was going to say because she would have said it, too: He's not a soldier. Not yet, and if the Gods will it, never, never, never. "Xanthe, take Astyanax now. Let him sit on your lap by the window."

Xanthe took the baby, and Hector turned to his wife.

"Andromache." He stroked her cheek and lowered his voice so that Xanthe could hardly hear the words he was murmuring into her hair. "Beloved wife. Beautiful love. Wait for me. I'll come back to you, if the Gods will it. I'll be victorious, and I'll hold the thought of your face before my eyes all day. Yours and the child's. Think of me."

Andromache smiled and put her lips on Hector's lips, and her hands behind his head. His arms were around her.

"You're trembling," he said.

"No, no," Andromache shook her head. "I'm chilly, that's all. There's no sign yet of Phoebus Apollo's chariot."

"I must go," Hector said. "Will you be on the walls to see the men ride out?"

"Forgive me," said Andromache. "I'll stay here till you return. I will work in my garden or at the loom. Others will wave at you from the walls. Your mother. Your father. Possibly Helen."

"They all mean nothing to me. Nothing. It's your face I want to see when I look back at Troy."

"I can't." Andromache stood very tall and straight. "We've spoken of this many times. I won't."

"You used to. There have been many days when I've seen you standing there, and it's given me courage."

"I know," Andromache said. "But I can't do it anymore. I can't see it. I'll wait for you here. Come back to me."

Hector left the room. As soon as he had gone, Andromache sank to her knees on the ground and covered her face with her hands.

"I'm sick of it . . . I'm sick to death of it, Xanthe. When will it end? I can't, can't be brave anymore. I want to weep and cry and tear my hair out by the roots and lie on the bed and never get up ever again, and what do I do? I stand there all stiff and smiling and being the wife of a soldier. I hate it. I hate the war, and that woman for starting it." She looked up at Xanthe. "Not a word, Xanthe. Not to anyone. They're always watching—all of them—to see if Helen and I are speaking or gouging one another's eyes out. Poor woman . . . It isn't her fault she's so beautiful. But I hate her sometimes for the way Hector looks at her."

"Lady," Xanthe said. "Don't say that. Lord Hector

loves you. He's a good husband. Anyone can see that. He loves you better than anyone in the world."

"That is true. It's true, but you're very young, Xanthe. It doesn't make any difference. He loves me, but he wants her in his bed. I know it. He's no different from the others. He hasn't touched her. Or I don't think he's touched her, but he *has* longed for her. I've seen it in his eyes. I used to care. Now I just want him to stay alive. That's all. I want him in this house again. And till he returns I shall stay in our rooms and in my garden. I won't go out. Not for anything. And tell the servants I'm busy. I don't want reports of how the battle's going. I wish I could forget all about it. I'm going to play with the baby under the fig tree, and later I shall work at the loom."

"So may I go, Lady? I should help Charitomene with the wounded."

"Yes, child. Go." Andromache rose to her feet and made her way along the corridor to her bedchamber.

THE BLOOD ROOM

Xanthe couldn't concentrate. They were supposed to be getting the room ready for the bodies everyone said would be arriving after the big battle. Anyone with wounds that were almost healed, anyone who had the use of his legs, was sent away to be tended by relatives in his own house.

"I'm sorry," Xanthe found herself saying over and over again, "only they say there's going to be fighting, and we have so little room."

"But I'll fade away and die without your care, little Xanthe," said one man.

"Your face is the best treatment," another cried. "Don't say we have to go. My wife's mother's moved in . . . She's enough to kill a man. Rather face Achilles than her any day."

Xanthe did everything she had to, but made sure that she was never far from Alastor's side, and when he woke up, she was beside him.

"Did you sleep?" she asked gently. "Are you feeling better?"

"I'm much better," Alastor said. "I could fight. If you went to my house and got my armor, I could go and help Lord Hector."

"You're being silly," Xanthe said. "You're still feverish. I'm going to wash you down now, with cool water."

Alastor smiled. "I suppose it *is* silly of me. Most people would prefer to be bathed by a lovely young woman, and I would as well, only imagine missing a chance to fight the great Achilles!"

"What's so great about him?" Xanthe asked. Of course, she'd heard all the stories—everyone had—but her hands were trembling so much as she moved the wet cloths over Alastor's upper arms, then his legs, then his face; she felt such a weakness in every part of her body as she looked at him; her face was so hot with blushing as she touched him that she was doing everything in her power to distract herself. If I'm thinking about Achilles, she said to herself, then I won't be concentrating on anything else.

"He's fearsome," Alastor said. "Taller and more splendidly armored than any other warrior. And invincible, they say. And without mercy. He'll kill you as soon as look at you, whoever you are. He's protected by all sorts of Gods. Women love him, but his heart belongs to his cousin Patroclus. That's what I've heard. If we can get him, the war won't go on very long without him. It's so important. That's why Lord Hector is eager to meet him. Oh, I wish I could be there!"

Xanthe hardly heard what he was saying. She'd been hearing similar words for a very long time, and they simply floated past her ears and disappeared. She found all talk of the war boring and terrifying at the same time. It was so much more pleasant to pretend. As Alastor went on and on talking, Xanthe lost herself in a fantasy: He was her husband. She was bathing him, and soon they would go together to their bed-chamber. At this point in the daydream, Xanthe's thoughts made her drop the cloth she was using, and she hastily brought herself back to her real life, to what was happening all around her.

"I must go," she told Alastor. "There's much to prepare. And you must rest."

She stood up and made her way to the bowl of water that stood in the corner. A man in full black armor, some kind of soldier, was there, leaning against the wall. Xanthe stopped, unsure what to do. Should she ask him to leave? She shivered. He was so tall, and his face was hidden. Maybe he had come to visit someone, but who was he? She had never seen him before, of that she was sure. She turned to ask Charitomene's advice, but the question slipped from her mind, and when she turned back, the warrior was gone. Could he have slipped out behind her while she was thinking? Xanthe wondered briefly if she could possibly have imagined him and decided that no, he'd been real enough. I'll ask Charitomene if she knew who it was, she thought, but by the time the filthy water had been poured away, she had forgotten the strange warrior altogether.

Boros and his companion were lounging about outside the Blood Room, leaning against the wall. Xanthe had to pass them on her way to hang the wet cloths out to dry. She looked down at her feet and walked quickly.

"Look at this plump pigeon!" Boros said in a voice loud enough for her to hear. "Look at the figure on her! She's mine, my friend. Any day now."

Ignore him, Xanthe told herself. He's not worth the

trouble. He'll stop if you ignore him. She hung the cloths over a low wall and made her way back, still looking down.

"That," said Boros, pointing a finger in Xanthe's direction, "is as fine a pair of tits as any in the city."

Xanthe felt something like a fire burning behind her eyes, and the words were on their way out of her mouth before she could stop herself. She turned toward Boros, filled with a rage such as she had never felt in her life. She said, "The women down by the walls are telling every- one . . . They say that what you've got between your legs is about as much use to them as a piece of boiled squid."

Boros turned scarlet and raised his hand as if he were going to strike Xanthe, but she was gone, back to the safety of the Blood Room. Had she really said such things? She couldn't wait to tell Polyxena about it.

THE GOSSIPS

THE KITCHENS

War or no war, the work of women goes on. Early, early in the day, when the chariot of Phoebus Apollo had scarcely begun its journey across the sky, and when the warriors of Troy were only just beginning to strap themselves into their armor, Theano, Danae, and Halie were busy folding and smoothing the clothes that had been carried to the palace from the courtyard, where yesterday they had hung out to dry in the sun.

"Used to love laundry duty, I did," said Theano. "In the old days. Down by the river with the sun on your back, and then laying all the clothes out on the bushes to dry, and passing the time with the shepherds, and sharing their food. Remember that? Nowadays, it's nothing but scrubbing at bloodstains. And have you noticed? Even now, when things are hard, she manages to get through the same amount of linen? No making do for Madam, even when the whole city is doing without."

Halie and Danae didn't need to ask who "she" was. They almost never called Helen by her name. At first it was out of a kind of awe for the strange and beautiful princess who suddenly appeared in the citadel one day at Paris's side, but now it was out of habit.

"I like her," said Halie. "I don't care what anyone says. There's something admirable in not letting your standards slip. And she can't help being so beautiful. That's how the Gods made her, and her beauty is a kind of illness. Wherever she goes, she's got the women all eaten up with jealousy, and the men with their tongues hanging out."

"If beauty's an illness, I wish I could catch it," said Theano, and her companions laughed. Theano's teeth stuck out over her lower lip, and her hair was sparse and gray.

"D'you remember her robes, and how we all gawped at them when she first came? We're used to them now," said Halie, "but in those days we'd never seen beads and gold pieces woven into the fabric. And that perfume of hers! They say she got it from an Egyptian sorcerer . . . It made you think of burning trees and sweet herbs and roses all at once. Smell it on the air, you could, long after she'd walked past. And her clothes made a musical sound as she walked. All those bits and pieces sewn into them, I suppose, but there were eyes out on stalks all over the place, and men following her through the corridors of the palace as if she were a tasty bone and they were a pack of dogs."

Danae said, "I've never known what to think. Did she come of her own accord, or did Paris take her by force? You hear one thing one day and something else another."

"Honestly!" Theano sucked her teeth in exasperation. "Have you not been looking at them these last ten years? Can't get enough of one another. Bleeding obvious."

"But it might not be real," Danae persisted. "Aphrodite might have cast a spell on her, or something. Deep down, she might be missing her husband and her little girl, mightn't she? I ask you: How could she have left her own little girl behind? Could you?"

"To get my hands on Lord Paris as he used to be? I'd leave anything in the world. Have you forgotten? Those blue eyes? That hair like spun gold? That nose? And don't let's start on his thighs, or I might fall over with my head in this pile of sheets. I'd have followed him to the ends of the earth. Most women would."

"Not me," said Danae. "Not if it meant leaving my child. I think she only did it because she was enchanted, that's what. I think one day she'll wake up and regret it all."

"And want to go back to that skinny, redheaded, freckled husband of hers? Never."

"His treasure isn't skinny or redheaded or freckled. Some say he's rolling in gold," Halie said.

Theano laughed. "That's the best bit! Not only did Paris run off with Menelaus's wife, he also remembered to pack the contents of his treasure-house. Or she did. Quite happy to spend the rest of her life up here in this windy citadel, but not without a bit of wealth, thanks very much. All the gold the ship could carry, all her jewels, and as many wooden chests full of gorgeous dresses as she could stack up on the deck without the ship sinking beneath the waves. And we've been washing them and folding them ever since."

"It's a privilege," said Halie. "To be of service to her."

"You just suck up to her, that's all," said Danae. "You're dazzled by her. You never stop to think that all this misery, all this washing and washing of blood-stained clothes . . . it's her fault."

"It's not," said Halie. "I've never really believed that. It's as much Menelaus's fault as Helen's."

"Menelaus?" Theano's mouth was hanging open. "I've heard a lot of nonsense in my time, but that really *is* ridiculous. How on earth could it be Menelaus's fault?"

"He left them alone together," said Halie. "What a fool. Imagine . . . You've got a young wife who looks like she does, and then this prince comes visiting one day, and not just any old prince, but Paris, and not only Paris, but Paris as he looked ten years ago, and you sit about in the palace with him for a bit, but then you say to your wife: *You* look after this fellow, dearie, and show him all the hospitality you can while I go off to an embassy or something, somewhere or other. Mad, that was. Begging for trouble. My husband would never have done such a stupid thing, I know that much."

"There's got to be more to it than that," Theano said. "I don't think we'd have been besieged by those Greeks for so long just on account of Helen, or of her and her husband, come to that."

"It's too complicated for the likes of us to understand," said Halie. "But it's to do with property and taxes and power and men things, and she's just an excuse. That's what my late husband, may the Gods grant him peace in Elysium, used to say."

Theano and Danae nodded and continued to fold the dry clothes.

HELEN'S PALACE

Marpessa was alone at the loom. That was the one good thing about a battle: Everyone went down to the walls to watch it, and the silence and peace were left to those like her sister and herself who kept away. Xanthe hates to see the blood, she thought, but I don't. I don't mind watching, but it's hot down there when the sun is at its highest, and here the thick walls keep it cool, and later on I can sit in the courtyard under the pomegranate tree with no one bothering me. When the sun is lower, she thought, when the shadows lengthen, I'll visit Xanthe, and meanwhile there is the weaving. She stopped for a moment with the shuttle in her hand and looked up at the wall where her favorite hanging told its story.

"Such a ghastly thing," Helen always said when she passed it, and turned her head away. So why, Marpessa wanted to ask her, did you put it there, where everyone can see it? I know why, she realized now. It's there to remind her. To show everyone that it isn't only Trojans who have suffered—are suffering—in this war. Agamemnon is her brother-in-law. King of Mycenae, a city rich in gold.

When Marpessa was a little girl, Helen had spent much of the day playing with her. "Just as I used to play with Hermione," she'd say. She would put glittering jewels around Marpessa's neck: ornaments hung with moons and suns of gold beaten to the thinness of new leaves on young trees. And Marpessa, whenever she thought of Helen, would connect her with gemstones and precious metals. Always, around her neck, Helen wore a ruby the size of a pigeon's egg. She told Marpessa, "Everyone calls it the Star Stone, and they tell silly stories about it. Some say that it drips scarlet liquid onto my skin, which is nonsense, because if it did my clothes would be horribly stained, and of course I'd never wear anything that did that, but people are very strange."

Marpessa hadn't answered, but even as a child she'd understood how such stories came to be told. The Star Stone caught the light and made small red shadows on Helen's skin that spread over the whiteness of her flesh like drops of blood, and sometimes Marpessa was allowed to wear the jewel around her own throat. Then Helen would look at her and say, "I helped myself to all this stuff when I ran away with Paris, and what use is it to me now? Where's my baby? Where's my sister?"

Marpessa sighed, remembering those days, and touched the threads of the wall hanging. Clytemnestra . . . That's her sister's name, she thought. And Helen showed me once how they were all related by scratching a family tree in the dust outside. The young girl in the wall hanging was her niece. Poor Iphigenia. Marpessa shivered, and felt a little ashamed of thinking such a picture a thing of beauty.

The Sacrifice of Iphigenia

The background: fawn for sand; peacock blue for the
ocean; pale blue for the sky; yellow for the sun
  The ships: black
  Agamemnon's cloak: purple
  Achilles' robe: dark red
  Calchas's robe: brown
  The sacrificial fire: orange and yellow
  Iphigenia after her transformation: white

The ships of the Greek fleet had gathered in Aulis, in
the bay, waiting for a favorable wind to speed them
to Troy. Agamemnon and Ajax, Nestor and Odysseus,
Menelaus, Helen's own husband: all of them pacing
the beaches, fretting and fuming at the outrage.
Paris, a young prince from Troy across the Aegean
Sea, had come as a guest to Menelaus's palace, and
then stolen away when the King was away from
home, taking with him Helen, the most beautiful
woman in the world. No one could tell with any
certainty whether she had been forced by the Tro-
jan prince or had gone of her own accord, blinded
by Aphrodite. And as if this were not horror
enough, the lovers had helped themselves to the
contents of Menelaus's treasury, and the ship that
bore them sat heavy in the water because of the
weight of gemstones and gold bars and carved ele-
phant tusks, brought to Menelaus as gifts by kings
from the lands that lay beyond Egypt.

Menelaus, bereft, called on his brother Agamem-
non from Mycenae of the Lion Gate and reminded
him of the oath sworn by all the Greek chieftains at
his wedding: how they had promised to come and

help him if ever anyone should come and steal Helen away.

Now there they were, with their armies gathered in tents on the shore, eager to make war on the Trojans and force them to give Helen back. But the sea was as flat as a pond and there was not a breath of wind to fill the sails of the tall ships that floated at anchor in the harbor at Aulis.

Then Calchas the priest came to Agamemnon and said, "The Goddess Artemis is angry because you boasted that you were a finer marksman than she. She demands a sacrifice. You must summon your daughter, Iphigenia. Pretend that Achilles seeks her as his bride, and Clytemnestra will bring her here. When they are in Aulis, I myself will cut her throat as swiftly as though she were a young calf. She will feel nothing. We will lay her body upon a funeral pyre, and the Goddess will smile on you and send winds to blow your ships to Troy."

And so the king's daughter was sent for and she came. The agonized Agamemnon had to obey and do what Calchas advised. When the time came for the ceremony, Clytemnestra, shrieking, raised her voice against her husband, and would have stopped the priest by force, but Iphigenia herself stepped forward and said, "I am not afraid, Father. Artemis will protect me. I am happy to lay down my life to help you and my country."

The pyre was built on the shore. Calchas took the young girl by the hand and led her to the altar. He raised his arm high, then brought it down. Agamemnon hid his head in the folds of his cloak, so that his soldiers should not see him weeping womanish tears.

The knife flashed in the light, and a great mist fell over the altar. And then a wind sprang up from the west and blew the mist away, and there lay the body of a white doe, with a gaping wound at her neck.

"The Goddess has shown pity for your daughter," said Calchas. *"She has taken her to the Elysian Fields and left this creature in her place. And, see, the wind is blowing. Omens are favorable for our expedition."*

There was great rejoicing in the ranks of the Greeks, but sorrow in Agamemnon's heart. And in the heart of his wife, Clytemnestra, not only great sorrow, but fury and a bitter longing for revenge.

Marpessa looked up from the loom and saw Hecuba at the door of the chamber. She stood up at once and bowed her head.

"Lady Hecuba," she said. "Come in."

Hecuba staggered to the chair that Marpessa had pointed to.

"Thank you, child." She sat down heavily. "Don't stop your weaving. I won't make you speak to me, do not fear. I know what a quiet little thing you are. But come, come here, child. I never see you. You always manage to place yourself in the shadows, away from prying eyes. Let me look at you." Hecuba looked carefully at Marpessa. "How quickly the moons have waxed and waned since we found you both, you and your sister. You have grown."

She stared at Marpessa.

"You're lovely, child. And you won't be a child for much longer, but a woman. Is he giving you trouble?"

Marpessa looked down at her hands and shook her head. Hecuba was talking about Paris.

"Let me know if he does. There's no real harm in him, but he finds it difficult to control himself when there are pretty girls around. As if you need to hear this from me!" Hecuba sighed deeply. "He's been nothing but trouble since the day he was born. I had a dream when I was carrying him that I would give birth to a torch that would set the whole of Troy on fire, and I sent him up to the mountain hoping that the Gods would take him, but it was not to be. Some say that while he was on the mountain he lived with a nymph called Oenone, whom he loved dearly, but he won't talk about that time to anyone, so how do we know whether these stories are true or not? In any case, what's happened has happened and now here he is in Troy after all. It's a long story, how he came back, but there's nothing we can do about it now. We are all in the hands of the Gods."

Marpessa said, "Will you drink something cool? Helen always asks for pressed pomegranate seeds with honey and water."

"No, no," said Hecuba. "I'm on my way home. I saw Helen down on the walls, and Paris was there for a while, but he disappeared. I couldn't stay. I couldn't watch a moment longer. The smell of all that blood in the heat was too much for me. I'll go to my own chamber, child. You're very kind. I will see Paris tonight in the Great Hall. I wonder where he can be."

The old lady left the room, and Marpessa smiled. She could guess where Paris was. He was in a bed somewhere, with someone. Maybe the wife of some poor soldier sweating on the Plain; maybe a serving girl, or someone from one of those houses down in the city where women were kept to pleasure men. She shivered. So far, she had managed to avoid him, but things had changed a little since the night when he had almost pinned her to the wall. At first she thought that he'd forgotten all about it. He had been drunk, after all. But these days he sometimes looked at her like a cat catching sight of a particularly plump mouse. The shuttle moved in her hand. When this thread was finished, she would go down to that horrible Blood Room and find her sister.

"You said what?" Marpessa could hardly believe her ears. Her own sister, so quietly spoken, so gentle, so shy. How did she dare?

"You've never seen Boros," Xanthe said. "He brings bodies to us in the Blood Room, from the Plain. He always smells of blood. Well, I suppose he can't help that, but he's hideous. He says he wants to marry me. He says he'll get me. He's horrible. I couldn't help it. The words just came flying out of my mouth."

Marpessa started laughing, and soon the two sisters were helpless, giggling like small children, weak and wiping the tears from their eyes.

"Boiled squid . . . ," Marpessa said. "I don't know how you found the words."

"I should have said more," said Xanthe. "I should've said the squid was bigger."

"You should be careful," Marpessa said, smiling in spite of herself, "if he's as horrible as you say he is."

"I'm not frightened of him. He knows very well that I'm under Lord Hector's protection. He wouldn't dare do anything to me."

"Still," said Marpessa, "I'd keep away from him if I were you."

"I don't go looking for him, you can be sure of that. Let's not talk about him anymore. Let's talk about something else."

"Everyone says there's going to be trouble down there." Marpessa shrugged her shoulders in the direction of the Plain.

"Not the war!" Xanthe said. "Please let's not talk about the war. What did we talk about before all this fighting started?"

"I can't remember. We were too little. I don't think I even knew how to talk properly when it started."

"Think of something else then. Tell me about Helen and Paris."

Marpessa was silent for a moment, and then smiled. "Less use than a boiled squid!" she said.

The girls burst out laughing all over again.

AT THE FISH MARKET

Halie had been chosen. She'd grumbled and moaned and said, "There's about as much chance of finding fish at the fish market as of eating a peach and finding a jewel in the middle of it. Even if there were any fish to be had, the stalls'll all be closed. There's going to be a battle, haven't you both heard?"

"Get on with you," said Theano. "You know you like flirting with the stall holders. Was a time when you did more than that, but we won't dwell on that now . . ."

"Stitch your lips together with a bone needle." Halie laughed. "I'll go. I'd rather be down there than here with a filthy-minded crone like you!"

She'd taken the basket, just in case. You never quite knew what you'd find down there among the sea smells and old fish bones. Some of the men still went out at dead of night, farther up the coast, and brought their catch to market. It didn't do to let more than two or three days go by without looking to see what was on offer. How would it be if there *had* been a catch, and the royal household didn't get to share in it?

But now Halie walked through the market sniffing. She'd been right after all, and Theano wrong. Wait till

I tell her, she thought. Everyone's on the walls, gawping at stupid men hacking one another to bits. Everything's closed. She was just going to turn back and make her way to the citadel when a silvery gleam caught her eye. Could it be? Yes, there, in the distance she could make out the figure of a man, and that looked very much like a huge silver fish on the slab in front of him. She quickened her pace, and soon found herself face-to-face with a fisherman she'd never seen before. Funny-looking old codger, too. Much older than he'd seemed from a distance, with a beard that glittered blue and silver in the sunlight, as though there were fish scales caught up in it. And such a long beard! It fell over his chest and almost to his waist. His eyes were the color of deep water, and his hair was wet. Perhaps he'd only just come from his boat. Still, there was a fish in front of him.

"Greetings, old man!" Halie said, and smiled the smile that used to work wonders on fishmongers in the old days. "You're not down on the walls like the others, I see."

"No, I'm not. Even though they're my walls," he said. "I made them. Shook the earth about and pulled the rocks together to create a barrier around the city."

Halie sighed. Just her bad fortune, to meet a lunatic. Better humor him. Maybe he'd part with his fish for less gold if he didn't have his wits about him. She was just about to ask the price, when the man went on:

"Don't you recognize me? Poseidon, God of the Ocean."

Yes, Halie wanted to say. And I'm the Nymph of the Waterfall. Words came flooding from the old man's mouth, and there was nothing to do but listen. Never mind, there might be a good slice of fresh fish at the end of it all. Halie continued to smile.

"It's all coming to a head down there, on the Plain," said the old man. "There's a man in shining armor, and they all think it's Achilles. It isn't, though. Don't you want to know who it *really* is?"

"Astonish me," Halie said wearily. The sun was growing hotter and hotter, and if this old bore went on for much longer, she would faint.

"Achilles isn't fighting today. There's been some quarrel with Agamemnon, and he's on strike. That's someone else wearing the great hero's breastplate and helmet and carrying his weapons and riding behind his white horses. I know who it is, but the Trojans have yet to find out. Hector, behind his coal black horses . . . He doesn't know yet. The person who is wearing Achilles' armor thinks it's enchanted. He thinks it will make him invincible, but he's wrong. Hector will find a space between one piece of metal and another, and that's the end of him."

"You haven't told me who he is, though." And how can you know all this when you can't even see the Plain from here? Silly old thing!

"I've changed my mind. You can wait and see like the rest of them. And get ready for what happens when Achilles finds out what Hector has done. I'd not like to be in Hector's shoes, for all the gold that glitters under the mountains."

"What about the fish?" Halie asked. "Will you sell me some fish?"

"Take it, and welcome, my dear." He lifted the whole fish and put it into Halie's basket.

"How much?" Halie asked, her heart beating faster. Fish. Real fish, roasted over coals with herbs rubbed into the skin . . . She could almost taste it.

"A kiss from a handsome woman like you will be fine payment."

"Pleasure's mine," said Halie, and she leaned over the slab to kiss the old man. Perhaps he wasn't so bad after all—a whole fish! Just as she was putting her lips to his wrinkled cheek, he turned his head and Halie found his lips on hers. Her mouth was suddenly filled with the taste of salt, and her nose with the smell of the weeds that grew along the shore. And because she had put her hand out and touched his shoulder, to steady herself as she kissed him, she could feel that he was wet. Soaking wet, as though he'd stood there floating in salt water. In spite of the hot sun.

"Good-bye, sir." She'd forgotten his name. Never mind. Get this fish home, she said to herself. She couldn't wait to hear what Theano and Danae said. She hurried through the empty market, then turned to climb up to the Palace. She glanced down for a moment, savoring her triumph, and nearly dropped her basket in horror. The fish had disappeared. Could she have dropped it? Because she was hurrying so much? She retraced her steps through the market, all the way to where she was before. Or where she thought she was before. There was no sign of the stall, nor of the strange old man who stank of the ocean. And no sign of her fish. Halie sighed. The sun had addled her wits, she decided. She was getting old. Imagining things. If I ever catch him, she thought, he'd better watch out for his beard. I'll cut it off with a kitchen blade. Silly old fool! I should have known he was not to be trusted. Calling himself . . . whatever he called himself. Whatever next?

When she arrived back in the kitchen, Theano said, "Well, any luck?"

"Nothing at all." Halie sighed. "The whole place was closed up." Somewhere at the back of her mind, there was a dim memory of someone talking to her, but as she didn't recall anyone at all being in the market, she decided she must have dreamed it. The sun could do funny things to you, and no mistake.

ON THE WALLS

"When the Greek ships first sailed into the bay down there," said the Singer, leaning on his granddaughter and pointing a shaking finger in the direction of the sea, "I had such good eyesight . . ."

Polyxena continued the sentence under her breath in unison with the old man. She'd heard it many times.

". . . that I could almost tell whether the men standing on the decks had blue eyes or brown."

Aloud she said, "You shouldn't complain. Many men of your age can't walk as well as you can, and no one in the world can talk as well."

She'd repeated the same words over and over again, but still they pleased the Singer. She could tell by the way he gathered his robe around him and stuck his chin out bravely. It was exactly the same posture he always took up when he stood beside Priam's throne to recite one of his old stories of monsters and heroes.

Polyxena pulled her scarf over her head to shade her eyes from the sun. The Plain shimmered in the fierce heat, but all along the wide walls people crowded together for a good view of the battle. Men too old to be fighting, young boys and women . . . hundreds of them straining their eyes for a glimpse of someone they knew; someone of their blood; someone close to their heart.

"We're late," said the Singer. "I like to arrive before the others . . . pick out the best place, where you can see everything. If I had my way, I'd be down here before dawn."

"Some of us," said Polyxena, "like our beds a little more than you do. Some of us are still having sweet dreams when you fancy striding out all over the city."

"Poor Polyxena," the Singer sighed. "I make so much work for you. But you know how grateful I am. I couldn't manage without you, even though I'm a selfish old man and never praise you enough."

Even as he was speaking, Polyxena could see that his attention was on the noises coming from the Plain. He pointed down from the walls and said, "Listen, child! Listen to the music of Ares, the God of War. Hear the bronze clamor of spear on armor and weep at the sorrowful sound of men's groaning, like a thousand rams' horns blown loudly enough to deafen them on Olympus."

"No need to practice your epics on me, Grandfather. I don't think it's music at all. What I hear is misery. *You* listen. Can't you hear them? Every other woman standing here on the walls is weeping. Look at them. I don't know why they come down here. I wouldn't if it wasn't for you. I hate it."

"And yet," said the Singer, "you want to tell the stories after me. How will you speak if you have not seen? How would you thrill the company with tales of great bravery? Raise their hearts in their breasts so that they long to fight?"

"I wouldn't," said Polyxena. "I'd tell the truth. I'd

98

tell the company what they all know and don't want to admit. Dead flesh stinks in the sun, whether the creature is a horse or a soldier. Blood brings the vultures down from the mountains. The groans of wounded men and the cries of their mothers are ugly. They plunge knives in the breasts of all who hear them. I would banish Ares and Hades from any tale I told."

"Then you would find your audience falling asleep," said the Singer. "You're young—and don't look at me like that. I know you hate it when I say that, but it's true, you *are* young. I wish I could say the same about myself. What *was* I saying? I've forgotten."

"Never mind," said Polyxena. "I know what you were about to tell me. People love hearing stories about Love and War."

"Exactly!" said the Singer. "That was exactly what was in my mind!"

Polyxena sighed. Being with the Singer was like having to look after a child. Only, unlike a child, her grandfather knew how to talk and never wanted to stop. How did Xanthe stand it, taking care of Astyanax? Having to repeat everything a thousand times and still not be sure that he'd understood? Iason didn't know how lucky he was to be tending horses, who couldn't speak.

"Look," she said, remembering what Xanthe had once told her about distracting a baby's attention when it was becoming too demanding. "I think that's Hector—yes—he's chasing someone in a chariot drawn by two white horses. I can't see the Greek's face, but his armor is made of gold. It's shining so brightly that Hector has his arm raised in front of his face."

"Achilles . . . ," whispered the Singer. "It must be. He's the only one I can think of who has armor that shines like the sun."

"Maybe," said Polyxena, suddenly aware that the name *Achilles* was being whispered all along the wall by a thousand tongues, so that the whisper sounded like a sea wave breaking and sweeping up the sand. "Everyone thinks so."

"What are they doing now?" The Singer was hopping up and down. "Tell me—don't keep anything from me."

"I can't see. There are men all around the chariot. The Greek has fallen, I think . . ."

"Yes, I can hear," said the Singer as a great roar echoed all around the walls. "Achilles has fallen. A day of great rejoicing. I must put the finishing touches to my triumphal poem. Come, child, let us go home. We've seen enough."

"Wait," said Polyxena. "Something's happening down there . . . There's someone riding to the walls. His horse is exhausted, poor thing, and still he spurs him on . . . He's saying something to that man by the tower . . ."

"What? What's he saying?"

"I can't hear," said Polyxena. "Wait." And stop talking so much, and let me listen, she thought to herself. Then, "It's not Achilles," she said finally, and sure enough from all around them, voices were raised in amazement, saying the same thing, *Not Achilles. It isn't Achilles.*

"Who then?" said the Singer. "Really, this is too

irritating for words. How am I supposed to tell the stories if I don't have the information? Go and find out who's dead. I'll tell you one thing: He was wearing Achilles' armor. I'd recognize that breastplate anywhere."

Polyxena looked at her grandfather and opened her mouth to speak, and then decided to keep quiet after all. What was the point of telling him that he hadn't seen the armor himself, and that she had told him about it? Nothing would change.

"It's a Greek trick," said a man standing near them. He was so old that his whole body was bent over and his limbs looked like the ancient branches of an olive tree. The Singer pulled himself up to his full height, feeling suddenly like a young sapling next to this person. And from the walls came the name, passed from one mouth to another, until it reached Polyxena, who repeated it to the Singer.

"Patroclus," she said. "It's Patroclus."

"Cousin to Achilles," said the Singer. "And more, much more. He shared Achilles' tent, and some also say his bed in that tent. Oh, Achilles will avenge him. I tremble for Hector. Come, child, let us return to our own house and weep."

"Why should we weep?" Polyxena said. "Hector is triumphant."

"Hector has been tricked," said the Singer. "He will not rest until he has met with Achilles."

"And if Achilles won't fight?" Polyxena wanted to know. "What then?"

The Singer shook his head sadly and said nothing, but the wizened old man who had been listening, it seemed, to the entire conversation, cackled like a hen and said, from between toothless gums, "He'll fight now, my pretty child. Oh yes, he will. Hector has made sure of that. There'll be a fight such as the Plain has never seen. Mark my words. Wait and see. Just as soon as Achilles has gathered his strength and got some new armor from who knows where . . . Chopped meat, that's what Hector is."

"Don't answer him," said the Singer. "It is disrespectful to be rude to someone as old as that. He's a fool, that's all. Let's go home now." They made their way slowly down the wide stone steps that led from the walls into the city.

"Sometimes," the wizened ancient said as he settled himself on a conveniently shaped rock, "people recognize the Father of All the Gods, and sometimes they don't. Never mind."

He watched the ebb and flow of bodies, the dance of war going on beneath the walls. The whole thing would soon be over.

THE BLOOD ROOM

"Nobody cares!" Alastor shouted. "You all creep around, pretending to do everything you can for me, but you won't do what I want. Nobody listens to me. I want to know what's happening. Why will nobody tell me what's going on?"

"Hector has killed Patroclus, and now everyone is saying that Achilles won't rest until his cousin is avenged. Some people are betting on Hector to come out victorious, but not many."

"Who told you? How do you know? Did you see the battle?"

"I don't need to see it. Everyone talks. In the kitchens. In the bedrooms. In the halls and the courtyards. We all know what's going on."

Alastor lifted his head from the pillow and turned over to lean on his elbow. He looked at Marpessa. He said, "Who are you? I've never seen you before."

"I'm Xanthe's sister. My name is Marpessa. You must be Alastor. My sister has spoken of you. I don't know why you're so angry, but it can't be doing you any good. Aren't you wounded? Aren't you supposed to be resting?"

"Damn resting and damn wounds. There's nothing wrong with me. A scratch here on the side of my neck, that's all, and they're treating me like a young girl who can't do anything except faint and lie around moaning."

Marpessa said nothing. Men thought women were weak, which amused her. She had seen girls screaming in the agonies of childbirth and wondered how men would manage if the Gods had arranged it for their bodies to be torn nearly in two.

"I want to get down there," Alastor continued. "She won't take me—your sister. She says I'm not to be moved, but I think she's just trying to get out of seeing what's going on. I feel so useless here."

"You wouldn't be much use on the walls, either. It'd just make you feel worse because you couldn't join in. And in any case, they've stopped fighting until sunrise tomorrow. The light is going. Can't you see? The sky is red: bloodstained like the earth. The gates have been closed. Hector is camped outside the walls, I know that much, because that's why I'm here. My sister was called to Andromache's chamber and asked me to come and sit with you so that you shouldn't be alone."

"I'm never alone," said Alastor. "My mother keeps coming and going with bits of this and that to feed me. I feel like a chick in a nest. I asked her to take me down there, but she wouldn't. And now there's you. You're not like Xanthe said you were. She said you were silent, and never spoke."

Marpessa smiled. "I don't. I can't think what's come over me. Usually there's nothing I want to say."

"She also didn't tell me you were beautiful."

"Rubbish. You're talking nonsense. I live in Lord

Paris's palace, and words coated in sugar don't impress me at all. Close your eyes and go to sleep."

"I'll dream of you," Alastor said, and soon he was breathing deeply.

Someone was watching her. Marpessa glanced over to the corner of the room, and sure enough there she was: Aphrodite, floating a little way off the ground, trailing robes of palest yellow, like spun light.

"You're wondering," said the Goddess. "You're asking yourself what I'm doing here. Well, that should be obvious. I'm bored. Everyone else is busy . . . Helen, Paris, all of them, down there fascinated with the comings and goings of a lot of sweaty warriors. It's tedious. So I thought I'd come and see how this Alastor is recovering. Don't you think he's pretty? He's struck with you, isn't he?"

Marpessa sighed. "Don't," she said. "Please don't, Lady. Don't tie your ribbons around my heart. Eros has already hit my sister with his arrow."

"How intriguing, then, if you were rivals!" Aphrodite giggled. "Your sister doesn't quite believe in my power. Perhaps I shall teach her a lesson. Nothing like a bit of competition between sisters to spice life up a little."

"No, I beg you," said Marpessa. "I couldn't bear to feel anything but love for Xanthe. Please. Go somewhere else. Do something else."

"It's a little late for him," said Aphrodite. "I'm afraid I got to him before you saw me. You're already in his dreams, I fear. Perhaps I will not put his image in your heart. Or perhaps I will. I'll see how things go."

She drifted up toward the ceiling. Marpessa knew

that Aphrodite was the most powerful of Goddesses, with her own strange laws. What, she wondered, will I say to Xanthe? Nothing. Not a word. That was best. Maybe tomorrow she would come here and help Alastor down to the city walls. . . . She shook her head. What was she thinking of? She should stay away, and have nothing more to do with this young man. Marpessa stood up and made her way to the door. There she turned around and looked back at Alastor's sleeping body, and felt something like a pain between her heart and her stomach; a kind of cramp that she would have called agony, were it not for the intense pleasure she felt as it came over her.

THE FORGE

Whenever he couldn't sleep, Iason walked in the city. When others were in their beds, when there was no danger of anyone pointing at him, or mocking him for being young and not a warrior, he made his way through the streets at the foot of the citadel. It was always quiet at such times. No lamps burned, so Iason picked his way by the light that Artemis allowed to come down from the sky. Sometimes her whole face was showing. Sometimes she hid it behind clouds, and sometimes she turned away altogether, but then a lesser radiance from the bright stars was enough to show him the path. On this night, everyone in the royal household was talking of the death of Patroclus. What, they were all wondering, would Achilles do? Iason looked up. He had arrived, without really notic-ing, at the forge where the blacksmith worked to keep Hector's horses shod in iron shoes. The blacksmith should have closed up for the night long ago, but even from a distance Iason heard the wheeze of bellows and a fiery glow came from the doorway. He hurried to see what had happened to keep the man working when the rest of the city was asleep. The heat coming from the smithy was so great that his skin was immediately wet with sweat, and the blacksmith was nowhere to be seen. In his place, a small, black-bearded man was sitting on the floor, hammering what looked to Iason like an enormous golden shield.

"Who are you?" said this man, without looking up.

"Iason is my name, but I should ask you who *you* are. I've been bringing my horses here for a long time, but I've never seen you before."

"Never been needed before."

"Why are you needed now? Where's the blacksmith? What do they call you? Where have you come from?"

"Like asking questions, don't you?"

"What are you making? That's not for a horse, is it?"

"Another question. Don't you do anything but ask and ask?"

Iason said nothing. Perhaps this man was right, and what happened in the blacksmith's shop was not his business. He was just about to make his apologies and leave, when the man said, "Name's Hephaestus."

Iason laughed.

"How did your parents know when you were a baby that you'd be working with metal in a forge? Hephaestus is the name of the blacksmith God, who works in the forges of Olympus."

"Right," said the man. "That's me. Hephaestus."

He must be drunk, Iason thought. He decided it would be best not to mention Gods and names again. He said instead, "What's that you're making? It looks extraordinary."

"New shield for Achilles."

Not drunk, Iason decided, but mad. He said, "Why

are you making a shield in Troy for one of our enemies?"

"Better facilities in this forge, that's all. I don't give
a fig for who's fighting whom. Not my business. My
business is making sure everyone has suitable equipment."

"I see," said Iason, though he was beginning to feel
as though *he* were drunk. "Mind if I look?"

"No skin off my nose," said Hephaestus.

Iason stared at the shield. He had never seen anything like it before.

"Layers and layers of tin and bronze . . . ," said Hephaestus. "That's what I've done there. And a sheet
of gold for extra protection. D'you know the power of
gold? Amazing, that's what it is. And notice the or-
namentation. Not bad, eh?"

The surface of the shield was embossed with the
figures of men, and dancing girls and animals and cit-
ies and landscapes, and all around the edge, waves and
more waves. Hephaestus pointed at them.

"The ocean," he said. "Surrounds us all. When you
see Achilles with this shield, after sunrise, he'll be a
sight to terrify every Trojan watching."

"How will you get it to him?" Iason asked.

"Thetis, his mother, will come and take it to him.
Also the helmet I've made him out of pure gold, with
a crest that stands as high and proud as any tree. Achilles'll avenge Patroclus, and then he'll bury him. He'll
cull a few of your blokes in the process, and no mistake,
they won't die easily, but that's nothing compared
with what's going to happen to Hector. No indeed."

The man chuckled, and Iason was suddenly angry.

Even if he *had* lost his reason, that didn't give him the right to speak disrespectfully of Lord Hector. He said, "You don't know what you're talking about. My Lord Hector is the bravest of men."

"Doesn't alter what we've got lined up for him." The man's black eyes met and held Iason's.

"We!" Iason scoffed. "Who is *we*?"

"You're a fool, boy. The Gods. I'm talking about the Gods on Olympus. You'll make your way back to your own bed, and in the morning you won't remember much at all. Go now. Dawn's almost here."

Iason made his way to the citadel. He reached the stables and fell into a deep sleep on a pile of straw. All through the next day, bits and pieces of a dream would not leave his thoughts. There was a fire burning in the forge, he recalled. Hephaestus was making a golden shield for Achilles. Iason smiled to himself. What did it mean, to dream of the Gods? He turned to his task of feeding the horses.

ON THE WALLS

Xanthe looked around her and wished she hadn't agreed to come. Alastor had forced her, and there was nothing she could have done.

"Your sister will take me if you don't," he'd said, and indeed, there was Marpessa, sitting a little way away with Helen and Paris. She hadn't said very much to Xanthe about the conversation she'd had with Alastor. Perhaps she should ask her what, exactly, had been said. Everyone who could be here was here, from the lowliest servant to Priam and Hecuba with their attendants. Cassandra stood alone, away from the rest of the royal household, and stared at her feet. Xanthe almost smiled to see that Theano, Danae, and Halie had found a good spot just above the gate. Of course, they wouldn't want to miss anything. Only the temple maidens and the very aged and infirm were not on the walls. And Andromache and Astyanax.

"I've brought you here," she said to Alastor, "even though you are still weak and probably still have a fever. I don't know why I did . . ." You're a liar, Xanthe, of course you know why. How could you resist it? The chance to spend almost the whole day at Alastor's side. You'd have done anything, admit it. Anything just to be near him. "But I don't think I can watch, Alastor. I shall hide my eyes. Or look down. And in any case, I find it all a muddle. Everything goes so quickly, I can't work out what's happening. I hate it. I wish I hadn't come."

"I'll tell you what's going on. That man . . . That's Achilles. Oh, Xanthe, you must see this! Have you ever set eyes on such armor?"

Xanthe looked down onto the Plain. Her eyes fell on a tall warrior dressed entirely in black armor, standing all alone. Somewhere, surely, she thought, I've seen him before. She peered down to try to catch a glimpse of his face under the dark helmet, but saw nothing but shadows, and when she looked again, he was gone. And she forgot about him almost at once, because suddenly, there was Achilles, not in a story anymore, but right in front of her, glittering and tall, like a giant made all of gold. Achilles, after all this time. You could see him coming from far away, driving his chariot over the earth, with clouds of dust around his wheels. They whispered his name all along the walls, and people stirred and moved closer to the edge to get a better view.

"He's attacking . . . Lord Hector is rallying . . . They're riding around the walls to the springs . . . There, beside the oak tree . . . Achilles is throwing his spear . . . Oh, no . . . By the Gods, that was close."

"Is he hurt?" Xanthe found that she was trembling all over. She couldn't say *dead.* The word wouldn't pass her lips.

"Achilles has taken up the spear again . . . Oh, Lord Hector!" As Alastor spoke, a heartbroken cry went up from the crowd gathered on the wall, like the sound made by an animal wounded in the hunt.

112

"The neck! Lord Hector is hit in the neck . . . But he's speaking. Can you hear what he's saying? Oh, if I weren't wounded, I'd be down there in a minute. I wish I had my sword with me. Why is no one going to help him? Where is everyone?"

Xanthe looked all around for someone she knew, and sighed with relief when she saw Polyxena.

"Polyxena!" she called to her. "Polyxena, I need you. Can you come here?"

Polyxena left the Singer's side and made her way through the crowd.

"What is it? What's the matter?"

"Will you wait here with Alastor? Will you take him back to the Blood Room when . . ." Xanthe found she couldn't finish the sentence. When Hector is dead. That was what she meant to say, but her whole mouth was filled with a bitter liquid, and she would have vomited if she had spoken one word. She swallowed, and breathed in and out deeply. Then she said, "My place is with Andromache. I have to go."

"Of course," said Polyxena. "I'll take care of Alastor. It'll make a nice change from baby-sitting my grandfather. Go. This is not the place for you."

Xanthe fled. She ran through the empty streets, with the sun burning down on her head. She ran past houses with their doors standing open. She ran up and up to the citadel, and just as she was passing into the first of the royal courtyards, she heard it and stopped, with her heart beating and the breath leaving her body in loud gasps. Part of her had been waiting for just that noise, and although she had never heard anything like it before, she recognized it at once. It was like a huge, towering, sorrowful wave of sound; a blending of sighs and sobs and groans that curled up and up through the hazy air of the late afternoon and broke over the city. And it went on and on. It grew louder, and soon there were other sounds added to it. A thousand throats were open and shrieking. Xanthe began to run again. It was impossible to believe that Andromache hadn't heard it. And of course, she would know exactly what it meant.

The screaming crowd that had been watching the battle since it started fell silent all at once. Hector and Achilles were there, close enough for all to see, close enough for their panting and their groans to carry up to those who were watching. No one breathed. The sun burned down on the men, struggling under the walls. Marpessa tried to turn her eyes away. It was too close, too painful even for her, but suddenly she saw a woman standing on the sand, and a chill ran through her. This was the Goddess Pallas Athene, dressed in garments of shimmering bronze. Even from this distance, Marpessa could see her clear gray eyes turned on Hector, and she shivered. Achilles' spear had fallen out of his hands, and the crowd on the wall began to shout, "Kill, kill him, Hector! He's yours! Kill the Greek! Kill him!"

Hector raised his sword above his head and ran toward his enemy. Next to Marpessa, a small boy cried out and covered his face with his hands, too frightened to look. Marpessa saw the Goddess bend down and pick up Achilles' spear from where it had fallen and hand it to him. He rushed forward then and found the one place where life can run out of a man in an instant: the soft place where the neck meets the head. The silver spear disappeared into Hector's flesh, and a fountain of red blood sprang up and spilled over his shoulders.

"Hector!" came the shout from the walls. "Hector has been wounded! Kill him, Hector! Don't let him get away!"

Hector fell. He lay on the ground, and above him Achilles stood with his sword drawn. On the walls, everyone had frozen into stillness, and now they leaned forward to catch what their hero was saying.

"Achilles . . ." Hector's words bubbled from his mouth in a froth of blood. "I am dying beside my city walls. Let them bury me. Let them take me within the gate. Don't leave my body to rot. The birds will peck it. The dogs . . . Let them bury me, or the dogs will suck at my bones. My father will give you gold. My mother will throw her jewels from the walls for you . . . I implore you, give them back my body."

"You killed Patroclus," Achilles replied, out of breath, panting in the heat. "You killed him, and I loved him. I can't forgive that. Never. Die. And I wish the dogs joy of your carcass."

He turned to all the soldiers who had gathered around to see, to protect their leader in case the Trojan hero suddenly managed to spring up again. . . .

"Do to him whatever you will," Achilles said to one, under his breath.

Marpessa heard him and began to weep. Others along the wall began screaming, shouting, crying, wailing.

"Remember me," Hector shouted with his last breath, as Achilles looked down at him. "Remember me when my brother Paris kills you in the shadow of the Skaian Gate."

When there was no more movement from Hector's body, Achilles came right up to it. He took out a small, sharp dagger and lifted one of Hector's legs from the ground.

"What's he doing?" someone next to Marpessa whispered.

"Wait. Shut up and watch," said his friend.

Marpessa watched, too. Achilles—could it be true?—was digging into the soft flesh of Hector's calf with the point of the dagger. Why? What was the reason? When he'd made a hole—that was what it looked like—in one leg, he let it fall to the ground, and picked up the other. No one stirred on the city walls. The sun suddenly vanished behind a bank of cloud, and a livid darkness spread over the Plain. Holes dug out with a knife. One in each leg. Then Achilles took two leather thongs and threaded them through the torn and ragged flesh. He tied the ends to his own chariot, and climbed into it.

"He can't . . . not even Achilles. He wouldn't . . . Would he?"

"Capable of anything . . ."

"Shameful . . . May the Gods come down from Olympus and strike the bastard dead!"

Marpessa stared. The only Goddess that she could see was Pallas Athene, who still stood on the Plain, calmly watching out of her gray eyes as Achilles' chariot dragged the body of Hector three times around the walls. Bloodstained earth filled his mouth. His long black hair was yellow with matted sand. Someone gave a cry that sounded like a bird tearing its own feathers from its breast. . . . Hecuba, writhing on the ground above the gate. Priam was roaring. He was like a lion with a spear in his side, in agony, in torment, twisting his head from side to side, as though to shake from it the terrible sight before his eyes. And Achilles? Marpessa looked at him, and saw that the Goddess had made him deaf. All he could hear was the beating of his own heart and the rush of his own blood, rising up under the golden helmet and filling the whole of his head.

Iason felt cold, even though the sun was still beating down on his head. The blood in his veins had turned to ice, and he couldn't move. Lord Hector was dead, and worse than dead. How could Achilles call himself human, when he had treated Hector's body with less respect than most people would give a dead sheep? A weight of sorrow sat on Iason's shoulders like a yoke, and he wondered if he would ever feel lighthearted again. And there was the horse, Aithon, standing bewildered in his chariot traces, with the mare that was his companion. What would become of the horses? Would Achilles take them back to the Greek lines and use them to draw a Greek chariot? Or would a stray spear from one soldier or another find a place in their beautiful flanks? At the thought of it, Iason felt bile fill his mouth, and he began to climb down from the walls. Xanthe had fled, long ago, and he knew she was on her way to comfort Lady Andromache. My place is with the other horses, Iason thought. I must go to them. I must go home. That's where I belong. In the stable, with them. When I get there, I'll tell them everything. I must hold on to my tears until I'm alone with them. They'll understand. Poor Aithon! Poor Hector! Woe to all of us, now that he is dead.

ANDROMACHE'S
CHAMBER

Andromache heard her husband dying. Long, long before the wailing floated from the Plain and broke against the walls of the city; long before the women's screams came flying through the air and into the windows of her chamber, she heard him. His voice sounded in her ear so clearly that she looked around to see whether Astyanax had heard it, too, but he was happily playing with his collection of carved horses, making them gallop, around and around and up and down in an endless series of races. *Andromache, I'm dying. Andromache, think of me . . .* The words were somewhere in her head, a thin, high sound that made her catch her breath. She put her shuttle down and listened. There. There it was. They were all weeping now, all of them, but not as she would weep. She felt a solid lump of anguish like a stone travel from somewhere near her heart and burst out of her mouth in a scream that filled all the spaces in her head, and after the scream came the tears, like a torrent. Even as they fell, she thought, part of her thought: I'll never be able to stop. I'll drown. I'm made of tears. There's nothing in me at all but pain. She saw her child, looking at her in amazement, and he seemed to be very far away,

118

and however much she wanted to pick him up and hold him, she couldn't. There was nothing she could do but weep. Stand there and weep. Her hands were tearing something. . . . What was she tearing? She neither knew nor cared, only she was aware of her fingers like claws in the fabric, and the sound of something from far away. A voice. Words coming into her ears through a thick mist that hung before her face. Arms around her, holding her. Who was this? Which of them had come to hold her? For one glorious moment, a blissful thought came to Andromache and she was happy: Mother. It's my mother. My mother's arms are around me, but the moment passed, and she knew everything again. She thought: My mother is dead. My husband is dead. I wish I were dead with them. But the voice was speaking. Xanthe. Kind little Xanthe was holding her, and speaking.

"Lady! I'm here. I will hold you while you weep. Lord Hector is dead and the sun is dark, but you must be brave. For Astyanax's sake. Poor little baby. Think of your son."

"Xanthe! I can't. I can't stay here. I must see him . . . I must go to him."

"No, Lady. Stay here. You don't know . . . Please stay here."

"I want to go. I can't leave him down there all alone. I was just thinking. I must find Theano and Halie and ask them to heat water for his bath . . . I want to be with him, don't you understand? I promised when I was a young girl to stay with him always. I must go to him now. How will it be if the whole city sees him in his death agony and not his wife?

They're all there, aren't they? Helen, too. I'm going. Stay with Astyanax. Wait for me till I come back."

Xanthe made out the words, even though every syllable was bubbling and drowning in tears. She went on holding Andromache in her arms, until at last her sobs subsided a little.

"Drink some wine to give you strength, Lady. Wait. Calm yourself before you go."

But Andromache had torn herself away from Xanthe and run out of the chamber and into the sun. Xanthe picked up Astyanax and said, "Poor baby. Never mind, little one, never mind. She'll soon be back."

"Da-da!" said Astyanax, and Xanthe started crying quietly. She glanced around the room. Andromache had obviously been working at her weaving. There was the shuttle, lying on the ground, but the cloth she had been making had been torn off the loom, and there was a ragged hole in the center of the fabric, as if a giant bird had attacked it with long sharp claws, leaving threads hanging in the dust.

"Let's play with the horses," she said, wiping her eyes with a corner of the baby's dress, and she thought of the white horses that had pulled Achilles' chariot, dragging Hector's body over rough ground.

ON THE WALLS

Polyxena looked at the Singer. He was standing a little way away from where she was, next to Alastor, and weeping. Never, in all her life, had she seen her grandfather cry, and the sight made her tremble and feel sick; worse than she felt about Hector, although it was true she had had to stifle a desire to vomit when she saw what Achilles had done to him.

"Alastor," she said, in a voice that was not like her own at all but seemed to belong to some quavering weakling. "Alastor, I must go to my grandfather . . . He's in a dreadful state . . . Look. I'll bring him back here. I'll come back to you at once."

"No," said Alastor, and his voice, too, was not the one Polyxena had heard before. "Go. I'm well enough to be on my own. I won't go anywhere. I'll just sit here. It's better if I'm on my own. I'm not . . . I can't speak to anyone anyway."

"If you're sure, then," said Polyxena, and Alastor nodded. She hurried through the crowds to where the Singer was standing, his face quite wet with tears.

Marpessa looked along the walls. A silence had fallen. After the storm of weeping and howling, everyone was quiet, gazing down on the Plain, wanting to turn their eyes away from the horror of their prince's body being dragged over the ground. Paris had shouted till he was hoarse. Priam had shouted, too. Unforgivable things: how he wished any other one of his sons were lying there dead, instead of Hector. But no one blamed him. Hecuba's maidens had carried her away to the Palace, to grieve in the darkness of her own chamber. Helen was white and trembling. Her tears flowed from under closed lids, and left not a mark on her face. Other women grew red eyed and swollen from weeping, but not Helen.

"Listen," she said to Paris. "There's Andromache. I can hear her . . ."

Everyone turned away from the Plain and watched as Hector's widow approached the walls. They let her pass, opening up a clear passage as she ran. What, Marpessa wondered, did you call the sound that she was making? A heartbroken wailing, a groan torn from the depths of her throat, a cry such as no one had heard before, and a cry that made the hair rise on the back of Marpessa's neck.

"Andromache . . . ," Helen began. "Sister, come . . ." And she stepped toward Hector's widow with her arms open to hold her.

"No," Andromache shrieked, and threw herself out of reach of Helen's embrace. "Not you . . . How do you dare? Whore! Trollop! Bringer of death to good men . . . Why do you come to comfort me now? Why did you ever come here to charm the men into a war they can never win, and never survive? I don't want you to touch me. I know—don't think I don't know—I do . . . Hector wanted you. I know that. He never said, but I could see. How he looked at you. How they all look at you. And you . . . I don't want to touch you. Leave me. Leave me here, and maybe a kind God will come and turn me into a bird, so that I can fly away into the sky and never come back . . ." Andromache flung herself to the ground, where she lay with her fists beating the earth.

Helen knelt down beside her, and only Marpessa heard the words she whispered: "Beloved sister . . . wife of the best man who ever trod this Trojan Plain, stop. It was only you. Hector loved you. No one but you in the world. You're his widow. You must mourn him fittingly. He's the father of your son. For Astyanax's sake, stop your weeping and hold it in your heart. You must be brave. Hector would expect it."

"I don't care," Andromache said, but more quietly. "Why should I care what he wants or doesn't want when he leaves me? Didn't he promise to be with me forever? I'm young, Helen. How could he break his promise to me? He can't have loved me. He wouldn't have fought if he'd loved me. He knew I hated this war and everything about it. I had the house all ready for his return. I was just going to find someone to heat the water for his bath . . ."

She struggled to her feet and made her way, with Helen holding her by the arm, to where she could see Hector's body. When she saw it, and what had become of it, every drop of blood left her face and she swayed as though she was going to faint. Then she put her hands in front of her face and pressed her fingers over her eyes. She stood like that for so long that Helen said, "Andromache, it's late. The sun is going down.

Come with me. I'll take you back now. You must rest. And Astyanax will be waiting for you."

"I'll go alone. My thanks to you, Helen, but I'll go alone. Xanthe is there, and she'll help me. See, I've stopped crying. I won't cry ever again, I promise you."

"Don't promise that," said Helen. "Never promise that. Tears are good sometimes. They clear the heart of sorrow. Cry. When you're in your own house, cry then."

"I haven't got a heart," Andromache said. "Not anymore. I've got a rock where it used to be." She beat her breast with a fist. "A rock bound with metal bands. I mustn't cry. Enough for my baby that he's lost his father, but the Gods are merciful and he is young, and doesn't need to know . . ." She pointed to where Achilles' chariot was disappearing over the Plain toward the Greek lines and shuddered. "If the baby sees me being the same as I always am, his life can be unchanged, can't it? He doesn't have to know. For as long as I can keep it from him, I will."

Marpessa, who was standing a little way away from Helen, watched Andromache walking, silent and upright, through the crowds, who stepped to one side and put out comforting hands to touch her robes as she passed. Then she turned to look for Alastor, and saw him at last, sitting on the ground farther along the wall with his head on his knees. She said something to Helen, who nodded, then Marpessa made her way to him through the crowds. Strangely, she felt as though all the other people on the walls had faded somehow and had no more substance than shadows. Maybe Aphrodite was responsible, even though she was nowhere to be seen. Soon Marpessa was at Alastor's side, and although often in her life she had been so uncertain what she wanted to say that she said nothing at all, now the words came into her mouth at once.

"It's me. Marpessa. I've come to help you. Where's Xanthe? She told me she was looking after you today."

The young man glanced up at her. "She went back to help Andromache. I don't need help."

Marpessa did not contradict him but sat down at his side and took his hand. Even though the tears were still wet on his cheeks and his voice sounded hoarse with weeping, of course, being what he was, he would never admit to the sorrow he was feeling. Why was it that certain men had a horror of being thought womanish that was stronger than the strongest pain?

"I want to go," he said at last. "Not to that awful room, though."

"To your mother's house?" Marpessa asked. "Shall I take you there?"

"No, anywhere but there. Even the Blood Room would be better."

Marpessa thought for a moment. Then she said, "Paris and Helen have many guest chambers in their palace. I'll take you there."

"Really?" Alastor was beginning to sound almost normal. "Won't they mind?"

"Everyone will be with King Priam tonight," said Marpessa. "No one will know, and even if they did, Helen is more hospitable than anyone else in the city. We'll be alone." A shiver went through her body as she spoke, and Marpessa wondered what she was feeling.

"Thank you," Alastor said. "You're good to me. You and your sister both. Kind hands, you both have."

"Stand up," Marpessa said. "Lean on me."

"I don't need to lean on anyone," he said, and gave her his hand. But as they began to walk from the walls and through the streets of Troy, the pain in his neck grew worse, and Marpessa put her arm around him and took much of his weight against her body. The sun was nearly in the sea, and it was cool to walk in the shadows of the houses, but where his flesh touched hers, Marpessa felt herself burning, and stronger than ever was the sensation of being part of a dream and not in her real life at all. They made their way through the city and up the hill to Paris and Helen's palace. Most people were still on the walls, and those who were not were in their houses, grieving. Silence lay on the stones and in the shade of every tree.

When they reached the threshold, Marpessa said, "Come, I'll show you to the guest bedchamber."

"Where," said Alastor, sounding breathless, "do you sleep?"

"In a small chamber next to the weaving room."

"Show me," he whispered. "I want to see it."

"Why?"

"I want to be able to picture you in it, when I'm not here."

MARPESSA'S
BEDCHAMBER

Marpessa said nothing. They walked, still entwined, through the corridors. No one had lit the lamps, and a purple dusk had spread through the house. At the door of her own bedchamber, she paused. Alastor said, "May I come in?"

Marpessa tried to speak, but her tongue seemed to be swollen and wouldn't move when she wanted it to. She nodded. They went into the narrow room.

"It's tiny," Alastor said. "Nothing in it really but this bed. May I lie on it? Do you mind? My neck is troubling me."

"Yes, yes of course," she said. "Lie there, and I'll go and find you some water. I'll dress your wound, if you like. Or I can go and find Xanthe."

"Water, yes," Alastor said, and lay back on the covers of the bed with his head on her pillow. "How can I ever thank you?"

Marpessa found herself staring like an idiot at a flower she herself had woven into the fabric somewhere near his arm, halfway down the bed. She forced herself to stand up and leave the room, and make her way to where the water pitchers stood in the courtyard. Where was everyone? When would they come home? She found a small jug and filled it, then carried it back to her room. All the time she was gone, a picture of Alastor lying on her bed filled her mind, and she made her way through the corridors like a sleepwalker.

"There you are," he said as she came into the room again. "I was wondering when you'd come back. I've missed you."

"Drink," Marpessa answered. "It's cool." She poured the water into a cup and held it to his lips. Alastor's hand closed over hers.

"Come and lie down beside me," he said, taking the cup out of her hands and putting it on the floor next to the bed. "I'm sad. I haven't been as sad as this since my father died, when I was a small boy. Lord Hector—he spoke to me last night. Comfort me, Marpessa. Hold me, so that I can weep with no one to see me."

Marpessa looked at him and a dizziness came over her, so that she almost swooned. Without a word, she lay down beside him and put her arms around him. His head was on her breast. She stared over his shoulder at the wall. Oh, Lady Aphrodite, she said to herself, help me. What is happening to me? She was trembling all over.

"Look at me," Alastor said, lifting his head level with her face. "And open your mouth."

Marpessa did what he said, and her heart . . . something . . . everything . . . melted like a honeycomb held near the fire, and she felt her whole body grow limp and heavy, and her mouth was filled with sweetness. She closed her eyes, and a wave of darkness washed over her as she fell back against the pillows with Alastor's weight and heat upon her. Night seeped into every corner of the little room.

THE STABLES

Iason had done everything he could think of for the horses, to comfort them. By some good fortune, someone had cut them loose from Hector's chariot and led Aithon and the mare, Aithre, back to the city, and to their own stable. They'd been brushed and fed and watered, and so had all the other horses, and Iason had covered all of them with the soft woolen blankets that Hector had brought down from his own home especially for his beloved animals. Now they were quiet, and the stables were swept and clean and there was nothing else for him to do. He should eat, but he knew that food, even if it had been proper food, like they used to eat long ago, would taste like ashes in his mouth. He looked out and saw torchlight flickering in the Great Hall of the Palace. You could go there, he said to himself. No one would mind. They will be mourning Hector and helping one another with their grief. Iason turned away from the doorway and went to sit in a pile of straw where no one could see him crying. This, he thought, must be what they feel—all the boys who lose fathers on the battlefield. Iason couldn't remember his own parents. And now, he thought, I am an orphan all over again. He thought of Xanthe, because thinking of her always made him feel better. She would be with the baby. Lady Andromache, he knew, would never again lie down in ease and comfort. However long she lived, and whatever happened to her in the rest of her life, that picture (the one that Iason wished beyond anything he, too, could scrub from his head) of her husband dragged behind that cursed chariot like a broken doll . . . that image would be branded on the inside of her eyes as long as she drew breath.

"Iason?" It was Polyxena. "I've come to see how you are. Have you eaten?"

Iason shook his head. "You are kind to think of me. The Singer . . . where is he?"

"I've left him with the king. Oh, Iason, you cannot imagine the sorrow. I had to come and find you. They're all weeping. I'm weeping. There's nowhere to go. Everyone, everywhere, is unhappy. I thought that here . . ."

"No, Polyxena, I'm weeping, too."

She sat down beside him and put an arm around his shoulders.

"At least we'll weep together."

Polyxena wondered if the Gods would forgive her for finding a small measure of happiness in being near Iason. Was any happiness allowed at such a sorrowful time? Perhaps, she said to herself, if I weep more bitterly, Iason will have to console me. Immediately she felt ashamed of herself for having such an unworthy thought at such a time, and she wiped her wet eyes on a corner of her skirt.

"I must go now and find the Singer. Sleep if you can. Dream of good things."

Iason nodded but said nothing.

PRIAM'S PALACE

In the Great Hall, the company was silent. Polyxena knew that even if the food in front of them had been ambrosia, no one would have been able to eat it. Everyone was there. They could have stayed hidden in their own palaces, but tonight was a night for all the princes of Troy and their households to come together under Priam's roof to mourn. To weep for Hector. Silence filled the spaces under the carved ceiling. Hecuba's face was covered with a black veil, and Priam, who only this morning had been an upright and tough-looking old man, a man in whose face you could still see the handsome youth he once was, that person had vanished, and what was left in his place was a shaking, red-eyed, and wild-bearded vagabond, like those who sometimes came into the city from the lands beyond Mount Ida. Cassandra sat alone, apart, staring in front of her. Her white face was stiff, and two spots of red stood out on her cheeks. Andromache had come in after everyone else. She was dressed in her finest robes, and even though her features were swollen with weeping, her eyes were dry. She walked the length of the Hall and stopped in front of Hecuba. Without a word, she knelt down and put her arms around her mother-in-law and whispered something in her ear. A groan of anguish came from Hecuba's throat as she clung to her son's wife until one of the princes—Helenus, Cassandra's twin brother—came to lead Andromache to her place beside Priam. Polyxena looked at Hector's widow, for once sitting at the table without her son. Astyanax must be asleep, she thought, and that's where Xanthe is: watching next to his bed.

"I think," she whispered to the Singer, "that they're waiting for you."

The Singer nodded and stood up. He walked up to the throne and bowed to Priam. He, too, Polyxena thought, had changed. He was smaller, frailer, and his voice, when he began to chant, wavered and dipped, and sounded as though it was full of tears:

"I have no lyre and no drum.
I have nothing but an old man's voice,
and I sing of Hector, fallen on the Plain.
A son to his father and to his mother also:
the child she suckled grown into a man.
Husband to his wife.
Leader to his warriors.
Companion to his brothers.
To all of us, a prince, tall as the oak that grows
south of the Skaian Gate, spreading green
branches, sheltering the citizens of Troy.
Now he is felled in the earth
like a tree splintered under the ax,
and sounds of weeping fly to the ears of the
Gods, where they watch us, high on Olympus.

The horses he loved wait in their stable
for gentle hands that stroked them every day.
His widow will lie on her marriage bed,
all her fine garments torn from her white
shoulders; her face running with tears.
Pour wine on the dry earth to honor Hector,
and the dry earth will drink it as it drank his blood.
The bird that sings to greet the dawn
sits silent now, grieving among the leaves.

Noble Greeks, and Achilles cruel in victory:
Return to us the body of our prince.
We will bring fragrant oils to anoint him.
We will cover his body in purple robes,
and flames will turn it to ash.
We will set him floating in Charon's boat
across the River Styx
and speed his journey to the Elysian Fields,
where he will stand with Herakles,
with Theseus and all the other heroes:
loved and revered forever."

When the song was finished, the Singer bowed again and made his way back to his place next to Polyxena. A murmur of approval filled the Hall, but no one spoke, and Priam and Hecuba had bowed their heads. Under her veil, the hero's mother was sobbing, and cries of anguish rose up and up into the vaulted roof. Only Andromache sat staring into the space in front of her eyes, seeing nothing; looking into the darkness of the farthest corners, as if there she would find the shadow of her dearest love.

HECTOR'S PALACE

THE SLEEPING QUARTERS

Astyanax was asleep at last. Xanthe had lost count of all the songs that she had sung to soothe him and calm him and persuade him out of her arms and into his bed. He lay there now, with his mouth half open, and the curls on his forehead were damp with sweat. The night air was sticky and heavy, even though the sun had gone down long ago, and there was for once almost no wind at all. Xanthe walked into the courtyard and looked down at the city. Usually at this time, all was dark. Every household went to sleep as early as possible, to preserve oil, and also (this was what Charitomene said) to try to find good dreams in the kingdom of sleep and forget about what was happening in the real world. Tonight, though, many windows showed light. The citizens of Troy lay awake, each one knowing that Hector was unburied out there on the Plain. Xanthe tried very hard not to think of what she had been told, but a vision of her dear master's body being dragged behind Achilles' chariot was there behind her eyelids like a fresh wall painting. What happened to the body at night? Did Achilles put a Greek soldier to guard it? Had he taken it back behind his own lines? Was there a dead Trojan prince lying in a tent down there? And how was he lying? Covered, with dignity? Or naked, like a piece of rubbish thrown out to feed the dogs? And what would happen tomorrow? Priam and Hecuba would want to burn and bury their son within the walls of Troy. Who would bring him through the Skaian Gate? Xanthe shook her head to try to rid herself of such questions and turned her mind to Alastor. How sad he must be, down there in the Blood Room. Hector had been more than his general in the field. Later, she thought, when Andromache returns from the Great Hall, I'll walk down there and spend the rest of the night, till dawn comes, sitting at Alastor's side.

She turned and went to sit beside Astyanax's bed again, and she began to cry, her tears running silent and unchecked over her cheeks. Poor little fatherless baby, she said to herself. What will become of you? Still sitting upright, she closed her eyes, and at last a kind of sleep came over her, and she heard and saw nothing.

Suddenly a sound disturbed her, and she was awake at once.

"Is that you, my lady?" she whispered. She had heard someone walking in through the outer courtyard.

"It is the Lady Andromache," said a voice that Xanthe recognized at once. Helen . . . Why was she here? Xanthe knew that her mistress's feelings toward her sister-in-law were sometimes less than friendly.

"I've brought Andromache home," Helen said to

Xanthe. "She should not be alone on such a night. I will sit with her."

"Xanthe is here now," Andromache murmured. "You can leave me. I'll wait here until it's light."

Helen didn't answer. She took Andromache's hand and led her to a couch.

"Bring cushions, Xanthe, please," she said. "And a cool drink, if you would, and we will sit here together and talk."

"I don't want to talk," said Andromache. "I have nothing to say. To you or anyone. I have nothing to do. Hector's body . . ." Andromache's voice wavered and filled with sobs, but she swallowed and made herself speak slowly and calmly. "My husband's body cannot feel what is being done to it. Only we can feel it: the pain and the shame. My body, too, is harnessed to a chariot, and every morning when Phoebus Apollo begins his journey across the sky, that's where I'll be: dragged through the day until the night releases me. And this torture will continue as long as I go on waking up each morning. It will never end. The Gods are punishing me, but I cannot think what I've done. Why don't they punish you?" Andromache turned her gray eyes on Helen. "You have done so many things . . ."

"Shh," said Helen. "Who can speak of the Gods and what they do and do not make us suffer? My heart aches for you, but you have your son to follow his father. You must be brave for his sake."

"Why have you come with me?" Andromache said suddenly. Xanthe, standing beside the couch, saw her flinch and pull away from Helen, whose arm was around her shoulders. "I have never . . . I did not . . ."

"Don't speak," Helen said. "I know that we've

never been the best of friends. Well, that's my punishment. I would have liked to know you better, but . . ."

"I saw how he looked at you," Andromache whispered. "Every man has the same look in his eyes. They are full of desire."

"Hector was always kind to me," Helen said. "From the very first day. No one else was. Even you wouldn't speak to me properly. And Cassandra . . . She actually ran away and hid from me, as though I were a plague carrier. Hector made me welcome. That's all. Nothing more than that, truly. Also, you forget how much in love I was at that time."

"And later? Were you still in love with Paris later?"

"Yes, of course I was . . . I am. There is no one but Paris for me. You know the story. That's how Aphrodite has arranged it. We are all in all to each other."

Silence fell. Xanthe realized that both Helen and Andromache knew this was not quite true, and yet neither of them was saying a word. The truth was: Paris tried his luck with everyone, and because he was so handsome, many, many women lay down for him. There wasn't a child in the city who didn't grow up knowing that. It had been common gossip as long as Xanthe could remember, and Marpessa had told her things . . . So Helen was lying to comfort Andromache. And if she is lying about that, Xanthe thought, she could be lying about Hector. Hector and Helen . . . Her mind refused to accept it. But anything was possible. Those arrows, like the one that had struck her when she laid eyes on Alastor . . . Those arrows were everywhere, and there was little a person could do to avoid them. Xanthe turned her thoughts to Hector, trying to imagine him alive and with Helen, but the image of his bloodstained corpse sprang into her mind again. Whatever his feelings for Helen had been, they were no longer of any importance.

"I loved him," Andromache said. "If he could be alive again, I wouldn't even mind him leaving my side and lying with you."

"You would," said Helen. "Of course you'd mind."

"Yes," said Andromache. "I would. I couldn't bear it." She made her hands into fists and ground them into the sockets of her eyes. "However I imagine his body, it is a torture to me. I can't stop seeing him . . ."

Helen put her arms around Andromache. "I'll stay with you. I'll stay all night, and all tomorrow, and for as long as you need me. You'll never be alone."

The shadows lengthened in the room. Andromache was still lying silent on the couch. She had not moved for a long time. When darkness filled every corner, Xanthe went to fetch a torch to light the lamps.

"Poor creature," Helen whispered. "She's completely exhausted. I'll sit with her till she wakes up. She will dream of him alive and her waking will be terrible."

"Will you take a drink, Lady?" Xanthe said, and Helen shook her head. Golden light from the lamp shone on the ruby that hung around her neck, and it stained her skin with scarlet. She said, "You're my Marpessa's sister, aren't you? I can see it now, although you're much fairer than she is. I should go back to Paris and see how he is. After all, Hector was his brother." Helen sighed. "They all think we're so happy, don't they? Isn't that what people say? You can tell me, child."

Xanthe hung her head. "They say that you love each other, but no one says you're happy. Many say that you miss your country and your child."

Helen took the fabric of her skirt between two fingers and began to twist it.

"He thinks I know nothing. He thinks I see nothing, but I've always known. He has little bites of everything that takes his fancy, like a boy at the fruit market. Before I even met him, while he was living on Mount Ida, before he even came to Troy, he loved a nymph called Oenone. Did you know that? Do people talk about that? They're all so preoccupied with the war that they've forgotten all about her, but I haven't. Sometimes I wonder about her . . . how she feels seeing me with him. And sometimes I look at him and ask myself whether it isn't Oenone he's thinking about. The person who told me about her was very clear that he truly did love her."

"Perhaps," said Xanthe, wanting Helen to go on, wanting her to know that she was glad to listen, "the person who told you wanted you to be jealous of this nymph. Perhaps they wanted to hurt you. Lord Paris has lived with you for ten years, after all."

Helen smiled. "You're a clever child. Of course you're right. It was Queen Hecuba who made sure that I knew all about it. She still disapproves of me, even now. Paris is her little child, who was taken from her at birth and was then restored to her. She's besotted with him. And do you want to know what the very saddest thing is?"

Xanthe nodded. Helen continued. "I don't really

care anymore. Isn't that dreadful? My love, this love that has nearly drowned the city in blood, is fading. It's nearly gone. There *are* times when he sets my flesh on fire . . . Forgive me for speaking so frankly . . . And then it's like it was at the beginning, but more and more often I look at him and think: Is this what I left my country for?" Helen shook her head, as if to clear it, and grasped Xanthe by the arm. "Please say nothing. To anyone. I'm ashamed to be so loose tongued. Promise me."

"I promise. I won't say a word to anyone. Not even to my sister."

"She knows. Your sister, I sometimes think, knows everything."

Xanthe smiled. "She has never said a word to me. She loves you, Lady."

"And she's been like a daughter all the time I've been here. She reminds me of Hermione, even though she looks nothing like her." Helen laughed. "But how do I know what my own child looks like anymore?"

She turned her face to Xanthe, and there were tears streaming down her cheeks. "I will stop," she said. "I don't know what . . . It's grief, that's all. Grief speaking through my mouth."

From the couch, Andromache moaned in her sleep, and Helen said, "She'll wake up soon. I must be ready when she does, with no tears to be seen anywhere." She wiped her eyes with the edge of her scarf and smiled. On her white skin, there was no sign at all of sorrow. She was smiling, as she almost always did, and beauty shone out of her eyes, more radiant than any lamp.

MARPESSA'S
BEDCHAMBER

Marpessa stood by the door and looked at Alastor lying in her bed. The night was nearly over, and she hadn't closed her eyes. Paris and Helen had not returned. Well, that was to be expected. They had probably stayed with Priam and Hecuba, to comfort them. Sleep would visit very few people tonight. She shivered in the cool night air. What had happened? What had she done? Part of her, most of her, knew that she should feel shame. She had let a man know her and was no better than the serving maids and silly girls who let themselves be pushed up against a wall by the first drunken lout who fancied them. And I can't, she said to herself, blame him. I could have done many things: Got up out of the bed. Turned away. Kicked him. Alastor is wounded, and I am stronger than he is, at least for now. She made her way to the courtyard and sat on Helen's seat under the pomegranate tree, and remembering how she had felt filled her once again with a sort of sweet longing in all her limbs, and she was washed all over with what seemed to her like a fever.

"And this is just the beginning," someone whispered.

"Love is like a drug. The more you taste, the more you need."

"Lady Aphrodite," Marpessa breathed. "I knew you were there, but I couldn't see you at first. Why have you done this to me? What will I tell my sister?"

"I have done this to you because everyone else is busy. They're involved with Hades and ignoring me. That's not something I'm used to. Besides, your sister, as I've told you, needs to be shown the power of Love. And this Alastor is not her fate. Say nothing to her. She doesn't need to know."

"But she loves him," Marpessa said. "And I have never, ever lied to Xanthe."

The Goddess shrugged. "Perhaps you will have to begin now. It's almost impossible to be in love and tell the truth to everyone. You'll see. Do you love him?"

"I want him. Is that the same thing?"

"Sometimes it is. Sometimes it's an illusion. I haven't decided which, in your case . . ."

"Have mercy, Lady Aphrodite. Please don't let me suffer."

"Suffering is part of it. You know that. And as for mercy, I have no idea what that is. It'll be light soon. Go back to your bed."

Marpessa gazed at the Goddess as she melted into the shadows, with her gauzy robes billowing around her like smoke. Alastor. She remembered in every part of her body his long, hard legs wrapped round hers, his breath in her hair, and his mouth open. Marpessa was breathless as she ran to her room. This, she thought, this is like being a fish on the end of a line: I am being pulled and pulled and I'm gasping for every breath, and I can do nothing at all.

THE BLOOD ROOM

Soon the dawn would be here. Already, behind the mountains, there was a pale glow in the sky. All the better. Xanthe tried not to be frightened of the darkness (*there's nothing to be frightened of, Astyanax darling . . . it's only that Phoebus Apollo's horses are resting for the night, that's all . . .* That's what Andromache always said), but it was more comfortable to walk around in the light, and even though the sun wasn't truly up, at least now the air was pearly, like the inside of a shell, and there were fewer shadows to worry about. Xanthe made her way silently out of the courtyard and walked toward the Blood Room, past the palace where Paris was probably waiting for Helen and wondering where she was, past the kitchens, past the bathhouses and the stables, where she knew Iason would be spending the night, tending to the horses. He said they knew everything, and if that was true, then they must be sad, too; just as sad as many people in the city who hardly knew Hector but still felt his death as a wound somewhere in a hidden part of themselves.

The Blood Room was still dark. Xanthe looked over to Alastor's pallet and gasped aloud, and then covered her mouth with one hand, so that none of the other men lying there asleep should waken. Alastor's bed was empty. She went over to it and bent down to touch the bedclothes, saying to herself: You're mad, Xanthe. You could see from the door that he isn't here. What are you doing feeling about among the covers, as though he had flattened himself to nothing? She sighed. Where could he be? His mother, Xanthe thought, the frightful Phrontis, has probably come and gathered him to her bosom, and forced him to go home with her, and I don't even know where his house is. Polyxena knows, though, and I'll ask her. Xanthe turned to leave. Suddenly the smell of wounds and sweating bodies overcame her, and she hurried out into the early morning. Someone was striding quickly down the hill toward the city. She looked after him: a tall man, still wearing black armor, even before dawn. I've seen him before, Xanthe thought. I remember. I saw him here once, in the Blood Room, and then again on the Plain, just before . . . She shivered, remembering Hector's death. I must find out who he is, she thought. I must ask. And as she turned her head, all memory of the Black Warrior left her. She breathed the cool air. Very soon now, the sun would be visible. The bulk of the mountain was black against a sky the color of ripe peaches. Xanthe stared at her feet as she walked, and because she was weary, the rhythm of her own footsteps lulled her, so that she was almost dreaming as she walked. Then, suddenly, out of a doorway that she hadn't noticed, came a hand, and it gripped her own arm just above the wrist.

"Little Xanthe," said a voice thick with drink. "I bin waitin'. Knew I'd find you if I waited long enough. Don't you rec-rec—er—nize . . . It's me . . . B'ros."

144

Xanthe felt cold flooding through her veins, and she trembled with terror. Boros. Drunk and slobbering and holding on to her wrist. She looked down at his thick arm covered in black hairs, like an animal's pelt, and shuddered.

"Let me go," she said. "I shall scream. I have to go home."

"Nonsess. Don' scream. No one'll take any no'ice. Think you're crying for 'Ector. Like the rest of 'em. Come o'er 'ere and gissa kiss . . ."

"No," said Xanthe. "I'm home. Let me go."

"Na," said Boros. "You come over 'ere and gissa hug. I wanna hug. Thassall."

He pulled Xanthe to him, and his arms were around her. I'll die, she thought. If I can't escape, I'll die. She wondered if anyone had ever died of disgust before. He's drunk, she thought. He's stronger than me, but I don't care. She brought her knee up and rammed it as hard as she could there, where she knew all men were powerful, and where, too, they could be sorely hurt, and Boros howled and his meaty hands fell away from her flesh. She didn't stop to look behind her, but ran as fast as she could up the hill to Hector's palace.

In the courtyard, she stumbled and half fell, half threw herself onto the ground and began to weep. She cried for a long time, and the salt of the tears she shed fell on her lips like balm. The tears were cleaning her heart from the inside, and at last there were no more to be shed, and Xanthe dried her eyes on the edge of her robe. It was filthy anyway, and even if it had been the cleanest garment in the world, she would have found a fire somewhere and burned it. Xanthe thought about what had happened and marveled at what she had done. It was not something she would ever have imagined herself doing . . . actually hurting a man. A very big man, too. When she knew she had to run, to flee, there was no fear in her at all, but now that the danger was over, a picture of exactly what could have happened came into her mind, and she began to shiver with the horror of it. The memory of Boros's hands on her body . . . She felt slimy all over, as if night creatures had walked on her skin. Wash, she thought. I must wash and wash and wash and scrub him from me. Quickly, before Astyanax wakes up and calls for me. The sun was over the rim of the mountain: golden and new. Another day.

MARPESSA'S
BEDCHAMBER

For much of the night, Marpessa had lain awake, aware of the warm body beside her. When they were tiny girls, still living with Charitomene before they were old enough to be sent to work for Helen and Andromache, Xanthe had shared her bed, and Marpessa had forgotten how comforting it was to hear another person breathing in the dark, how safe she had felt when she woke from a bad dream, knowing that her sister would listen and speak to her and make all the terrifying night shadows that lived in the corners of the room look quite ordinary again. Now the window was showing light, and soon the sun would wake Alastor. She pushed back the covers and left the bed.

"Come back," Alastor said. "Please come and lie next to me again."

"Shh!" said Marpessa. "I thought you were asleep. You must be silent. Paris and Helen will wake up and find us. Come, I'll help you up, and you must go back to the Blood Room."

"I refuse to go back there. Let me stay here, with you."

"No." Marpessa spoke urgently, kneeling down beside the bed and shaking Alastor a little to make him see, to stop him dreaming. "You don't understand. You have to go. What happened last night . . ."

"You didn't mind then. I thought . . ."

"I know. I didn't mind, but I was somewhere else. I wasn't thinking properly. It mustn't happen again. And you must say nothing about it to anyone. Promise me."

"Why? Why should I? Are you ashamed?"

"Yes. I wanted it then, and I don't . . . I will remember it always, but please, I can't see you again, and you must forget all about me."

Alastor laughed. "I don't see why. I don't see why I can't have some pleasure in my life. After all, we don't know how long the war'll go on, and as soon as I go back to the fighting, I might be killed at any time."

Marpessa smiled. The old women were right. They'd told her: All young men use those words as a spell to pull young girls into their beds.

"You won't catch me like that," she said. "And I don't want to hurt my sister. She mustn't ever, ever know what's happened between us."

"Why not?"

"Because she loves you. She told me so. If she knew what we'd done, she'd be more unhappy than I could bear."

"But I've never said a word, never done anything to show . . ."

"I know. And I also know that your mother has probably singled out a young woman for you to marry. Am I right?"

Alastor groaned. "I may die first. But you're right. There is someone. She's from beyond Ida, where her father owns vineyards and fields, and the Gods know how much money she has, but my mother has decided on a wedding. And what my mother decides on comes to pass every time. But that shouldn't make any difference to us. I don't love this person my mother's found. I've only met her once or twice. Please, Marpessa. Please don't turn me away. Meet me sometimes. I won't tell anyone. I won't breathe a word to your sister. I'll find somewhere safe where we can be completely alone. Say you will."

"I'm not saying anything. You must go. Can you walk? Quickly, before they all wake up and find us."

Alastor struggled out of bed.

"I'm going. Kiss me before I leave."

"I mustn't."

"Only one kiss. I promise. Then I'll go, and you may never see me again."

"Very well. Come outside."

They tiptoed through the house, still shadowy in the early dawn. They went through the courtyard and to the gate with Alastor holding tight to Marpessa's hand.

"Farewell," he said, and bent his head to kiss her. She turned her face to him, and his mouth on hers filled her with longing. Would they ever lie together again, as they had last night? I mustn't, she thought. Nothing but harm can come from it. She closed her eyes and filled her nostrils with the smell of him, and drew him to her with her hands so that his body was close to her once more. Fear filled her suddenly, and she knew that if he summoned her, if he found a hidden place where they could be safe, she would not be able to stay away.

"Silence," she said, letting him go. "Remember to say nothing."

He smiled and turned and made his way down the hill toward his mother's house. Marpessa closed her eyes. Aphrodite, help me, she thought. Help me forget him.

ANDROMACHE'S GARDEN

Andromache walked to the seat under the fig tree without knowing quite where she was going. She had to remind herself over and over again of where she was, and who was with her, because otherwise she felt herself to be a moving mass of pain. Every word that was spoken hurt her, and her skin was bruised by every kind glance that fell on it. Meals were a torment, with silence filling the Great Hall. How could she eat? She sat and stared at the food set in front of her, and could not even bring herself to lift it to her mouth. Cassandra and Hecuba also had not eaten for three days. Cassandra's face was white and thin, and spots of livid color stood out on her cheeks. Her eyes were dry, but purple shadows stained the skin beneath them. I am better away from all of them, Andromache thought. I am better alone. And the darkness covers me a little; keeps my agony hidden from everyone. She sat wearily down on the seat and closed her eyes. Sleep was impossible. Every night, for as long as she could, she roamed about the house, because when she lay down, there was nothing she could do to stop the tears falling from the corners of her eyes and soaking into the pillows under her head.

"It's too much," said a voice next to her, and Andromache looked around, surprised. Who was this who must have accompanied her from the Great Hall without her even being aware of it?

"Who are you?" she said after looking closely at the woman sitting next to her. Could she have been waiting for me here in the garden? Andromache wondered. I've never seen her before, but she seems to be a person of some standing. Her blue robes shimmered in the feeble light that came from the open doorway. Her face was lined, but in her youth she must have been beautiful.

"Never mind me," said the woman. "Listen while I tell you what I think."

Part of Andromache thought: Why should I do what she says? And why don't I ask her again what her name is and where she comes from? She closed her eyes while the woman went on and on talking.

"You have suffered so much, my dear. Your pain is terrible. It's all been too much. This is what happens when they fight . . . the men. Killing your husband: Well, that was bad enough, but to treat his body like that! Men don't even do that to the animals they hunt. I know . . . I know what you feel, with your husband's body unburied, but do not fear. Soon, soon all the rites will be performed, and meanwhile his body is safe. I am keeping it safe myself. No harm will come to it."

"Who are you?" Andromache whispered.

"I am the Goddess Hera. Wife to Zeus."

Andromache sighed. "I must be dreaming. This is a dream."

"Call it what you will. I only came to tell you that

what Achilles did today will not pass unavenged. Do you know of it? Have they told you?"

Andromache shook her head.

"They don't want to burden you, for you have enough to bear. But today Achilles slaughtered twelve Trojan prisoners of war. There are twelve widows in the city tonight, feeling as you do. He only did it to show his power, to show that he could. He has become too proud, and as usual it's left to me to put a stop to things when the men go too far. But Achilles knows that the end is coming for him, too. He heard your husband's words, torn from his throat as he died: *Remember me when my brother Paris kills you in the shadow of the Skaian Gate.* While he's awake, he can forget them for a while. There are drums beating and brave songs in the air, but when the sun goes down and he lies in his tent alone, those words are loud, loud in his ears. Paris isn't sleeping so well, either. For the first time since he came here with Menelaus's wife, he's beginning to realize what his actions will mean. He heard his brother's words, too, you know, and he's filled with anguish and terror, you may be sure. How? he thinks, and he tosses and turns in his bed. How will I kill the terrible Achilles? There's no rest for Paris."

Andromache stared at the blue-clad figure, and even as she tried to summon words that might be suitable to utter to the queen of all Olympus, the solid shape beside her on the stone seat began to dissolve and melt away, like smoke blown by a strong breeze.

"Wait, Goddess," she said. "Don't go—speak more of my husband. Tell me where he is—tell me."

Andromache looked around her. The whole garden

was empty, and her ears rang with the silence that filled the shadowy place. She had fallen asleep for a few moments and dreamed a dream. That was all. After a few moments, when she tried to think of what the dream was about, she could remember almost nothing. A woman in blue had come to sit next to her.

HELEN'S PALACE

One thread after another. Marpessa was finding it harder and harder to concentrate on her work. Since the time when she had let herself be wound around with Aphrodite's enchantments, there had been no rest in her mind and none in her body. Everyone, from those in the royal household to the very lowliest citizen of Troy, was wounded by Hector's death, and worse than that, by what Achilles was doing to his body, and the whole of Troy was in torment.

So it's unkind and selfish of me, Marpessa said to herself, to think of myself so constantly: the things that I did, and the feelings that come to my body and my skin so that sometimes I'm almost fainting. The next thread . . . I'll think of that. Red, the color of blood and death and war. It seems my hands are following my mind and choosing suitable colors.

"Pessa? May I come in?"

"Xanthe! Oh, Xanthe, it's been so long since we've seen each other." Marpessa left the loom and went to greet her sister. "Can you stay? Sit here. Can Andromache spare you?"

Xanthe sat down on a couch Helen used to lie on when she grew tired of the weaving. You could imagine her on it, she thought, stretched out on the yielding pillows decorated with elaborate patterns woven into the cloth: vines and flowers and birds.

"It's awful there. I've been longing to come and see you, but I can't leave them. Today I couldn't bear it any longer, so I've run away to you. Poor Andromache paces the rooms like a lioness and doesn't cry, but I can see the pain in her and I know she's holding it all in because of Astyanax, and then Helen comes and sits with her, and so does Hecuba, and I go down to the Blood Room, but that's worse now than it ever was. Everything I see there reminds me of Hector's poor body, and then I want to be sick. And Alastor isn't there anymore. That's the worst thing. I asked Charitomene, and she told me that he hasn't come back since I took him to the walls on the day that Hector died. She says he's gone back to frightful Phrontis. She says Phrontis is his mother, after all, and some people say she has stocks of food no one knows anything about, because of who she knows outside the city. Now I don't know if I'll ever see him again. Polyxena says his mother probably keeps him under guard, to prevent me from getting at him. I can't bear not to see him, Pessa. My whole body feels as if it's in pain."

Marpessa chose another thread from the basket and pretended to be concentrating hard on deciding exactly where it should go.

"You're very quiet. Why aren't you saying anything?" Xanthe continued. "Comforting me? What will I do if I can never see Alastor again?"

This question, at least, Marpessa could answer.

"Your life will continue as before. You'll be unhappy for a time, and then less unhappy."

"I suppose so. But do you think I should go to his house and try to see him? Would it be wrong to tell him how I feel? Why are men so stupid? Why don't they understand what our looks and movements mean? He must have felt my love for him coming through my fingers as I dressed his wounds."

"He did say that you were gentleness itself."

"Did he?" Xanthe smiled for the first time, and her face was bright with pleasure. "How wonderful! What else did he say? I asked Polyxena to look after him on the day Hector died . . . Did you take her place while she attended to the Singer? Try to remember every word he said. How long did you stay with him?"

Marpessa turned again to the wool basket and tried to look as though all her attention was on the weaving stretched on the loom before her. Her heart was beating, and a heat that was partly shame and partly fear rose up in her.

"Oh, not long. Not long at all. I just took him to a house belonging to a friend of his and left him there."

"What friend? He never said anything about a friend to me."

"I don't know. I didn't ask." Marpessa pretended to find a mistake on the loom and bent her head to hide her red face. How hard it was to tell such lies! How was she going to be able to keep on and on doing it? Fortunately Xanthe was still thinking about Alastor and not noticing her.

"Honestly, Marpessa. You're so vague. You never notice anything important. You knew I'd be interested. Do you remember at least where the house was?"

"No, I don't," said Marpessa. "It's no good getting angry with me. You've forgotten what that day was like—what we were all feeling. It's all right for you. You didn't watch. You never have watched. But I did. I saw it. Everything. The blood. Achilles standing over Hector, pushing the spear down—have you had enough? Shall I go on? Do you want to hear about how he slit the flesh above his ankles?"

"No, stop!" Xanthe was sobbing. "I'm sorry. I don't want to hear anything. Anything."

Marpessa ran to her sister and put her arms around her.

"No, it's me. I'm sorry. I know you hate all of that. I'm just angry with you for being angry with me for no reason. I was being childish." Oh, Gods, how will I do this? I can't even look at her, because I blush with shame at my own lies. How will this all end?

Xanthe's sobs calmed a little. Marpessa continued. "You're my big sister, but I feel older than you most of the time. You're so gentle. You're so soft that I worry about what will happen to you."

Xanthe sniffed. "I'm not as soft as you think. I can look after myself. You'd be amazed."

Marpessa laughed. "I would be amazed. I don't believe you. What would you do in a crisis?"

"I can tell you that," Xanthe said. "I kneed Boros in the groin the other day."

Marpessa's mouth fell open. "You didn't. You couldn't have. Did you? Truly? Why haven't you said anything before?"

"I wanted to forget all about it." Xanthe shivered. "He's so disgusting. I was on my way home from the Blood Room on the morning after Hector's death, and he jumped out at me and started pawing at me and hanging on to me, and I just kicked him where it really, really hurts. That's all."

"Well, I'm proud of you." Marpessa smiled. "But be careful. He'll be hurt now. His vanity, I mean, as well as his boiled squid."

Xanthe started to giggle, and soon she and Marpessa were weeping with laughter. Every time it faded a little, Xanthe said "boiled squid," and they began shrieking all over again, each of them knowing that the mirth was only a temporary relief from her true feelings.

THE SINGER'S HOUSE

"Wait!" Polyxena said. "Don't say a word. Come into this room before my grandfather hears you and decides to see what's going on. He's worse than any woman, and if he knows there's a story unfolding somewhere in the house, he'll come sniffing around to see what it is."

"You are talking about me again, child," said the Singer, shuffling out of a darkened chamber and smiling at Xanthe. "Greetings, Xanthe. My granddaughter thinks I should rest. She doesn't understand that it does me good to see and speak to young people. I need to be up-to-date with all the gossip. Have you got a good story for me?"

Xanthe shook her head. "I'm afraid not. I wanted to ask Polyxena a favor."

"Go on then, don't let an old man disturb you. I'll just sit myself down"—he lowered himself stiffly onto a stool— "and you girls can just forget all about me."

"Come over here," said Polyxena, and when Xanthe came closer to her, she whispered, "He doesn't realize that people might want a bit of privacy sometimes. Are you all right?"

Xanthe shook her head. "Alastor's disappeared. I don't know where he could have gone. Marpessa said she took him to a friend's house on the day Hector died, but she can't remember anything about where it is, or what the friend's name is, and I'm afraid I've left it too late. We are still mourning in Andromache's house, and Astyanax knows there's something wrong, and doesn't exactly know what it is, but it makes him naughty, and fretful at night, and I'm so tired . . ."

"Alastor's probably back with his mother by now. The frightful Phrontis. I'll take you there and we'll find him, you'll see."

"Just as long," said the Singer from his corner, where he had been sitting with his eyes closed, pretending to sleep, "as you keep Phrontis well away from me. That woman's voice can singe a person's ears. And there's a history between us."

"You're a nosy old man!" Polyxena smiled. "Xanthe didn't want you to hear what she was saying. What history? You must tell us. It's the least you can do."

"Well, she's always been frightful, but long ago she wasn't the most unattractive woman in Troy. And she was a widow. One night when the wine was flowing rather freely, I'm afraid I let my hands get a little carried away—you know how it is—and from that day on, she pursued me. That's the only way to put it. I was forced to hide from her many times. She understood that I wasn't interested, in the end."

The Singer chuckled, and Polyxena said, "Go back to sleep, dear Grandfather. You men are all the same. It doesn't matter if you're young or old. Led by your desires."

"She's the one," said the Singer. "She was led by *her* desires. But of course you're right, child. You're wiser than your years. We are all creatures of the flesh. All of us. I could tell you some things that would surprise you. When Helen first came to the city, for instance, there wasn't a male in the Palace who didn't lust after her. Even Hector . . . but perhaps I should not speak of the dead in this way."

"What about Lord Hector?" said Xanthe. "You can't start a story and not continue. Please tell us."

The Singer said. "There you are. That's a good sign. You have room for something else in your head apart from this son of Phrontis's. You are clearly not about to rush down and visit Mother Poison and buy some concoction that will end your suffering."

"Please tell us about Lord Hector," Polyxena said.

"It's nothing, really. Or not much, or I would have told you the story before. Also, I never saw any sign of its being true. I once heard someone . . . I forget who . . . It was during a feast of some kind, a very long time ago. Deiphobus, perhaps."

"It doesn't matter who it was!" Polyxena laughed. "Are you going to tell us the story or just torment us?"

"It's nothing much," the Singer said. "Only that Deiphobus said Lord Hector was as dazzled by Helen as the rest of them, and hadn't been slow to show her how *strong* his feelings were. Those were his exact words, and he kept emphasizing the word *strong* then making all sorts of rude gestures—I'm sure I don't have to demonstrate exactly *what* gestures—and everyone nodded and made even worse gestures and laughed into their wine."

"I don't believe it," Xanthe said. "Deiphobus is jealous of his brothers, everyone knows that. *He's* the one who wants Helen for himself. Even I've noticed how close he stands to her, whenever Paris isn't there . . . Not Hector. Hector loved Andromache. You know he did."

"Of course he did, but it doesn't make any difference. You don't understand, child, because you are still very young. I know about such things, because Love and Desire are such wonderful subjects. I've been making up poems about them for years and years. You girls should learn that just because a man loves one person, that doesn't mean he can't desire another. Or even many others."

"Of course we know that, dear Singer," said Xanthe. "And even though we're young, we're not stupid, and we *have* been walking around in these palaces all our lives. But I need Polyxena to take me to Phrontis's house. I don't even know where it is."

"I do," said Polyxena. "We'll brave the monster in her lair. Hercules himself would quake, but I'm not frightened. I'm curious, that's why. Nothing to do with you. I want to see whether she's got someone lined up for her beloved son."

"When can we go?" Xanthe asked.

"As soon," Polyxena answered, "as Lord Hector is buried."

"Poor Andromache," Xanthe said. "My own pain made me forget her, and now that I think of her, I feel her pain instead. I'm going. I should have been there long ago."

"And will you admit that I've made you feel a little better?" Polyxena put her arms around her friend and hugged her.

"You always make me feel better, Polyxena. You're my friend."

"And I, too, have helped to make you happier," said the Singer. "Admit it, child, and flatter an old man who has the thankless task these days of composing nothing but elegies or songs to rouse an army to battle. I wish I could be writing love poems instead."

"Yes, Singer, you have been very kind. I thank you both."

Xanthe stepped out of the shadowy room into the last of the afternoon light. Phoebus Apollo's chariot was rushing toward the cool waves of the ocean, leaving a trail of scarlet and gold in the sky behind it.

THE GOSSIPS

PRIAM'S PALACE

Theano, Danae, and Halie worked almost in silence. Instead of talking freely, they could only whisper, because of where they were and what they were doing. Queen Hecuba had summoned them to the storehouse, where all the ceremonial linen was kept, together with what remained of the wealth of the royal household.

"What d'you think she's up to?" Theano muttered, and Halie said, "Shh, here they come. Both of them, not just Hecuba. We'll know soon enough."

They could hear Priam raging from far away.

"Anyone else . . . any single other one of my useless children . . . I would give anything for Hector to be alive now, even the life of another of my offspring. Why him? Why the best? Answer me that, woman."

"Calm yourself, husband," Hecuba said, "for the Gods tell us what must happen, and now they have shown themselves most clearly. The meaning of your dream was plain."

"It wasn't a dream, I keep telling you. I saw her. Iris, the messenger of the Gods. She spoke to me and told me exactly what I have to do. And though it makes me ill to think of begging at the knees of that dog Achilles, I will do it for Hector. But we need to empty our coffers and give him all our best treasures."

"That's it," Danae whispered. "We're here to open chests and boxes and whatnot. The queen, poor thing, can't do it on her own. Have you ever seen inside them? Last time I looked was years ago, but there are things in there to make you weep with longing. No one does work like that nowadays. Wool that fine you'd think some spider Goddess had the weaving of it. And there's decorated linens in there as well, dyed all the colors you can think of."

"Theano, Halie, Danae," Hecuba called to them. "We're preparing the ransom for Hector's body. Take everything you can see that's worth anything at all"— she waved a hand toward the boxes—"and pile it up over there. I'll send for some men to carry it to the wagon." She turned back to her husband and spoke to him gently. "I'll tell you something else I have arranged, my dear. You will not cross the Plain alone at dead of night . . . a man of your age."

"How dare you arrange things without consulting me first, woman? I am not only your husband, but still the king while there's breath in my body. How dare you change the conditions that were laid down? Achilles specified. I must come alone, he said."

"You may be king, but you're a fool all the same. He didn't mean 'alone' as you think he did. He meant: No soldiers. No advisers. No ceremony. Achilles won't lay eyes on the people I've asked to go with you."

"People! More than one . . ." Priam was lost for words.

"Iason—you must have seen him—a young stablehand from Hector's household. Someone has to help you unload. I don't want Greeks doing it. And the Singer's granddaughter, Polyxena, to look after you. Don't pretend you don't know who she is. You've often remarked on how sensible and intelligent she seems."

Priam shook his head. "Children, both of them. Nothing but children."

"You're never happy!" Hecuba was dangerously near tears. "It's obvious that Achilles wants no one of importance. He doesn't want to feel threatened by you. Imagine what he'll think if you arrive there with a proper royal retinue! I found you young attendants on purpose, don't you see? No one could possibly fear either of them. In any case, it's all organized, and I don't want to hear another word about it."

She went over to the chest and opened it.

"Meanwhile, here's the gold. Cups, tripods, all sorts of things that I used to think were important. Take them all and add them to the pile." She sat down suddenly on a stool, and covered her head with her veil and began to weep.

"You start moving all this," muttered Theano to her companions. "I'll look after the queen."

Halie and Danae could hear her talking soothingly as they worked. King Priam fingered each garment as they brought it, and smoothed it down carefully.

"Twelve mantles," he muttered. "Tunics, blankets, cloaks . . . how will we cover our bodies when all this has gone?" He shook his head, then turned to Halie.

"Shall I tell you what Iris told me?"

Halie lowered her gaze to the floor. The king had never spoken so directly to her before.

"She said that Hector's body had been protected. That was her word. Hera herself has anointed it with fragrant oils, so that . . . so that no harm has come to it. Do you understand? It will be as though sleep has taken Hector in its arms, and not one single mark will be visible on his limbs of . . ." Tears stood in King Priam's eyes. "Of what happened to him at Achilles' hands." He wiped his face on a corner of his cloak and went on. "Nor of the time that has passed, nor the heat. It'll be as though he'd died yesterday."

"Yes, Sire," said Halie comfortingly to the king, but when she returned to the chest where Danae was busily folding the last garment she sucked her teeth and murmured, "He's wandering, poor old thing. It's been many dawns since Hector died. Dogs, rats, birds: Who knows what creatures the bastard Greeks have allowed to gnaw at his flesh? And even without that, the heat all by itself will have made the body smell so dreadful that they'll be holding their noses on Mount Olympus."

"Shh!" said Danae. "He'll hear you. Poor thing! If he wants to believe that Goddesses come to him in the night and tell him things, then let him. Bear our sorrows as best we can, all of us, don't we?"

At last the work was done. Theano, Danae, and Halie closed the doors of wardrobes and the lids of chests, as the menservants took the treasure to the courtyard ready to load onto the wagon.

"You may go now," Hecuba said. "And we thank you for your help."

The women made their way to the kitchens.

"Doesn't help, does it?" Theano said. "Being grand and owning lands as far as the eye can see. When your child is dead, he's dead, and that's a pain in your heart as long as you live."

"Hector's worse than dead," Halie pointed out. "He's unburied. King's right to go and ask Achilles for the body. Burying his son is more important than war and pride and silly things like that."

"What if Achilles refuses? And what about Hector's body? You said it yourself. It'll be rotting by now, whatever the poor old king thinks. What'll seeing *that* do to him, d'you think?" Danae asked.

"Always expecting the worst, you are," Theano said. "Why can't it all be true? Iris visiting the king, and all that stuff about the body."

"If you expect terrible things," Danae said, "then they don't surprise you, and all good things are like wonderful gifts."

The three women found some baked dried corn-cakes in the kitchens left over from the last meal, and they ate them silently, dipping the hard crusts into a bowl of olive oil as the Goddess of Dawn stepped over the dark mountains in her pink robes and into the sky above the city.

ON THE PLAIN AND OUTSIDE ACHILLES' TENT

Polyxena fixed her eyes on Iason's back. He was sitting up in the front of the wagon with the driver. There was only one seat at the back, and Priam, wrapped up in a warm cloak, sat in it and stared at the darkness with his lips firmly closed. Polyxena perched on one of the chests of treasure and listened to her heart beating with excitement and something like terror. When Queen Hecuba had summoned her and told her the plan, she'd made it all seem easy.

"Look after him as if he were the Singer" were her words. "Make sure he doesn't do anything stupid."

But the Singer talked all the time, and the king said nothing. He was heartbroken, of course, but that wouldn't have stopped the Singer. Perhaps he didn't consider a young girl worthy of conversation. I don't care, Polyxena said to herself. Iason is here. And maybe I'll see the great Achilles himself.

The wagon made its way slowly across the Plain. The black sky seemed to press down on it as it crossed the landscape. Polyxena wondered who the driver was. She didn't recognize him. He was very thin and dressed in gray robes. His skin was gray, too. Surely there should be some light from somewhere? This darkness was thick and hot, like a blanket thrown over the wagon. Polyxena peered into it, trying to make out the lights of the Greek camp. You could see their watch fires from the wall, so why were they invisible now? Priam, Iason, and the silent driver were nothing but blacker shapes in the night. Suddenly they stopped, and if she hadn't seen it with her own eyes, Polyxena would not have believed it. The darkness thinned, and out of a dissolving fog everything became visible again. There was the line of tents, and the fires in front of them, and men crouched beside them. Greeks. Two armed soldiers were waiting for the wagon, and they took hold of the horse's head.

"King Priam?" said one of them.

"I am here," said the king in a breaking voice. His hands shook and trembled as Polyxena helped him down from the wagon. They were cold. She had wondered what Greek soldiers would look like when you were very close to them, but they were no different from Trojans. Men, that was all. Ordinary men.

"King Priam is to come with us," said one of them. "We'll see to the unloading of the wagon."

"I'm supposed to unload it," said Iason, and Polyxena thought how brave he was to say such a thing to a man twice his age and nearly twice his size.

"Suit yourself," said the Greek. "But my fellows will take the stuff away. Does that meet with your approval?"

"It does," said Iason gravely, and Polyxena smiled to herself. Iason wasn't very good at knowing when people were being sarcastic.

"You," the Greek turned to Polyxena, "can wait

here. I'll see that they bring you some warming drink."

"I don't want a warming drink, but I thank you," Polyxena said. "I can't stay here, though. I promised the queen that I'd go with King Priam to Lord Achilles' tent."

The Greek sighed and said, "Suit yourself. Follow me. You can't go in, though. Not right into the tent. You do know that, don't you?"

"I'll sit outside and wait for the king," Polyxena said. She turned to Priam and put a hand on his arm, just as she always did with the Singer. "Come, Sire. It's time to go."

Priam, with Polyxena to help him, walked slowly behind the soldier who was leading the way to Achilles' tent. She knew, from his silence and his trembling, which she could feel because she was so close to him, that the old man was afraid. Only his love of Hector drove him to face his son's killer. Achilles was unpredictable, everyone said. Was Priam frightened for his own life? Whatever his feelings, when they reached the tent, he became someone quite different. Later, when she spoke of it to Iason, Polyxena called it "a transformation." The old king drew himself up to his full height and strode into Achilles' tent as though he had come to discuss some treaty. Once again he was the ruler of a great city.

The tent flaps fell closed behind Priam as he entered, and Polyxena sat down to wait on a wooden seat close by. Two Greek soldiers guarded the entrance, with spears in their hands.

"You're wondering what's going on in there, aren't you?"

Polyxena started. It was the driver of their wagon. Where had he come from? Where was Iason? Was this person going to be difficult? Polyxena was not really frightened, because there were people near, and she could scream as loudly as any wild creature, if she had to, but this gray person made her feel cold. Perhaps the night air was unusually chilly, but she felt as though she were sitting, quite suddenly, in an icy place. She nodded. "I'd like to know. I'd like to make sure Achilles is treating the king properly."

"He is. He will. Priam is on his knees in front of him. Appealing to him, in the name of his own aged father, to be merciful to an old man and release Hector's body for burial . . ."

"How do you know? You can't see in the tent any more than I can."

"I see everything. I am Hades, the God of Death."

Polyxena thought, I knew there was something wrong with this wagon driver. The poor queen probably couldn't find any normal drivers willing to risk crossing the Plain at night. I must find Iason. What's happened to him?

"He is tending to the horse," said Hades. "And Achilles is raising Priam to his feet. The old man has moved him. He's reminded of his own father, far away. He is giving orders that Hector's body be bathed in the finest oils and prepared for burial. *Take a purple cloak*, Achilles is saying, *to wrap the body in*. And servants will bring food and drink for the two men."

"He won't eat," Polyxena said. "He hasn't eaten since Hector died. And he hasn't closed his eyes in sleep, either."

"Now that the rites can be performed," said Hades,

"Priam's heart is easier. They are drinking wine. Soon they will come out, and you must be ready for him. Go and stand near the tent."

Polyxena went. By the time she reached the tent, she had forgotten what the wagon driver had said to her. Perhaps she had closed her eyes and dreamed it, but she thought she remembered him saying his name was Hades. She stood and waited. When Priam came out, followed by Achilles, she went up to him and took him by the arm again.

"Come, Sire," she said.

"Hector's body is being brought to the wagon," Priam murmured, and to Achilles he said nothing, only nodded his head. Polyxena couldn't help staring at this huge, handsome man with the fair hair who stood in the entrance to the tent. Achilles. Terror of Troy. Killer of Hector. He had tears in his eyes, and Polyxena wondered whether Hector's dying words, *Remember me when my brother Paris slays you in the shadow of the Skaian Gate*, went around and around in his head every time he lay down to rest.

On the way back to Troy, because of the presence of Hector's body (which seemed to Polyxena smaller than the living person had been, as though Death had shrunk him), no one said a word. Dawn was coming up over the mountains, and the sky was growing lighter. Priam was not a king now, but only an old man with eyes reddened by tears. He looked surprised at his own womanishness and the pain he felt, and tried to cover his face with his cloak. Polyxena thought: Men are fathers just as women are mothers, and must also feel the pull of the blood that is their blood. Hector was his favorite son. How will he continue in the world without him?

Suddenly Iason said, "There's Cassandra up on the walls. They'll all come out to bring Hector's body into the city for the funeral rites."

The gates opened for the wagon, and Polyxena saw the crowds running out to meet it. They were groaning and shedding tears and tearing their clothes as they followed the progress of Hector's body to the place where the pyre had been built. The priests were waiting, and Hecuba, with her face veiled, and all Hector's brothers and sisters. Polyxena looked for Xanthe, and there she was, with Astyanax in her arms. Andromache had her head bowed, and her face was streaming with tears.

"Her bed will seem as wide and empty as the Plain tonight," said a voice in Polyxena's ear. It was the driver, Hades, who had left his seat when the body was taken off the wagon, and now suddenly appeared beside her. "I could comfort her. I could say, *You will meet your beloved husband again one day, in the Elysian Fields, where heroes live forever*; but I will say nothing. The God of Death never speaks of what will come to pass."

Polyxena turned around to tell him to take his drunken ramblings elsewhere, thank you very much, and how dare he interrupt a funeral as important as this, when she saw that he had vanished completely. She looked for him in the crowd, and for a moment thought she saw the gray robes standing at Andromache's side, but then he was gone. Iason came through the crowd toward the wagon.

"Will you come with me? I have to take this horse back to the stable."

Polyxena nodded.

"Is anything wrong?" Iason asked, noticing how solemn she was. How silent.

"No, nothing. Can you remember what that driver's name was?"

"He didn't say. I thought he'd told you."

"No, no he didn't," Polyxena said. She was ashamed to admit that she had forgotten every word the man in gray had uttered. Even his name had gone from her memory altogether. There was something very strange about it, but Polyxena was tired after the events of the night and could think only of her soft bed.

THE STABLES

As Iason brushed the coats of one horse after another, he wondered about the passage of the days and nights, and about the way that life returned to being ordinary after even the most horrifying of events. It didn't matter that men died and women wept for them; it didn't matter that every day the stories grew and spread and people muttered under their breath about omens and oracles and how the city was sure to fall soon. Ordinary things had to be attended to. Horses needed food. They needed someone to care for them. And the stray dogs and cats, although sometimes they vanished and Iason suspected they'd been caught and killed for food, still came to the stables to hunt for mice and lizards and lie in the shade next to him whenever he stopped from his work to rest. For a while after Hector's death, there was less fighting, and then the warrior women, the Amazons, had come to help their ally King Priam, and everyone in the city, even Xanthe, had stood on the walls to see their queen, Penthesilea, riding tall and beautiful on her enormous horse at the head of her troops as she came toward Troy over the Plain.

Tears came to Iason's eyes. Penthesilea was dead now, killed by Achilles. No longer beautiful, no longer brave, but gone forever, like so many others. I don't know, Iason thought, moving his brush over the flanks of a fine chestnut mare, whether there really is such a place as the Elysian Fields, or the kingdom of Hades. No one comes back to tell us what it's really like, so it could be that this life is all we have. He knew he couldn't say so to anyone, because they all believed in Gods and Goddesses, and Marpessa, Xanthe's sister, had seen them and talked to them, and there were temples all over the hills set aside for their worship, but still Iason wondered. He himself had never seen even so much as the shadow of a God.

"And if they're so wonderful," he told the mare, "why have they arranged the world so badly? Why do they allow wars to be fought? Why do we have to die at all? And why is love so complicated? Look at Xanthe. She's been walking around like a stunned sheep. All she can think of is that stuck-up Alastor."

"What are you telling that poor horse, Iason?" Xanthe spoke from the door of the stables, and Iason dropped his brush.

"Nothing," he said, stooping to pick it up. "What did you hear? I wasn't saying anything important, really. Did you hear anything?"

"Well," Xanthe settled herself on the blanket Iason used to lie down on sometimes. "I thought I heard you say something about Alastor."

"I did. I said he was stuck-up. He is stuck-up."

"He's not. He's very . . . well, not stuck-up anyway. He's rich, that's all."

"Same thing," Iason mumbled into the mare's neck, but Xanthe wasn't listening, he knew. *Why do you always come in here and torment me by talking about him?* was what he should have said, but he

178

didn't. I'm a coward, he thought. I'd rather have her come and talk to me about anything than not come at all.

"So what," he said to Xanthe, "has been going on in the wonderful world of the very rich Alastor? I wish . . ."

"What? Tell me what it is you wish."

I wish that you could love me instead of that mother's boy who will never look at you however long you moon about at his gate, Iason thought, but all he said was, "I wish you could be happy. I wish the war would end."

"We all wish that," Xanthe said. Iason nodded but said nothing, and only the horses' soft whinnyings stirred the silence of the afternoon.

"I'm going to his house. Alastor's house, imagine! Polyxena promised to take me after Hector was buried. They say his mother has arranged a marriage, but no one knows, not really. All I want is a chance to speak to him."

"What about? What's there to say? Why don't you take your heart and your feelings, Xanthe, and transfer them somewhere else? To someone else." He tried to keep the happiness out of his voice, but Iason's heart was pounding and his head was full of a glorious noise: If they've found Alastor some rich young thing, then he's gone. He'll never look at her again. She'll forget him in the end. I've got a chance. Maybe she'll look at me now. Maybe I can say something.

"Who else is there?" Xanthe asked, rising to her feet. "There'll never be anyone else like Alastor. Never. I'm going now. Good-bye, Iason."

"Come back soon," Iason shouted after her, trying

very hard to forget all that no-one-else-like-Alastor nonsense. He went to the barrel where the oats were kept and spoke over his shoulder to the horses. "Perhaps I'll try the Gods, eh? Perhaps I'll offer up a sacrifice to Aphrodite and ask her to help me."

The horses neighed when they saw the way the air was stirred as the Goddess of Love moved daintily among them.

"Silly Iason," she said, and only the horses heard her. "Fancy not believing in me! You're one of my faithful ones. Look at how much you love Xanthe!"

Iason wondered why suddenly the stable smelled so fragrant and decided that it was probably Xanthe's perfume. He closed his eyes and breathed it in.

"You're dreaming, Iason," said a voice, and he quickly opened his eyes. Polyxena stood in the doorway smiling at him.

"No, truly," he said. "I thought I smelled something, that's all. I'm happy to see you."

"Really?" Polyxena felt her heart leap up a little at his words.

"May I ask you to do something for me?"

"Anything, Iason. You know I'd do anything for you."

He nodded. "Yes, yes, I do know that. You are the best of friends, Polyxena."

Polyxena smiled, but she knew all of a sudden what Iason was going to ask her: Would she speak to Xanthe? Would she arrange a meeting? Something like that.

"Would you speak to Xanthe for me?"

Oh, Polyxena, what it is to be always right! She did not trust herself to say anything, but nodded and tried hard to smile encouragingly. This was difficult, because she was also trying not to let any tears fall. As soon as Iason spoke, every hope would be lost. She would no longer be able to dream or imagine or pretend that one day he would look at *her* and find her beautiful.

"Tell her I think of her all the time," Iason said, and Polyxena flinched. "Tell her I love her. Tell her that when this war is over, I shall ask Lady Andromache if I can marry her. Will you do this for me?"

Polyxena said, "Yes, yes, of course I will. But I must go now, Iason. I have stayed too long."

"How can I ever thank you, Polyxena?"

She ran out of the stables without giving him an answer.

ANDROMACHE'S
BEDCHAMBER

"Lady, may I speak to you?"

Xanthe stood beside the marriage bed that looked so enormous now that Hector was no longer there to share it. Since his death, Andromache had started to lie on it all day long, with her eyes closed. She got up every evening to take her place with Priam and Hecuba in the Great Hall, but she said nothing even there, and not a single morsel of food passed her lips. For the rest of the time, she lay on the bed, neglecting her child, speaking to no one, growing thin and wasted. Xanthe had seen death in the Blood Room. She knew what it did to bodies: how they grew cold and stiff, how they lost the glow of life and became greenish and pale and slightly glistening. She had heard the wails of the bereaved and seen the widows and sisters of soldiers throw veils over their faces and tear their clothes in anguish. This, though, she had never seen. Helen, Hecuba, and all the princes and princesses of the royal household came and visited and were sent away. *Lady Andromache is sleeping. . . . Lady Andromache's head hurts. . . .* Xanthe was finding it hard to think of excuses. It wasn't right. This withdrawal from everything, this refusal to talk to anyone; it was against the natural laws. Even wild creatures on the hillside took care of their young, but Andromache left the care of Astyanax entirely to Xanthe, who was patient and loving for the most part. Lately, however, she felt herself becoming irritated. *Want to play horses, Xanthe. Want ball. Xanthe do. Xanthe sing songs.* The words flew around her head so fast that she had once or twice found herself thinking: Go away. Leave me alone. Go and bother your mother. But she kept silent, because it wasn't the baby's fault that there was no one else but Xanthe to look after him and listen to his childish chattering. And always, always she remembered that he was fatherless. *But what of my other work?* she said often to Polyxena, who came sometimes to sit with her in the courtyard while she watched Astyanax scratching patterns in the sand. She wanted to go back to the Blood Room. She wanted to find Alastor, whom she missed. Where had he hidden himself? Marpessa, who came every evening at sunset, was more silent than usual. It was no good asking her if she knew anything about Alastor—she was scarcely acquainted with him, after all. No, Xanthe thought, it is definitely time for me to act, to say something. Otherwise I shall go mad.

"Lady," she said again, when it became clear that Andromache was not going to answer immediately. "We must talk. We must talk about Astyanax."

"Why?" Andromache sounded weary. "What's the matter with him? Don't you look after him as well as any mother? I can't . . . I can't think about him now."

"But I'm not his mother. You are. He asks me over and over where Lord Hector is and that's hard enough, but what am I to say when he asks me where you are, and why can't he come to you, and will you be singing him a lullaby tonight? He misses you, Lady."

"I can't bear it, Xanthe, and that's the truth. I can't bear to look at his face. He reminds me of his father, and I'm trying so hard to forget . . ."

Suddenly Xanthe was seized with a rage such as she had never felt before in her life, and a great heat rose up in her breast and words fell from her mouth before she could stop them.

"You're wicked—nothing but a wicked woman! The scrawniest cat in the stable looks after her young better than you. Why don't you think of him? He's little . . . What does he know of the world and of death? What's he thinking while you're lying here like a statue, weeping and wailing? Anyone would think you were the first widow in the history of the world and that no one had ever lost a husband before. Well, you aren't. What you are is selfish and lazy, and if Hector can see you from the Elysian Fields, he'll be in torment at the way you're treating his child. *His child.* The moment he's dead, the moment he's no longer here, you change completely. Where's the old Andromache? I know it's not my place, but you've been the only mother I ever knew, and how do you think *I* feel, when you push me away and won't talk to me, and won't listen, and won't let me hold you as you cry? I feel useless and stupid and I wish I could leave this sad place and go back to the Blood Room. There at least they have the kind of wounds I know how to do something about . . ."

Xanthe's voice faded away. Her anger had also changed, to a kind of terror. Who was she to talk to the Lady Andromache like this? She would probably be sent away immediately; exiled to another household, and not allowed anywhere near the child she loved. She said, turning away, unable to face Andromache, "I'm sorry, Lady. I should never have said those things. It's not my place to criticize you. Please forgive me."

"I forgive you," said a voice almost in her ear, and then, quite unexpectedly, she felt two arms around her, and she was being hugged, clung to, while her mistress's tears flowed over her hair. "Oh, Xanthe, how will you forgive *me*? And Hector . . . I pray to the Gods that he, too, will be able to pardon me. Do you think he will? I love him . . . loved him so much. Everything I've done has been because of that love, but it's no excuse, you're quite right. I will change. I will. I will look after Astyanax now, and take him to visit his grandparents, as I should have done long ago."

Andromache stepped away and let go of Xanthe, and sniffed. "Let me wash my face and put on new clothes and then bring him in to me. My poor baby!" She sank on to the bed and began weeping again. "What must he think of his mother?"

"He'll be happy now," Xanthe said. "Everything will be better. I've told him you were sick. And you were. But now you will be yourself again."

"Never," Andromache said. "Never the old me, but I should try at least to be a human being and not a living corpse."

"There's something else," Xanthe said. "I haven't mentioned it, but it's very important."

"Tell me," said Andromache. "Haven't I done enough?"

"No, Lady. You must promise me that you will eat. I can see every bone in your body."

Andromache sighed. "I suppose so," she said. "Or you will bully me till I do."

"You'll die if you don't," said Xanthe. "And I don't care how much you want to, you're not allowed to, because of us. Astyanax and I. We need you."

At this Andromache, who had begun to sound almost normal, burst into tears all over again, and this time it was Xanthe who came to put her arms around Andromache.

"We're useless," Andromache said, laughing and crying at the same time. "Useless weeping women. Is it any wonder the men think we are weak?"

Xanthe smiled. "I'll go and find the baby. Theano was showing him how to make barley cakes."

PHRONTIS'S HOUSE

"When?" Polyxena asked. "When will we be able to go? You nag me and nag me, and now look at you. Days and nights have gone by, and the moon has changed from a fingernail to a ball, and still you're making excuses. Do you want me to take you to Alastor's house or not?"

Part of her knew she should have mentioned Iason's words to Xanthe by now, but she made all sorts of excuses to herself. To him she'd said it would be better to wait until the mourning for Hector was over. Xanthe would be more receptive then. To herself she said, You promised to tell her but you never said when. Surely she'll be more likely to listen when she's not quite so preoccupied with Alastor. But she knew that she was delaying because to speak the words would make Iason's feelings real. If she said nothing, she could still pretend, at least when she was alone.

"Of course I do," Xanthe said. "We'll go this afternoon if you like. It isn't my fault. Things have been . . ." Her voice trailed away as she thought how things had been. Andromache had risen from her bed, that was true, but she was still walking around her house like a ghost, and even though she now looked after her son, it fell to Xanthe to play with him when his mother grew tired. This was often, in spite of all her brave words. Xanthe took Astyanax to see Iason and the horses in the stables, walked with him beside the river when it was cooler, put him on her lap for meals, and sang to him at night until the light had gone from the sky. When she was not taking care of Astyanax, there was work to be done in the Blood Room. It was only when she lay in her own bed at night that she had time to think of Alastor.

"Have been what?" Polyxena said.

"Difficult. Busy. I don't know exactly, but the time hasn't been right."

"But now it is?"

"Yes," said Xanthe. "Charitomene is coming to sit with Astyanax. The Blood Room is quiet."

And so when most of the city was resting after the midday meal, the girls found themselves on their way to Phrontis's house.

"How much longer?" Xanthe followed Polyxena down the winding street from the citadel. Phoebus Apollo's chariot had just started its journey toward the sea, but the heat still pressed heavily on the stones, and the girls tried as hard as they could to walk in the shadows of the houses. Suddenly Xanthe pulled at Polyxena's arm.

"There! Did you see him?"

"Who? What are you talking about? I haven't seen anyone."

"He was there. The Black Warrior. I've seen him before."

"Phoebus Apollo has baked your head . . . What are you talking about?"

"I see this warrior. I've seen him in the Blood

Room, and once I saw him on the Plain, and now he slipped in between two houses, but I recognized him. He's so tall . . . You must have seen him. All in black, like a long, walking shadow."

"You've never said anything about him before. Are you sure you're not just imagining him?"

Xanthe shook her head. "I forget about him. As soon as he's gone. If I hadn't spoken of him to you, he'd have been gone from my memory long ago."

"Then forget about him again," Polyxena said. "He's probably someone from a dream, and it's hot enough to make you think you see all sorts of things."

"Aren't we nearly there?" Xanthe asked.

"Not long," said Polyxena. "There it is. Not a bad house, is it? But the Singer says that Phrontis is eaten up with envy of all those who live in the citadel. She feels, he says, that that is where she belongs. I'm surprised she hasn't managed to wangle a betrothal for Alastor with someone related to Priam—the other Polyxena, for instance."

"How does the Singer come to know so much about her?" Xanthe peered into the distance at the white walls of the place Polyxena had pointed out.

"He says it was because he was a friend of her father's, but I think the frightful Phrontis quite fancied herself as the Singer's wife at one time, after her own husband died."

"But he's ancient!" Xanthe cried out, and then realizing how rude she must sound, she blushed and said, "I'm sorry, but you know what I mean."

"That's the whole point. You marry an old man, and in just a few years' time you're a rich widow with a house in the citadel. I wouldn't put it past her."

Xanthe smiled, but her mind was already full of thoughts of Alastor. What if he refused to see her? What if he had forgotten all about her after such a long time? What if he didn't want to talk to them? What would she say to him? Why had she come? All the days while she was imagining their meeting, she hadn't considered the words, or the very first moment. . . . Would he smile when he saw her? Or be angry? She shivered in spite of the heat.

Polyxena, meanwhile, had approached the gate. A man, rather younger than the Singer but still a long way from his youth, said, "Good day, young ladies! May I be of any assistance?"

Later, Polyxena would giggle at how long it must have taken Phrontis to teach him to talk in such a fancy style, but now she said, "We wish to see the Lady Phrontis. My name is Polyxena, and I am the granddaughter of the Singer, who sits at King Priam's side. He is an old friend of your mistress, and I'm sure she would like to hear news of him."

The old man went into the house, and the girls waited. Sooner than they had hoped, Phrontis herself came running out of the door, gathering her skirts about her and talking and smiling. "My dear, how lovely! The Singer! How grand a poet he is, and how delightful to meet his granddaughter! And how kind of him to think of me! Some would say he'd forgotten all about me. We used to be very close, a long time ago, but those were happier days. He was such a handsome man, and I was quite a beauty, if you can believe such a thing from an old prune!"

"We are very happy to see you," said Polyxena,

"and you are looking very well. I shall tell my grand-father how well you look."

"Come in, my dear, come in," said Phrontis, and then she turned and her eyes traveled up and down Xanthe's body. She frowned and looked puzzled. "Who is your friend, my dear?" she said to Polyxena. "Your face," she said to Xanthe, "seems vaguely familiar."

"This is my friend Xanthe," Polyxena said, and because Phrontis still had a puzzled look in her eyes, she went on. "She is nursemaid to the Lady Andromache, and she also looks after the wounded. She tended your son, Alastor, and cared for him well."

Phrontis stiffened. She pushed her face close to Xanthe's and said, "Yes, I do remember now. Of course, that terrible room, smelling of blood and dirt and who knows what other unspeakable things. I never understood why my son couldn't have been brought to my house straightaway, but there you are. All sorts of funny things happen during wartime, don't they? But I'm forgetting my manners. Please come into the cool of the house, and I will arrange for drinks to be brought."

Horrid woman, Xanthe thought, following Phrontis and Polyxena into the house. Phrontis had actually taken Polyxena by the hand and left Xanthe to trail after the two of them. And not one word of thanks or greeting, hardly even an acknowledgment of Xanthe herself. Never mind, she thought, looking around her at the room they were in, we are in Alastor's house. Soon, soon, she would see him, and then all the insults Phrontis could throw at her wouldn't matter.

"In the old days," Phrontis was saying to Polyxena (she spoke only to her), "there would have been home-baked pastries sprinkled with spices and honey, and sweets from the other side of the mountains, where they make them with rosewater and almonds . . . Mmm . . . But now a bit of pomegranate juice and a few figs from my tree is all I can offer. What dreadful days these are! How is the Singer managing, at his age?"

"He says that old men need very little food, and even less sleep," Polyxena said, and Phrontis laughed as though the remark was the wittiest thing she'd ever heard. Xanthe gazed at everything, thinking: That's where he sits, that's his chair, that's his wall hanging. She was trying as hard as she could to remember every detail so that she could bring everything to mind later on, when she was lying alone in her bed. She wondered when they would see Alastor, when she would dare to mention him . . . or maybe Polyxena would say something. She looked at her friend and mouthed "Alastor" at her. Polyxena made a soothing gesture with her hand and said, "Is your son recovered?"

"He's much better, thank you so much for asking. In fact . . ." Phrontis smoothed her hair back with a hand that looked very like a tree root. "He will be sorry that he's missed you. I've told him so much about the Singer, and I'm sure he'd have been quite thrilled to meet his granddaughter."

Xanthe felt all the breath leaving her body. She hadn't realized until that second that she'd been holding it, like someone swimming underwater. Then she felt misery falling over her, filling her with heaviness and making everything she looked at dark. She had never once thought that perhaps Alastor wouldn't be there. What was she supposed to do now? And where was he? Could they ask? Could they go and find him, wherever he was? They certainly couldn't visit Phrontis again.

Phrontis continued. "I just can't keep him away from the walls. All day long he'd be down there if he had his way. Looking at the fighting. He's so brave . . . too brave for his own good, I always say. Well, his father was the same. I wish I could keep him by my side forever, but it is not to be. Can you keep a secret, my dear?"

She spoke to Polyxena. It was as though Xanthe weren't even in the room. Polyxena nodded. Phrontis lowered her voice and said, "You know, of course, that he is already betrothed? No? I'm surprised he didn't tell you. I am in the process of arranging the wedding. Do you know Agamede, the daughter of Hypsenor?"

"No," said Polyxena.

"A lovely girl. A very good family, related—distantly, it's true, but still related—to the royal household. They are delighted with the match. I think that the wedding *might* have to wait until the war is over, naturally, but it can't last that much longer, surely? The bride's family lives beyond Ida. They're great landowners. You should see the dowry we've been promised . . ."

Words and more words came out of her mouth. Xanthe imagined them like black flies, buzzing in her ears, and she wanted to hit them, to hit Phrontis, to say something. She stood up.

"I think," she said, "that we should go now, Polyxena. It is nearly time for Astyanax to be bathed before bedtime."

"Yes," said Polyxena. "And thank you very much for your hospitality."

"And please send my best wishes to your grandfather, Polyxena dear," Phrontis said. "And I will make sure to invite you to the wedding."

Before she could stop herself, Xanthe said, "Please tell Alastor that Xanthe sends him greetings."

Phrontis looked at her as though she were a dog or cat that had suddenly been given the power of speech. She seemed astonished. She didn't, Xanthe noticed, say that she would pass on the message. Instead she made some silly remark about how late it was and how much she still had to do.

Polyxena and Xanthe passed through the gate and made their way through the streets in silence.

ON THE WALLS

Paris had not been sleeping well. Dreams tormented him. The hours of darkness were not quiet but filled with sighs and words he could not quite hear, and screams from the throats of dying men. One voice only came to him clearly, all the time, his brother Hector calling out as he died, *Remember me when my brother Paris slays you in the shadow of the Skaian Gate*. Paris thought sometimes that it was only when Helen spoke to him that Hector's voice in his head fell silent. He stood now on the walls and, although his eyes were turned toward the Plain, he saw nothing. Some men were riding about by the Gate, and he glanced down to see who they were. The sun shone straight into his eyes, glittering on someone's armor. No, it couldn't be . . . Could it be? Was that Achilles?

Paris raised his hand and blocked out the dazzle. It was. Him. Hector's murderer. Then he heard the murmuring and whispering of those watching from the walls. "Achilles! Oh, Gods, it's Achilles!" they said, and many hid their eyes, terrified of what would happen. Paris's mouth was suddenly dry, and he reached for his bow and arrow.

"Can you see me, Trojan Paris?" Achilles shouted. "Apollo's rays are blinding you, that's clear. I'm not hanging around down here for prophecies to come true, either. What chance do you reckon you've got of hitting a moving target? No chance at all. And even if you do hit me, don't you know I'm protected?"

Achilles' laughter rose and seemed to echo in the still air. Everyone on the walls had stopped talking, stopped moving, and stared at the golden-haired Greek. Paris took an arrow and loosed it from his bow without thinking, and it flew down and down from the high walls, and the moments that passed as it fell were the longest Paris had ever known. Later he would tell Helen that some God must have guided its passage, because the arrow traveled almost as far as the ground and then seemed to hover and turn and seek out the only vulnerable part of Achilles' entire body: his heel. The heel his mother had held above the level of the water when she dipped her son's body into the enchanted river. Between the leather and the bronze of his leg armor, Paris's arrow sought out the soft flesh, and the Greek fell to his knees on the sand.

"Bastard!" Achilles' dying cry bubbled from his mouth as his body twisted itself into a knot of pain. "You have fulfilled the prophecy and killed me, but I can still . . ."

The rest of what Achilles wanted to say was lost in the roar that came from every Trojan on the walls.

Paris looked down to where his enemy lay. The shadow of the Skaian Gate was like a coverlet of darkness spread over Achilles' body. His men were busy there now, picking him up, taking him away for burial. The crowds on the walls were joyous . . . shouting with joy.

"Sleep quietly now, Hector, my brother, and do not

come to haunt me in my bed," Paris murmured aloud, and his eyes filled with tears for all of them: those who were dead, and those who were waiting to die.

Polyxena said, "Alastor's probably not at the walls at all. He's probably just run away from that voice."

"But I didn't see him, did I? The whole visit was pointless. It's just made me feel worse. You heard. He's practically married. I can't bear it."

"You knew that was likely. Didn't you?"

"I suppose so," Xanthe said. She didn't tell Polyxena that she'd been secretly hoping for the impossible . . . for Alastor to have been missing her desperately, unable to sleep or eat for love of her. What a fool she was! How stupid love made everybody! She kicked a loose stone and was glad of the pain in her toe, which distracted her for a moment from the pain in her heart.

"Someone," said Polyxena, "has done something spectacular down there on the Plain. That racket is coming from the walls."

Xanthe listened for a moment, and heard it: a roaring, and shouting, and it wasn't at all like the noise that she'd heard as Hector was cut down.

"Come on, hurry up. Let's go and see what's happening!"

"Must we?" Whatever it was that had been going on, it was bound to involve death in some form or other.

"Yes, of course we must, or my life won't be worth anything. If it's something interesting, the Singer will never let me hear the end of it—*How could you go off and leave me at such a time,* and on and on. As if he wasn't sitting under the vine snoring his head off when we left."

As they made their way down to the walls, they passed bands of children and women with smiles on their faces, and men too old to fight were almost running along the streets.

"Stop!" Polyxena called out to them. "Tell us. Something has happened. What is it? Is it over? Is the war over? Wait, speak to us. Tell us . . ."

A woman did stop at last, and turned a radiant smile on the girls. "Has no one told you? It's a glorious day. He's dead. Achilles is dead. Hector's bloody murderer, lying dead as any chicken ready for the pot. Now let's see how brave the Greeks are! Our prince Paris has done what Hector said he would do. Killed the dog Achilles in the shadow of the Skaian Gate . . ." And she was gone before Polyxena could ask for details.

"Let's hurry," she said. "You must tell Andromache, and I must go and make up some story for the Singer."

All the way to the citadel, they passed groups of happy, singing people. Xanthe followed her friend, who was a faster runner than she was, and marveled, as she had marveled many times before, that someone's death could be the cause of such joy. She couldn't help thinking there was something a little wrong about such rejoicing.

After the girls left her house, Phrontis sat for a long while, thinking. That other one, the one who wasn't

related to the Singer, was in love with Alastor. It was
as clear as daylight. . . . How she had mooned about
the house staring at everything with cow eyes, soft
with devotion! Was she the one? Was it possible?
Phrontis had noticed that Alastor had often been absent from home during the past moon. She had as-
sumed that he was visiting those houses all young
men visited, down by the walls. She wrinkled her
nose, thinking of the women she sometimes saw in
the market: painted creatures who never, she was
sure, took proper baths, but applied fragrant oils to
filthy skin, to cover the stink of their depravity. It
hurt her that her little boy—and yes, she was foolish,
but that was still how she thought of him—wanted to
consort with such women, but why should he be different from every other man in the city? Now this dim
little child with her enormous dark eyes and light hair
had appeared out of nowhere, and Phrontis found herself wishing that whores were all she had to worry
about. I knew, she said to herself, I knew the minute
I saw her looking after him when he was wounded
that she was trouble of some kind, and I was right.
Phrontis was used to being right. She always was, in
her own opinion. And she wasn't afraid to take action.
If Alastor is besotted, she said to herself, then the wedding must be brought forward, war or no war. She
would send a message to the farm with one of the
servants and suggest a time for the ceremony. And the
moment Alastor came home, she would tell him of
her decision.

THE RUINS

At the exact moment that Xanthe and Polyxena were talking to his mother, Alastor was leaning on his elbow and looking into Marpessa's eyes.

"Why not?" he said.

"Because I hate . . ." Marpessa couldn't put into words her feeling of being on display, visible, even though these ruins, which she hadn't even known about, were full of hidden rooms and shadowy spaces behind broken walls. "I don't like this place. I think someone will see us. I feel as if we're being watched."

"Then where can we go? Your bedroom is just next door to all the comings and goings of Paris and Helen and their servants, and my mother rules our house, and walks into my chamber as if I were a child like Astyanax. And I can't bear it, Marpessa. I'm on fire. You are like a fever that has infected me. I can't bear to live if you're not in my arms, and sometimes I just feel like rushing at the first Greek I see, so that he can kill me and then my suffering will be over."

"Don't be stupid," Marpessa said. "You hardly know me."

"I know I want you."

That, Marpessa thought, was the truth at last. He

wanted her. He didn't love her. He'd never claimed to love her. His mother (and he'd mentioned this more than once) was busy arranging a marriage for him. He didn't say, *I'll marry only you, beloved Marpessa.* Of course not. What did she have to offer a young man like Alastor? Nothing. No money (apart from the few coins and pieces of old jewelry Helen sometimes gave her, which rattled around in her box of treasures), no land, no family, not even a proper name. She had thought and thought about these things until the inside of her head, she was sure, resembled a basket of wools, all tangled up together, difficult to sort into separate strands. Sometimes, when she was alone, she could do it. She could be sensible, and then all the different feelings lay quietly side by side in her heart, and she could think about each one in turn. At such times, she said to herself: I will tell Alastor I won't see him again. I will find Xanthe and tell her what I've done and beg her to forgive me. I will think only of my work.

Then a message would come from him. *Meet me at the ruins. Come to the ruins.* No one else, he said, knew about them. The house was a property that had belonged to his father's brother, who was now dead, and the whole place had been left to fall to pieces. And she went, every time. Now she lay in the curve of his arm and looked at him. Her whole body longed for him, she wanted only to take him in her arms and forget everything just for a short time, but she held back. Anyone could walk past the ruin and decide to explore it: a child, an animal, and Marpessa thought that she would die if anyone actually saw her in the

postures of love, which had about them so little dignity, so much of—she blushed—the ridiculous, when
you were only a spectator.

"We might as well go, then," Alastor said. "There's
not much point hanging about here . . ."

If we're not going to make love, Marpessa thought.
You don't want to talk to me. It's not enough simply
to sit by my side. There are better things to do than
be with me, if I'm not going to oblige. That's what
you mean, so why don't you say so? She was silent,
but in that second, she made up her mind. This would
be the very last time she came to the ruins. Let's see,
she said to herself, how you like that. Out loud she
said, "Let's go, then. It's getting late."

Alastor stood up and started to pick his way over
the broken stones of the ruin without even looking
behind to see whether she was following him. They
walked a little apart, not speaking. Suddenly from the
walls of the city came a shout of triumph, rolling
through the still air.

"Listen," Alastor said. "Something's happened.
I've missed it. I must go and see what it is. I could
kick myself. What if something important's happened? Will you be all right on your own? Do you
mind if I run ahead?"

"Perfectly all right, thank you," said Marpessa.

For a moment, Alastor looked at her and smiled
and touched her arm.

"Things can't go on like this," he said. "I'll find
somewhere for us. I know you hate meeting me here.
Don't worry. I'll send a message. But I must go now.
Who knows what's going on? Farewell."

"Farewell," said Marpessa. But he had gone, running toward the sounds of the shouting. I am no longer in his mind, she thought. I am unimportant. She watched him as he ran. The Black Warrior was running after him, and Marpessa recognized Ares, God of War. She'd seen him often, down on the Plain, the long, dark folds of his cloak making another night wherever he spread them.

THE GOSSIPS

THE KITCHENS

"What I want to know is: Who're we meant to believe?" said Theano, plunging her hand into an enormous terra-cotta jar and feeling around in it for whatever bits of grain were stuck to the sides or still hid right at the bottom, where they were hard to reach. "The way I heard it, he was immortal . . . His mother's Thetis, some kind of water deity or nymph or something, and that's why the Gods allowed him to be special."

"That's right," Halie said. She was putting all the food that could possibly be found on the table and wondering, with the part of her brain that wasn't occupied in thinking about Achilles, how she and the others were supposed to turn these leavings into a feast. Priam had called for a celebration. His son had avenged Hector. The terrible Achilles was dead. The whole city had been in an uproar for several days. Skins full of wine suddenly appeared out of thin air, as if by some enchantment, and for once the Singer had something other than funeral dirges to think about. There he was, for everyone to see, striding about the corridors, miraculously more upright than he had been for years, making up triumphal songs with a silly grin on his face, like a young man whose team had just won some games or other. Everyone was thinking the same thing: Maybe it'll be over soon. Maybe the bloodshed will stop. Maybe there'll be proper meals. Fools. Halie sighed. Things were bound to get worse before they got better. Cassandra wasn't taking part in all the rejoicing, and until *she* had a smile on her face, Halie wasn't going to take anything for granted. She turned her mind back to the question of whether Achilles was or wasn't immortal.

"They can't let a mortal escape Hades," she said. "Stands to reason. If they did, then he'd be a God, just like the ones on Olympus."

Danae, who'd been quietly scrubbing earth from a few wizened root vegetables that had come into the city through some tunnel or other—better, she always thought, not to ask questions—said, "Then what's all that about his mother dunking him in the River Lethe?"

"Ah, well," said Halie. "That's where the Gods are so clever! Had to hold him by his left heel, didn't she, so's he didn't drown . . . So that bit, where she held him out of the water, stayed dry, but then the magic from the river couldn't get at it, right? And Paris's arrow got him in that exact spot."

"Bit lucky, if you ask me," said Theano, who had managed to scrape together a few cups of grain. Maybe there *would* be enough for some kind of a cake. She'd have to look into how much oil there was. "Bit of a coincidence. Hitting just that tiny part of Achilles' body. Never a crack shot that I heard of, Paris isn't. You know what the men say: His best weapon's in between his legs!"

The women laughed together, happy that some kind of meal was beginning to take shape on the table. Danae said, "He was helped, though, wasn't he? The Gods had a hand in it, stands to reason. Some say they're down there on the Plain, guiding arrows and shielding people and all sorts of weird stuff."

"Still," Theano persisted. "Who ever heard of dying from a wound in the heel? Fishy business going on, if you ask me."

"Don't you know?" Halie said. "I thought everyone knew. Paris's arrow was poisoned."

Danae and Theano sucked the breath in through their teeth and shook their heads. Halie continued, "I was wondering why Mother Poison had been visiting. Didn't I tell you? She'd been here more than once in the days before Achilles' death. I wondered at the time what she was up to, because as you know, she hardly ever leaves that hovel of hers. Still, Paris must have summoned her, and she's probably no different from any other woman where he's concerned. But she gives me the shivers, I tell you. I'd have to be pretty desperate to consult her. Her teeth are enough to give you bad dreams, and as for her eyes . . . Well, I've seen eyes like that on an owl, but never on a woman." She shivered and looked over her shoulder as though Mother Poison might be lurking in a corner of the kitchen. She wasn't but someone was.

"Who d'you think you are?" Halie said. "And who gave you permission to come into this kitchen?"

"Apologies, ladies," said a young man, and he stepped forward out of the shadows.

"Our lucky day!" Theano chuckled. "Handsome

young men in very short tunics turning up to chat. What's your name, then?"

"They call me Hermes," said the young man.

"Don't tell me . . . The Gods have sent us a message," said Danae.

"Well, yes, as a matter of fact."

Theano, Danae, and Halie started laughing.

"Think we're soft, don't you, eh?" said Theano. "No respect for your elders, you young people . . . Well, what's this message from the Gods then? Spit it out, if you're going to."

"It's a warning. It's Paris. He will die soon, did you know that? Be warned."

"You're a troublemaker and probably a Greek spy, young Hermes. Why should our brave Paris go dying all of a sudden? He's lasted well enough so far. Aphrodite watches out for that one!"

"You mustn't forget what all the oracles have said, though," said Hermes.

"Remind us," said Danae.

Hermes sat down on a low stool and began to speak.

"Paris can only be killed by an arrow from the bow of the great hero Herakles. And that bow is now with someone called Philoctetes. D'you know about him? The Greeks had forgotten all about him. Well, you can hardly blame them. It's not an episode that reflects well on them . . ."

"Get on with it," Halie grumbled. Some people had no idea of how to tell a story.

"When the Greeks were on the way to Troy, they landed a hunting party on the island of Lemnos, and Philoctetes was one of the men sent to shoot deer for provisions. Unfortunately it wasn't a deer he shot but a dragon who was sleeping in a cave. The creature, in its dying agonies, bit Philoctetes on the foot. The wound festered. It suppurated."

"Good, juicy word, that." Theano nodded. "Suppurated."

"It wasn't a good feeling for Philoctetes. It was torture for him. He writhed and foamed at the mouth and cried and groaned, and his foot swelled and turned green from the poison and began to stink so fearfully that none of the Greeks would go anywhere near him."

"Charming people!" said Halie, not quite under her breath.

Hermes continued. "His constant shrieking was unbearable, and Agamemnon decided that he should be left on Lemnos while the army continued the journey to Troy. They left him some food and some skins of wine, and off they went and forgot all about him for years and years. But then, when Paris got that lucky shot at Achilles and actually killed him, the Greeks had to do some serious thinking. Someone reminded them that they needed Philoctetes because of his bow and arrows that used to belong to Herakles . . ."

"You've told us that already," said Danae. "Get to the point."

"The point is, they went to fetch Philoctetes back from Lemnos. They found a haggard, filthy, starving wretch sitting among the bones and feathers of nearly ten years' worth of dead seabirds. And the wound on his foot was still weeping pus, and the smell was more dreadful than they had remembered. At first Philoctetes tried to shoot them, but they quickly told him they had come to cure him, and took him off to the

Greek camp, where he was bathed and fed and looked after, and the best army surgeons tended his wound and cleaned it, and it soon began to heal. Now he's as good as new. And so Paris will die."

"Why didn't they bring that poor creature back when he was first hurt? Cruel, that was. I call it dreadfully cruel," said Halie.

"You can't ask questions like that," said Hermes. "Everything has to be done in the right order, or the whole narrative falls to pieces. One thing has to follow another. You can't skip over anything, or move things along faster. One step at a time."

"So why have you come to us? What do you expect us to do?"

"Nothing," said Hermes. "I don't expect you to do anything. I wanted you to know. That was all."

Theano blinked. She looked at Danae and Halie.

"Did you see a young man here a moment ago? Quite a good-looking lad in a very short tunic with some story about Paris and someone whose name I can't remember?"

"Yes, but where's he got to? He brought us something, didn't he? He told some story, didn't he? I can't quite remember what it was. Something about Paris." Danae shook her head.

"He said," Halie laughed, "that he was Hermes, messenger to the Gods!"

They laughed together, and Theano said, "They'll say anything for a bit of attention, young people. Now, where's the honey? There must be some left somewhere . . ."

By the time a sort of cake had been baked, Theano, Danae, and Halie had forgotten all about their visitor.

HELEN'S PALACE

Marpessa stood alone at the loom. Since the death of Achilles, Paris had been feeling happier, and that meant that Aphrodite was in the palace more and more often. She was here now. Marpessa glanced at her, where she hovered near the door of the bedchamber, wearing a dress like a silvery cloud, and the Goddess smiled.

"Just like the old days," she said. "Isn't it? Helen hasn't been feeling very affectionate lately, but I've fixed that for the moment. She seems quite transported today."

Marpessa bent her head to her weaving and tried to ignore both what Aphrodite was saying and the noises that she heard coming from the bedchamber.

"It isn't very tactful of me, I know," Aphrodite continued. "Making all this happen where you can hear it. Why don't you step outside for a while? Or maybe you enjoy reliving your adventure with the beautiful Alastor in your head?"

Marpessa wanted to ask the Goddess, *When? When will I be able to be with him again? What will become of us?* but didn't dare. Aphrodite, though, must have read her mind, because she said, "I will turn my attention to you soon, do not fear. I don't know what will happen . . . not yet. As you can see, I have other things on my mind."

Marpessa smiled at Aphrodite's words, and a weight of misery that had been lying on her heart for a long time lifted a little. She made her way to the door, thinking that there was time for a short walk up to the temple before Paris and Helen emerged into the house.

Paris had gone. No sooner had he left her bed than there was something urgent that he had to see to in Priam's Palace. Helen smiled as she arranged her hair on top of her head again. When he said things like that, he was usually lying, but after the exertions that they had just been through, she doubted that he would have any energy left over for anyone else. But, she thought, with men you never know.

"Marpessa!" she called. "Come in here and help me pick a dress for tonight's feast."

When Marpessa didn't answer, Helen went into the weaving room to look for her.

"Marpessa? Where are you?"

For a moment, she was irritated that there was no one to attend her at once. She would have to call someone else. I can't be angry with her, poor little thing, Helen thought. She goes out by herself seldom enough. I should be glad that she's found something of her own to do.

At just that moment, a young man burst through the door and said, "The Lady Helen? I must see her . . . Please tell me where I may find the Lady Helen."

"I am the Lady Helen. Who are you, and how do

you dare to burst in on me in this fashion? Shall I call out for the guards to come and have you thrown out?"

"No, Lady, I beg you. I have come to do you no harm. I have a message for the Lord Paris from my mother. My name is Corythus. I am Lord Paris's son."

Helen laughed, and the scarlet jewel that lay between her breasts caught the light.

"Don't be ridiculous," she said. "How can you possibly be? I am the Lady Helen. I know everything about Paris that it's possible to know, and he has no son. Who is this mother that you speak of?"

"She is a nymph. Her name is Oenone, and she lives on Mount Ida. She sent me here to make myself known to my father . . . to claim something of my birthright."

"Nymph!" Helen's voice rang with scorn. "Superstitious nonsense. Listen here, young man. If my Paris got himself involved with some feebleminded country bumpkin who puts her faith in spells and potions before he knew me, that's neither here nor there. Looking at you, I'd say it all happened years and years before he even met me. He must have been practically a child himself. It's all ancient history, and if I were you, I'd forget all about it, and get back to the mountain, before my husband gets home. He's very jealous. There's no telling what he'll do if he finds you here . . ."

As she spoke, Helen noticed Marpessa standing in the frame of the door.

"Marpessa, dear, I'm so glad you're back. This visitor is just leaving. Will you be so good as to show him to the gate?"

"No!" Corythus shouted. "I'm not going before I've spoken to Paris. I will cling to your feet until he comes, and anyone who wants to throw me out will have to pull me away from you, Lady."

"Stop!" Helen shouted. "Take your filthy hands off me at once, or I shall scream for help . . ."

Later Marpessa tried to remember the sequence of events. Everything happened too quickly. One moment there was Helen, shouting, and then Paris came in, and why did he have a knife in his hand? Still, there it was, shining in the light of the torches, and without asking any questions or waiting for Helen to say another word, Paris plunged the dagger into the young man's throat from behind and he fell forward. He was dead. That was bad enough, but what came later was even worse. When Helen told Paris what the young man had claimed, he didn't deny any of it. Helen turned white with fury and shouted at Paris.

"Go back to her, then. I don't want you laying one more finger on me. You're disgusting. A cowlike country girl who thinks she's a nymph is about your style. Why did I ever leave my poor husband who never treated me like this? I must have lost my reason. I can't believe I left my child for you, you bastard . . ."

The screaming and raging went on and on into the night, but then at last Helen withdrew to her room and silence fell. Paris was left to deal with the body: to arrange for it to be taken back to the mountain for burial. After it was gone, he sat for a long time in the dark garden, weeping. He caught sight of Marpessa on

213

her way to her own chamber and said, "That was my son, Marpessa. Do you understand why I am so plunged in gloom?"

"Yes, Lord Paris. It is a sad night."

"I never knew I had a son. Can you believe that? And no sooner does he announce himself than I kill him. A terrible sin . . . the worst sin in the world to kill your son."

"You didn't know he was your son," Marpessa said. Paris groaned.

"Everything is unraveling . . . Do you ever get that feeling? No, of course you don't. You're only a child. What do you know of such matters?"

Marpessa could have told him, but decided it would be wisest to keep silent.

ON THE WALLS

If Xanthe had reason to hate Boros because of everything he was and the way he had treated her, what he had just told her made her hate him even more. How dare he! How could he torture her in this way? Maybe what he'd said to Charitomene wasn't true. He'd made quite sure Xanthe was nearby and had spoken in an unnecessarily loud voice when he said it. "That young man who was here a bit ago . . . the good-looking chap that your little girl over there fancied the arse off . . . Excuse my language, but you know what I mean . . . He's got a girlfriend. Isn't that something? No one knows who she is, of course, but he's mooching about like a lovesick poet and doesn't seem in any hurry to get back to the fighting."

Charitomene made a *tsk*ing noise with her teeth.

"You don't know what you're talking about, as usual, Boros. Why don't you stick to dragging bodies about? That's all you're good for. Young Alastor is betrothed to a young woman from beyond the mountains. I know that for a fact."

"Who's saying a word about betrothals? That's got nothing to do with it. I'm not saying he's going to marry this one he's so smoochy about . . . just sowing his wild oats, if you get my meaning. Dipping his wick. Getting his end away. That sort of thing."

"You're disgusting, Boros. Go. I don't want to hear another sound out of your mouth. Bring the wounded and get out. I'm an old woman, and there's nothing you can say that I haven't heard before, but I can't have you infecting young ears. You're revolting."

Boros stumbled out of the Blood Room, and Xanthe was so relieved he had gone that it took her some moments to understand what he'd said. Could it possibly be true? It was so long. So many nights and days had passed since she had seen Alastor. Sometimes she dreamed of him, and then he was beside her, close to her, with his eyes looking deep, deep into hers, but when she woke up, his face had vanished from her mind, and she found it difficult to remember his voice. She knew that he spent hours on the walls, looking out over the Plain, spotting warriors that he knew, and staring out toward the Greek camp to see whether any of their heroes were riding out to battle. She had to know the truth, however painful it was. She would go and find him.

"Charitomene, do you need me?" Xanthe said.

"No, child. It's quiet today. Go. My greetings to the Lady Andromache."

Xanthe nodded but said nothing. She had no intention of going back to Hector's palace. As she left the Blood Room, instead of turning toward home, she made her way out of the citadel and through the streets, toward the walls. As she approached them, she could hear the shouting. That meant that something was going on; some fight or another. Xanthe felt her heart begin to beat faster, and sweat broke out all over her body. Only for Alastor's sake would she go anywhere near a place where men were hacking at one another, trying to kill and maim and wound; trying to win.

There were people standing all along the walls, but they weren't crowded, as they had been on the day of Hector's death. She stared at the backs of the old men, the grandmothers with young children, who brought them here to look at the battle as though it were a form of entertainment. Xanthe shivered. She knew how difficult it was to say no to the little boys, who nagged and nagged to be taken to watch the war. It wasn't surprising. If all everyone talked about was heroes and soldiers and skirmishes, then of course they'd be interested. They, too, wanted some of the excitement. Lady Andromache said nothing to Astyanax about the fighting, nothing at all; but still he'd heard about it somewhere and had begun to charge about the courtyard shouting "Bash the Greeks!" at the top of his voice and waving a small tree branch above his head.

Where was Alastor? Xanthe's gaze went from one back to another, and then at last she saw him: standing all alone, apart from the crowds. She clambered up to where he was. Lady Aphrodite, she murmured to herself, help me. Let this all be something Boros made up to hurt me.

"Alastor?" she said. He turned and saw her, and smiled. Xanthe thought he must be the most beautiful man in the world: handsomer even than Paris. Now that his wound was healed, his skin was like gold, shining and smooth, and she had to hold her hands

217

firmly at her sides to prevent herself from reaching out to touch him.

"Xanthe!" he said. "Where have you been? Why haven't I seen you? You're only interested in me as a patient, aren't you?"

"Oh, no. No. Really." Why are you being tongue-tied? Speak. It's your only chance. "I wondered what had happened to you. How you were. How are you?"

"Happy. I'm happy, Xanthe. Can't you see it?"

"I can. You look very well. I'm glad . . ."

"Come here. Come closer, and I'll whisper why it is that I'm so happy."

Xanthe hoped she wouldn't disgrace herself by fainting. She came and stood so close to Alastor that her arm brushed his. She found that she was holding her breath, and she let it out in a rush.

"I must whisper in your ear. It's a secret. Do you promise faithfully that you won't tell a soul?"

Xanthe nodded. "I won't tell anyone. I swear."

Alastor brought his lips to her ear. "I have found someone who sets me on fire when I'm with her," he said.

Xanthe closed her eyes and felt herself swaying a little. Maybe it isn't what Boros said. Maybe this is someone he's been to visit in one of those houses down by the walls, where all the young men go, they say. But it's the end for me. He doesn't love me.

"You mustn't be angry, Alastor, but I knew that already," Xanthe said. "We went to visit your mother, Polyxena and I, and she told us—me—all about the wedding. I hope you'll be very happy."

"Wedding?" Alastor grinned and then started laughing. Soon he became convulsed with laughter and made such a noise about it that nearby watchers on the walls, who were still absorbed in the battle, made faces at him.

"I'm sorry, Xanthe," he said at last. "Only it's so ridiculous. To imagine that I would burn with desire for someone my mother picked out for me. No, this is someone else. I only met her recently. All I do all day is think about her. I can't stop thinking about her, and that's the truth. The wedding is something else altogether. My mother threatens me that it will all take place soon, but I'm not thinking of that. Who knows whether it will or not, in time of war. Even my mother doesn't have the war under her control, and what I feel is, I'll worry about Agamede when and if I have to."

"Who is she then, this love of yours?" Look at me, talking as if nothing at all were wrong! Look at me behaving as though his words were just words and not little daggers piercing my heart! Now there are two of them I have to worry about.

"I'm sorry, I can't say. I swore to her I would say nothing."

"It doesn't matter. Do you love her?"

"You girls—you're forever going on and on about love. What does it mean? I know how she makes me feel in every part of my body. Isn't that enough?"

Xanthe thought about her feelings for Alastor. Were *they* only in her skin, in her flesh? Was that what love came down to, after all? She remembered Andromache, lifeless without her husband.

"No," she said. "It isn't enough. There's more."

"Well, it's enough for me, believe me. While this war's on anyway."

Xanthe sighed. War, always war. What the old women said was true, then. Men would always think about war before anything else. She imagined it like a great tree, spreading its roots into the earth, digging itself deeply into everything, throwing its shadow everywhere.

"I must go now, Alastor. I have work to do."

"You're angry with me. Why are you angry with me?"

"No, no, truly I'm not, but you know I don't like the battles. I'm needed in the Blood Room."

"But something's happening . . . You can't go now. Look. Look at that man down there. Do you know who he is?"

"I don't care who he is."

"Then you should. He's Philoctetes. They say he's out to get Paris. There he is, Paris, up there . . . He doesn't seem worried, does he? See Philoctetes' bow? It used to belong to Herakles."

"I DON'T CARE!" Xanthe screamed as though the words were being torn out of her throat. "Are you incapable of understanding a word I say? I don't care if the bow belongs to Ares himself. It's nothing but a weapon. I'm going."

"I'm sorry, Xanthe. I know you hate all this. Let's meet again, and talk again. I like talking to you. You're a good listener."

"Farewell," Xanthe said. She turned and made her way back through the city. The sun was at its highest, and yet she felt cold. Boros hadn't been lying. What Alastor had told her was the end. There was no more hope for her of love, or joy. Perhaps she should ask Lady Andromache if she could become a temple maiden? Then she could serve the Goddess and never have to see Alastor or any other young man ever again. But who was she, this unknown girl who had wrapped herself around him like a climbing plant? And how could she find out, without telling anyone Alastor's secret?

THE BLOOD ROOM
AND HELEN'S PALACE

Xanthe looked around her at the wounded lying on their pallets, and at Charitomene, sitting on her low stool beside the door. It was the time of day when the sun had just begun to slide down toward the sea, and a golden drowsiness filled the room. Some men were snoring. No one was badly hurt. Xanthe sat on the floor in the darkest corner and leaned her back against the wall. From somewhere far away came the sound of crying, but still, Xanthe's eyes drooped and closed. She thought of what Alastor had told her, and she felt a childish desire to cry. I'm like Astyanax, she thought. Weeping because I can't have what I want . . .

"Help! Someone help! Quickly . . . Come and help quickly! Is there a healer here? Someone who knows about wounds . . . Lord Paris . . . Come quickly . . ."

Xanthe opened her eyes. She recognized a servant from Helen's palace, who was shaking Charitomene by the shoulder and weeping.

"Get your breath back, man," the old woman said soothingly, "and tell me exactly what's happened."

"Lord Paris . . . He's hurt. An arrow wound in the side. But quick. He's dying . . ."

Xanthe stood up at once. Was it that man—she

couldn't remember his name—the one with Herakles' bow? Maybe he'd been lucky after all. Xanthe shivered. What a spectacle that would have been for Alastor. How pleased he'd be that he hadn't missed that! But surely Paris couldn't be dying?

"Come, child," said Charitomene. "Bring the oil. Bring the clean cloths. I have the herbs."

They gathered everything together and followed the servant up the hill. Heat rose from every stone and seemed to make the air shimmer, as though it were a moving veil of some fine, translucent cloth. Xanthe heard the cries long before reaching the palace, and the hairs stood up on the back of her neck and on her arms. Could a man shriek like that? It sounded like a tormented spirit from Hades.

Paris was lying on the tiled floor, just inside the door. Helen knelt beside him, with his head on her lap. Servants and other soldiers from the battle who had brought Paris to his house clustered around him, and Xanthe caught a glimpse of Marpessa in the corner, holding a jug of water, ready to hand a moistened cloth to Helen, but she couldn't even smile at her sister. The terrible crying went on and on and rose to the high ceiling of the room. Charitomene sat down next to Paris and spoke to him as if he were a little child.

"Let's see, lovey . . . What's this? . . . A bad gash on the side. It doesn't look too deep, though. I don't think there's anything to worry about . . . A little oil and a few of my magic herbs, and you'll be up to all your old tricks again in a few days, never fear."

Xanthe peered at the wound, and indeed, it *did* seem as though Paris was making rather too much of a fuss. She'd seen a lot worse. Even Alastor's wound

223

had been deeper, and he hadn't shrieked like this. Paris was now throwing his body from side to side, and foam flecked the corners of his mouth.

"He's saying something!" Helen said suddenly. "Listen for what he's trying to say, Charitomene, for the love of all the Gods." Tears were pouring down her face, and her clothes were crumpled and torn and stained with Paris's blood.

Charitomene bent her head and listened. Paris was delirious. His skin was burning with a fever—why was he on fire after such a small wound?

"Poison—he says he's poisoned." Marpessa spoke more loudly than she normally did, to be heard above the shrieking. Everyone turned to look at her.

"Are you poisoned?" Charitomene leaned close to his mouth. "Paris, answer me. Has someone poisoned you? Who? Tell us who."

Xanthe heard a commotion in the courtyard, and then Hecuba and Priam were there, too, and adding their weeping to the tears that Helen was shedding. Hecuba flung herself down on her son's feet.

"My baby! My darling boy! What's to become of us?"

Paris, hearing his mother's voice, struggled to sit up.

"Mother . . . Take me there . . . the mountain. Take me . . . Oenone . . . love . . . the only one . . . Save me."

The effort of saying the words was too much, and Paris sank back onto Helen's lap. She looked down at him for a long moment and then stood up, not even bothering to find a pillow for his head. She looked at Hecuba, still weeping and clinging to Paris's feet; at

Priam sitting and holding his hand; at all the servants looking grim; at Xanthe and Charitomene and Marpessa holding the jug with water. She pushed the hair away from her forehead and wiped away her tears. Her face was instantly pale and beautiful once more, as though she had never wept in her life. She smoothed her skirts and arranged a veil embroidered with sparkling silver pieces over her head.

"You all heard him. Do what he says," she said to them, her voice hard. "Take him to that little bitch up on the mountain and let her get on with it. She loves him, apparently. She's welcome to him. Good riddance. Come, Marpessa, we have weaving to do."

She left the room, and everyone stared after her. It was Priam who spoke first.

"There is no time to be lost. Bring a litter and four strong men. We are taking him to the nymph on Mount Ida. She has magic powers, they say."

HELEN'S BEDCHAMBER

Marpessa, the other servants, everyone in the household was asleep, but torches still burned in Helen's bedchamber. She sat on the bed, with all her tears shed. Around her neck she wore only the Star Stone. The funeral rites for Paris were over. They had been almost too much for her to bear with dignity, but she had managed. She had kept her head held high, and covered her face with a black veil. Hecuba and Cassandra were veiled, also, which was a good thing, because their hostile glances in her direction would have been like daggers. She felt them, of course, but as long as she couldn't see them, it was easier not to think about them. When the fire was put to the wood under his dead body, she had felt pain all through her flesh. Her Paris . . . How could he be dead? From a wound like that? She'd heard the gossip, the whispering in corridors. The arrow was poisoned. Philoctetes had dipped it in the Hydra's blood. It had been nothing but a scratch, but enough to carry the venom into the blood. And then there was Oenone. She had rushed through the crowd, pushing the strongest guards aside, and thrown herself onto the pyre. . . . Helen started up and looked around. Someone was in the bedchamber with her.

She saw her at once. A woman sitting calmly on the seat beside the window.

"How dare you!" Helen said. "I don't know who you are, but you must leave at once." Another of Paris's conquests, no doubt. Another Oenone. Will there be no end to them?

"You're quite right. I *am* another of Paris's conquests."

Did I speak? Helen wondered. I must have done, without knowing it.

"You didn't speak. I can read your thoughts. We all can, all the inhabitants of Olympus. I am Aphrodite, and I have loved Paris since before he met you. We Gods often love mortals . . . There's nothing new in that. Zeus has changed himself into all kinds of shapes whenever the fancy took him. You of all people should know about that, as you're his daughter. A swan . . . That was the shape, was it not, in which he visited your mother?"

"There's no need to bring that up," said Helen. "Some people say it's just a legend."

"More fools them, then," said Aphrodite. "You of all people believe in the Gods, do you not?"

Helen nodded. "But why are you visiting me now? I've never seen you before."

"That doesn't mean I haven't been here. I've come because I'm grieving for him. I loved him. I wanted to be near someone who would understand. I've fallen in love with mortals before, but Paris was the special one. No one loved him better than I did. And he loved me. All his life, he worshiped me. Everything he did, he did for my sake. Can you bear the truth? He loved me better than he loved you, and much better than he loved that sullen creature Oenone. Can you believe how badly she's behaved? Fancy coming back after all those years to say *I told you so*. I was there, you know. When they carried Paris up the mountain to her cave, or grotto, or whatever she calls it. He was half dead. She came out looking smug, and what did she say? I'll tell you. She said: *You left me for Helen, even though I loved you. Now go to your Helen, and see how much use she is to you. I won't save you.* What a bitch! She could have brought him back to life and chose not to."

"Thank you for telling me. I wondered what had happened up there on the mountain."

"She made widows of us both, that's what happened. I shall put aside my bright clothes, and cover my face, and mourn for Paris. As you will."

Aphrodite stood up, and Helen watched as she drifted across the room like mist and disappeared . . . Did she go through the door or the window? Had she been there at all? Perhaps, Helen thought, it is my grief and weariness speaking. Or the wine I drank. She glanced down at the Star Stone and the crimson light that fell on her white skin like drops of blood. Aphrodite faded from her memory like smoke blown away on the wind.

THE GOSSIPS

HELEN'S PALACE

"Dogs!" Theano's mouth was twisted with pain. "Ashes on Paris's pyre not yet cold, and look how they're all behaving. Fighting over Helen as though she were a bone. A meaty one at that."

"Dreadful," Halie agreed. "Dreadful to see. Paris's brothers squabbling over who's going to have her, and nagging Priam, and not even having the courtesy to ask her what *she* wants."

"She wouldn't want any of them," said Danae. "That's what I think. I wouldn't be a bit surprised if she's ready to go back to them. To the Greeks. What's the point of hanging around here now that Paris is dead?"

"Surely not!" said Theano. "Would they have her? That Menelaus'd strangle her, wouldn't he, after the way she's treated him?"

Halie shrugged. "But look at all this stuff. It's hard to blame the princes, when you come right down to it. Worth her weight in gold to any husband, isn't she, and that's before you put her beauty on the scales." She sighed. "Lived a long time, I have, but I've never seen riches like this before." She ran her hand over lustrous fabrics sewn with precious stones and looked up at a hanging woven in happier times, which showed Europa on the shores of a blue sea, placing a garland of scarlet flowers around the neck of a white bull.

"Zeus," said Theano, "looks very placid and docile, doesn't he? I don't hold with sneaking up on a young girl like that. I call it wicked. Girls love animals, everyone knows that, and it's taking advantage . . . I've often wondered . . ." Her voice faded away.

"What? What've you often wondered?" Halie asked, a little distractedly. She had begun to wrap the jars and plates in rags and was busy arranging them in the bottom of one of the huge wooden chests that stood ready to be filled with all Helen's belongings.

"D'you think the Gods change back into their own proper shapes? When they come to mortal women? When it comes to the crunch, if you know what I mean?"

Halie looked up, and so did Danae, who was standing on a high chair, unhooking the hangings from the walls. They were silent for a moment, then both spoke together:

"Of course they must . . ."

"Oh, yes, they must, otherwise . . ."

"Otherwise," Theano summed up what they were all thinking, "the whole business would be utterly revolting, and we'd have to vomit every time we thought about it."

"Imagine getting into bed with that!" said Halie, shuddering and pointing at the black face of the Minotaur in the center of his labyrinth, on the hanging that showed Theseus about to kill him. "Yeuch! A bull . . . and he wasn't even a God in disguise!"

"But," said Danae, "you've got to admit, men, some men anyway, *do* look a bit bull-like, or foxlike or doglike. Doesn't Deiphobus look like a horse to you? Perhaps this Minotaur was just a Cretan who was a bit darker and hairier than the rest . . ."

Halie and Theano began to laugh. It was true. With his thin face and long nose, the prince *did* look a bit like an inhabitant of the stables.

"We shouldn't laugh," said Halie. "Poor Helen! Fancy going from Paris's bed to his!"

"And from these beautiful rooms to Deiphobus's barracks of a palace, which hasn't seen a woman's touch for years." Danae clambered down to the floor, carrying the hanging and stumbling under its weight. She began to fold it carefully, with the back of the work on the outside so that the colors of the picture might be preserved.

"I was there yesterday," said Theano, "cleaning it up a bit. The floor looked as though it hadn't been swept since the beginning of the war. I don't know how Helen will survive there." She shook her head, and she and her companions continued to pack away the contents of the palace. Soon the woven pictures whose colors used to sing out and lift the hearts of all who saw them were closed up in the fragrant darkness of the sandalwood chests, and the walls themselves were as blank and pale as deserts.

THE MARKET

Marpessa wandered through the market, wondering what she could possibly find to take back to the kitchens. It's not my job, she thought. Why should I go to market for Priam's cooks? I don't know how to find the right person . . . the one who might have grapes from a secret vine outside the city. She shouldn't have sent me. In her heart, Marpessa knew that Helen was being kind. She doesn't really care whether I find anything or not. She's sent me out of the house because she knows how sad I am. She thinks it's because of Paris, and because we're all going soon to another house that won't be what we're used to, and to another master who is not kind and indulgent . . . who's the very opposite of his brother in every way.

Marpessa picked up a piece of dried meat and wondered whether, if she gave it to Theano, it might turn, by some enchantment, into something delicious.

"Buy it or don't buy it, young woman," said a wrinkled crone who was sitting on the ground nearby. "But don't finger it like that. No one else will want it if they see you handling it like that."

"Anything this young woman handles," said a voice behind her, "is turned into ambrosia. I guarantee

232

it." Alastor. Marpessa blushed and put the piece of meat down and turned to face him.

"What are you doing here?" All thoughts of food had left Marpessa's head, and at the sight of Alastor she felt suddenly faint and her head swam.

"I came to find you," said Alastor. "I wanted to speak to you. I asked at Helen's palace . . . They told me you were here."

"Whom did you ask?" Marpessa felt cold. One of the servants could easily tell Xanthe . . . but perhaps because everything was so upside down at the palace, no one would remember someone asking for her.

"I don't remember. An old man. What does it matter? I need to talk to you, Marpessa. Is there somewhere we can go?"

He looked grim and serious. What had become of his smile? Had something happened? She said, "There is a bench there, under that tree. We can sit there."

They walked in silence. They sat down together, and Alastor stared at the dust between his feet and spoke without looking at Marpessa.

"I don't know how to say this," he said. "I've gone over the words again and again, but now that you are here in front of me, I've forgotten what they all were and I see only your beauty and I want only to hold you . . . May I hold you?"

Marpessa shook her head. "Not here. Anyone might see. Tell me what you came here to say."

"I came to ask you to meet me. Tonight, after everyone in your household is asleep, meet me at the ruins. I implore you, Marpessa. I shall never ask you to come to me there again, but this once . . . I beg of

233

you. There is something I must tell you, but this is not a place where I can do it."

Marpessa glanced behind her for a moment and caught sight of Aphrodite leaning against the tree that was sheltering them.

"Do what he says," came the Goddess's whisper. "There will be a memory in your heart worth keeping, for I should warn you that there is little he has to say that will be a comfort to you . . ."

"Very well," Marpessa said. "I will be there as soon as I can. Wait for me."

She stood up and made her way out of the market without looking behind her. He is gone, she said to herself as she walked. He has asked me to the ruins to tell me that he no longer loves me. She felt a sickness come over her and leaned against the stones of the wall. Please, dear Aphrodite, help me! she said to herself. Let me not vomit here where everyone can see me . . .

The sickness left her at last, and she stumbled toward the palace. Just as she crossed the threshold, a terrible thought came into her mind suddenly, and she felt herself turn cold all over. Her bleeding . . . what had happened to the bleeding that came to her whenever the moon was on the wane? In the womenservants' quarters they spoke freely, and Marpessa knew that when a woman was carrying a child in her womb, her bleeding stopped. Could it be? Was it Alastor's child making her sick and weak? Surely, surely, when she told him what she was carrying in her own body, he would not cast her away? Hope, like a small bird, fluttered up into Marpessa's heart.

HELEN'S PALACE

"I realize that you are all heartbroken," said Deiphobus, looking around him at the servants of Paris's household, gathered in the hall of their master's palace. He sat on the chair his brother always favored, and Marpessa hated him for that and for being who he was: not Paris. Helen was in the seat next to him, and her whole body seemed to be pulled into itself, as though being close to him was painful to her. That, thought Marpessa, wasn't surprising. I wouldn't like to be sitting beside him. It was hard to believe he was Paris's brother. Deiphobus was thickset and dark, and shorter than Priam's other children. He had a long face, a square chin, and eyebrows that nearly met over his nose. He smiled and went on. "I am, naturally, heartbroken myself. I have lost too many brothers in this war, and the whole city is grieving both for them and for all the rest of the warriors who have gone to the Elysian Fields."

"Get on with it," someone muttered. Marpessa couldn't make out who it was, but she agreed with him. Everyone knew what was happening: The household was being taken apart, piece by piece. Priam had decided, and his word was law. Helen was being given to Deiphobus in marriage, and moving to his house, and all the servants were waiting to hear whether they were going to be dismissed. The question was: How many of them would Deiphobus take into his palace? And what would become of those who were forced to go home to their families, who could ill afford to feed them? Deiphobus continued. "The Lady Helen is doing me the honor of becoming my bride. It is my duty to care for her as my brother would have wished." He smiled at Helen. "I will do my utmost to make her as happy as she was with Paris."

"Little hope of that, my friend," came a whisper from behind Marpessa. "Not with your looks and character."

"An unfortunate aspect of this situation, however, is the fact that most of you will, I'm afraid, have to return to your families. I have servants of my own and, of course, I couldn't possibly let them go. My future wife says she will not come to my house without Marpessa—where are you, Marpessa? Please make yourself known. Ah, there you are! Lady Helen says you are like a daughter to her. You will help her prepare for the move. As for the rest of you, you will be paid some recompense. And I wish you all good fortune."

Marpessa found herself surrounded. Most of the servants were happy for her, and clustered around her to wish her well. A few kept away, saddened or jealous, but for most of the household she had been a kind of mascot or pet since the day she'd arrived in the palace as a small girl.

"Come, child," said Helen, standing up and turning toward the bedchamber. "Help me prepare."

Marpessa followed Helen out of the hall. As soon

as they were alone in the bedchamber, Helen sank onto the bed and covered her face with her hands.

"Oh, Marpessa, what is to become of us? Did you see him? Can you imagine what my life with him is going to be like? I can't bear it. I wish I could just lie down here and never wake up."

"Don't speak like that, Lady. I'll be with you. I'll take care of you."

"When the war is over, everything will change. I've dreaded the end of it for years and years, not knowing what would happen to me, or to any of us, but now, with Paris and Hector gone, I could almost wish for the Greeks to win."

"No, Lady, don't say that. What would become of our city and all of us in it?"

Helen looked up, and Marpessa hardly recognized the snarling features she saw.

"I don't care!" Helen was shouting, the words coming from a throat raw with sorrow. "It's not my city. It never has been my city. As far as I'm concerned, the whole place can fall apart stone by stone. If the Greeks win, I shall throw myself down at Menelaus's feet and beg him to take me back. And you can come with me. We can leave all this misery behind us and live in a civilized place once again. I sometimes forget how much I miss my home. Paris made me forget, but Deiphobus will make me long for it again. Why are you crying, Marpessa? What have I said? Speak to me."

Marpessa shook her head and wiped the tears from her eyes. "I've never thought of you leaving. And as for me, how could I go without Xanthe and . . ." She stopped abruptly. She had been about to mention Alastor, but caught herself before his name rose to her lips. "This is my home. It's the only home I know. I couldn't leave. Never."

"And me?" Helen was weeping now, too, and her voice wavered and shook. "What about me? You've been like a daughter to me, Marpessa. Without you, how could I have borne to be parted from my Hermione? And I thought you loved me . . ."

"I do. I do love you, Lady, but my sister . . . She's the only real family I know. How could I leave her here?"

"Then she'll have to come with us, that's all. I'll beg Menelaus. I'm sure he won't be able to refuse me anything." She laughed. "I'm sure I'll remember how to twist him around my little finger . . ."

But what, thought Marpessa, if Xanthe doesn't want to come? Do I want to leave Troy and all I've ever known? What if Alastor wants me to stay with him, when he hears that a baby is coming? And what if the Greeks don't win? What if we have to stay here, but not in these beautiful rooms? With Deiphobus. Helen, it was clear, had let her grief for Paris make her a little crazed.

"Let's prepare ourselves, Lady," she said at last. "We have to leave soon, and nothing is ready."

Helen flung herself back on the bed and covered her face with her scarf. "You do it. I can't think about it now. I'll come soon. Bring the jewels. We must pack them away carefully. I don't trust that man. We must wrap them in garments and put them in jars and bottles where he won't think to look."

"Surely he wouldn't?" Marpessa said.

"He would. They all would. The gold is coming to an end. Soon Priam won't be able to buy horses, or weapons, and then patriotic husbands will volunteer their wives' belongings. Wait and see. We must keep the jewels safe. There are some rags in that chest over there."

Helen's gold . . . Marpessa lifted each necklace, each bracelet and brooch, and laid it out, ready to be hidden. Light from the wall torches fell on filigree flowers and cunningly engraved discs that hung from finely worked chains like tiny suns. There were gemstones set into heavy rings: rubies from the East, turquoises the color of the sea, and amber like solid honey, carved into bird shapes, snake shapes, leaf shapes. Marpessa shook each piece as she wrapped it and listened to the bell-like music of the metal before muffling it with fabric. Helen, while she was working, sat up suddenly on the bed and began to finger a small bracelet made of coral splinters bound together with slender silver strands.

"Do you remember this, Marpessa? I gave it to you to play with the very first day you came into my service."

"And you said that it used to be your daughter's, but that I could wear it if I wanted to . . . That made me so happy. I wore it for days and days, and didn't even take it off to go to bed."

"You were such a tiny thing. Charitomene had been looking after the two of you, you and Xanthe, and then all of a sudden Hecuba decided that you were old enough to work for your living . . . poor little things . . . Scarcely more than babies, you both were, and yet so grown up. I never saw you crying, but you must have been so sad, separated from your sister and your nurse and everything you knew, and put into my house."

Marpessa bowed her head and smiled.

"I didn't weep, because I was happy. As soon as I saw you, as soon as I came into your courtyard, I knew that here I'd be surrounded by beauty in all its forms. I thought I must be on Olympus, among the Gods. And I knew that Xanthe was near. She told me. She told me that she would always look after me, and I believed her. I still believe her, whatever she tells me."

"There won't be much beauty where we're going, child. A different life awaits us, and I pray that it won't be for long. Here, take this and put it away. I feel like crying every time I look at it."

Marpessa wrapped the bracelet in a soft cloth and placed it with the other jewels.

"There, Lady," she said. "It's done. Everything's safe now."

Helen lay on the bed with her eyes closed and said nothing.

"She's not really asleep," said a voice from the corner of the room. Marpessa looked into the shadows and saw Hermes. She recognized him at once, by the feathered wings on his heels and his staff wound around with snakes.

"She's planning something," the God continued. "Everything is different now. She's going to do everything in her power to help the Greeks. She could have done it years ago, of course, but now it's become a matter of urgency."

"What can she do?" Marpessa asked. "She surely wouldn't dare to leave the city?"

"They wouldn't let her. But there are ways in and out, don't worry. The Greeks know what's going on.

They'll reach her. Things will start happening now, wait and see."

"Who's that?" Helen said from the bed. "Who are you talking to?"

"No one, Lady," said Marpessa. "I've finished the jewels."

"The robes, then. I feel like dressing myself in a sack for that horse-face Deiphobus, but I'm not leaving any of them behind."

Marpessa folded each garment gently, and laid it in the chest.

"You look pale, child," Helen said suddenly. "Are you sick?"

"No, Madam," said Marpessa after a long moment. She thought: How wonderful it would be to tell Helen everything! What would she say? Would she let me stay if she knew what I had done? I can't tell her. Not now. Maybe later, when we have settled into the new palace. She said, "I'm sad, that's all. I think of Lord Paris, and of how our lives were, and I'm afraid."

Helen picked up a skirt that seemed woven out of moonbeams and held it up to her face.

"I'm frightened, too," she said. "Only I don't know what I'm frightened of, and I refuse to let them see it. Deiphobus and all his people. We have to remember who we are."

"You are a queen, Madam," said Marpessa, "but who am I?"

Helen smiled. "You are a queen's dear child," she said. "And I shall look after you."

"Thank you," Marpessa said. Soon, soon, the night would fall, and she would be on her way to the ruins to meet Alastor.

HECUBA'S CHAMBER

"On my own? I'm to take Astyanax to his grand-mother all on my own?" Xanthe tried not to sound worried, but she couldn't help it. She'd never been to Hecuba's chamber all by herself. Usually she followed Andromache and carried everything. Babies seemed to need more equipment than a royal prince on a long voyage, and Xanthe, whenever they visited, had her arms full of carved animals, and Astyanax's special cup, and several soft cloths that he needed to cling to whenever he lay down for a rest. How was she supposed to take care of him and look after all his possessions at the same time? And was she meant to talk? Generally Andromache did that at least, answering Hecuba's questions and keeping up the chatter as best she could.

"Hecuba won't want to talk to me, Lady," she said to Andromache, trying to persuade her to come. "And it's good for you to go out sometimes. You are too much alone."

Andromache dragged herself off her bed for some part of every day, that much was true, but she was still—Xanthe didn't know how to express it—still *absent*, and she had taken to looking at people, not straight in the eye, but over their shoulder, as though there were something behind them that was more interesting than they were. *It's almost as though* (this was what Xanthe had said to Polyxena) *every single person Andromache sees is hiding her husband from her.*

"Going to see Hecuba is not good for me." She shook her head. "It's good for Astyanax to see his grandmother, and I want him to grow up knowing who he is—a king's grandson—but it's awful for me. She stares, Hecuba, she stares all the time, and wonders—even after all these years, she wonders, I can tell—what it was that Hector saw in me. She'd never say so, but that's the truth. And then there's Cassandra. I've never known how to speak to her, but now she's impossible. I can't find a single word to say. She's always been peculiar, and now, from all I hear, she's worse than ever. Please, Xanthe, I beg you. Please go for me."

So Xanthe did as she was told, and now here she was, sitting on the floor of Hecuba's room while Astyanax played next to her, with his carved animals about him. Cassandra sat on a chair like a small throne. Its arms and legs were inlaid with flower patterns in mother-of-pearl, and there were cushions on it embroidered with silver thread. She paid no attention to Xanthe at all, but from the moment the two of them had come into the room (Xanthe with her arms full of toys and bits and pieces, and Astyanax clinging to her skirt), she had started to stare at the baby, and her eyes were still fixed on him. Hecuba had sent a servant to the kitchen, and drinks of crushed lemons and water mixed with honey were brought, and there were even some small cakes.

"Take a cake, Astyanax, my lovely boy," Hecuba said, sounding like a dove cooing. "War or no war, there's always something tasty for my little darling. And come over here and give your grandmother a big kiss."

Xanthe led Astyanax by the hand, and the child let himself be enveloped in the curtains of black cloth that Hecuba had taken to wearing.

"Horsies," he murmured. "Want horsies."

Hecuba wiped a tear from her eye. She said, "He's like his father. Just like my poor Hector. Have I told you . . . Xanthe? Is that your name? Of course it is . . . I remember now. I'm getting old and forgetting everything. Hector had a whole collection of creatures made from the tusks of elephants, and the horses were always *his* favorites, too. I must see if I can find them somewhere. I've been hiding things away for so many years now that I scarcely know what's left to us. Yes, darling, go and play with your horsies. Play here, where I can look at you."

Hecuba turned to Xanthe and said, "Why has Andromache not come to visit me? Has she no respect for the mother of her late husband?"

"Oh, no, Lady," said Xanthe quickly, horrified. "She speaks of you with love and honor, but today . . ." (What can I say? Xanthe thought. What excuse can I give that won't get Andromache into trouble?) "She is troubled with pains in her head." Inspired, she went on: "My mistress has slept very badly since Lord Hector died. She dreams he is alive, and then the pain she feels when she wakes up is terrible."

"I know . . ." Hecuba shook her head sadly. "I suffer in that way myself. I dream of him sometimes, and

244

he is no older than Astyanax. Nothing but anguish for the mother of a warrior from the day that he's born. Anguish." She reached out and helped herself to a cake. Xanthe racked her brains for something to say, and gazed around the room. Cassandra had stood up, and Xanthe looked at her more carefully. She was making her way over to Astyanax. . . . She was squatting down near him and staring and staring in that mad, unsettling way that she had. Astyanax took no notice. He was holding his favorite horse, Blackie, who was carved from dark wood, and galloping him up one row of tiles and down another. Blackie eventually came to rest at Cassandra's feet, and Astyanax looked up at her.

"Horsie," he said. "Blackie."

Cassandra held out both her hands, cupped as if she were waiting for water to be poured into them.

"Will you let me hold him?" she asked Astyanax. "Just for a very short time? He's so beautiful."

Astyanax nodded and placed the toy in his aunt's hands. For a long moment, Cassandra stared at it, and Xanthe saw her grow pale. Her mouth began to twist, and soon tears were gathering in her eyes. She sprang up suddenly, and, putting her hands as far away as possible from her body, she began to scream. Her mouth became a cave, a dark cave, and the sounds that came from it sent a shiver of dread through Xanthe's body. It sounded as though Cassandra were being torn limb from limb.

Hecuba leaped up and ran to her daughter. She put an arm around Cassandra and murmured in her ear while calling for the servants over her shoulder. Astyanax went to Xanthe and buried his face in her lap.

Xanthe wanted to move, too. She, too, wanted to run, just like the baby, and hide her eyes, because what she was seeing was so dreadful. The princess was still holding the toy horse, and over and over again she shrieked words that Xanthe could scarcely make sense of. Something to do with fire and flames. She threw the toy horse away from her at last, and then brought her hands to her face. Both the palms were scarlet, as though they'd been burned, but how could that be? The horse was lying on the tiles. Perhaps Cassandra had been clutching it so hard that the wood had hurt her in some way. Xanthe picked Astyanax up and went to fetch the toy from where it had fallen. Cassandra had stopped shrieking. Hecuba took her over to the bed, and she lay on it, twisting from side to side and murmuring quietly. Xanthe couldn't help hearing her words:

"Burning . . . my hands burning . . . Run. Take them away . . . Take the flames away . . . The fire's coming. It's coming . . . the fire."

Hecuba turned from the bedside and said to Xanthe, "Don't worry, child. She's just . . . tired. Overwrought. She . . . takes everything very hard. This siege is trying for her."

"I understand, Lady," Xanthe said. "But Astyanax wants to go home now. To his mother."

"Yes, yes, of course. Thank you for bringing him to me. And please send my fond greetings to Andromache."

Xanthe and Astyanax made their way out of Hecuba's chamber. Cassandra's moaning followed them along the corridors and out into the courtyard. Her mind is wounded, Xanthe thought. Something has pierced her heart, and she feels as much pain as the men lying in the Blood Room torn apart by spears. She shook her head, trying to forget how the princess had sounded, trying to scrub from her mind the memory of Cassandra's voice. The baby was sucking Blackie's foot as though nothing had happened.

"Mama," he said to Xanthe. "Want Mama."

"Yes," Xanthe answered. "We'll soon be there. Soon be home."

⊙꘠꘠꘠꘠꘠꘠꘠꘠꘠꘠꘠꘠꘠꘠꘠꘠꘠꘠꘠꘠꘠꘠꘠꘠꘠꘠꘠꘠꘠꘠꘠꘠꘠꘠꘠꘠꘠꘠⊙

THE RUINS

⊙꘠꘠꘠꘠꘠꘠꘠꘠꘠꘠꘠꘠꘠꘠꘠꘠꘠꘠꘠꘠꘠꘠꘠꘠꘠꘠꘠꘠꘠꘠꘠꘠꘠꘠꘠꘠꘠꘠⊙

Everything is transformed at night. Artemis, the Goddess of the moon, is the best of enchantresses, Marpessa thought as she looked around her and saw the
buildings that were so familiar to her changed and
made beautiful in the silver light that flooded the sky.
The air was warm, even though Phoebus Apollo's
chariot had plunged into the sea a long time ago; and
silence so thick that it almost hummed lay over roofs
and streets and stones. She walked to the ruins as
quietly as she could, holding her sandals in her hand
because her bare feet made no sound at all. I ought to
be frightened, she thought. There may be evil spirits
abroad in the darkness, but I don't care. They can't
touch me, because I'm on my way to see him. She
looked toward the Greek camp and saw, far, far away,
the scarlet glow of their watch fires burning. Down on
the walls, she knew, there were sentries posted in case
their enemies should take it into their heads to attack
at night, but everyone knew these men generally
dozed with their backs against a rock, and relied on
their dogs waking up and barking at any sign of movement on the Plain.

"Alastor!" she whispered. "Are you here?" She

stepped into the shadow of the broken wall, picking her way carefully through the rubble on the ground.

"Here, Marpessa. I'm here. Come to me."

Marpessa noticed that he had come prepared. She had grumbled and complained about the hardness of the bare earth, and here was a blanket: thick, hand-woven, probably the best Phrontis's house had to offer. Surely she hadn't allowed him to rifle through her chests?

"Sit here," he said. "Sit beside me."

"There is something I should tell you," Marpessa began.

"Later," said Alastor. "Kiss me first."

Marpessa turned her mouth to his. It's an enchantment, she thought. Part of the darkness and the silence and the silver light: It melts me, and changes me, and I can't remember what was in my head before, nor what I wanted to say. She closed her eyes and let herself sink backward to the ground. Part of her knew. Part of her was saying, Why are you doing this? It won't help you. It will hurt you in the end. But now it's like honey and like silk.

"Marpessa . . . ," Alastor breathed. "I can't bear to think of my life without you." His hands were on her breasts, and he was lifting her skirt. Stop him, something in Marpessa said, but her limbs had a life of their own and wrapped themselves around him as though they were ivy tendrils clinging and clinging. Her mouth was open, sucking him into her, and she pushed herself against him, wanting every part of her skin to fuse with his, wanting to become one creature, intertwined and breathing the same breath forever.

She closed her eyes, and the whole universe was only him, Alastor, panting against her neck until at last she felt herself trembling and drowning; her whole body shivering into bright pieces, like the sparks that fall from a flaming torch.

They lay quietly for a long time when the loving was over. Marpessa turned to look at him, and his eyes were closed. Perhaps, she thought, he is asleep. Should I wake him? She knew that soon they must leave this place, but she didn't want to move. We could stay here forever. She smiled at the silver stones, at the black shadows that moved among them. This could be our house. We already have a blanket.

"I'm not asleep," he murmured. "You can speak to me, beautiful Marpessa."

"No," she said. "You must speak to me. You asked me here to tell me something. Or at least that was what you told me this morning. Perhaps it was an excuse, and you simply wanted to lie down with me."

"Of course I wanted that. I haven't been able to stop thinking about you. There's a fire burning in my body, and only you can put it out."

Marpessa said nothing, but she smiled inwardly. Paris, when he was alive, said things like that all the time. And he meant them, too, just as Alastor meant what he said, but it amounted to so little. All he was saying was: I desire you. Your body calls to me. Paris had found many, many women who made him feel like that. Maybe Alastor was the same. Maybe all men were. I wish, Marpessa thought, that I knew more about them.

Alastor sat up and moved away from her a little.

"The things I have to say to you are not easy," he

began. "I wanted you to hear them from me rather than from gossiping servants."

Marpessa lay like a statue, staring at the air in front of her. Something heavy and dark was coming toward her, like a boulder rolling down a mountainside. For one wild moment she thought: I'll get up and run away, and then I won't have to hear it, but almost at once, she *knew*, better than she had ever known anything in her entire life, that there was no escape from what Alastor had to say. She struggled upright and then rose to her feet and went to sit some way away from where they had been lying.

"Speak, Alastor," she said at last. "I'm ready for whatever you have to tell me."

"I'm to be wed," he said, staring at the ground between his knees, and in such a low voice that Marpessa had to lean forward to catch his words. "My mother has arranged for it all to take place in a few days. My . . . my betrothed has arrived from the country, with her father, and everything is being prepared. I can't avoid it, Marpessa. My father's dying wish was that I should marry her . . . Agamede."

Marpessa said, "Very well. I'll go now and never speak to you again. I wish you and your bride all the good fortune in the world." She began to walk toward the entrance to the ruin.

"Wait, wait, Marpessa, I implore you!" Alastor ran after her, catching her by the hand and pulling her to his side. "I can't let you go like this! Will I never see you? Will you not come to me again?"

"The moon has made you take leave of your senses," Marpessa hissed at him. "What do you think I am? Just because I have no family and work for the

251

Lady Helen, you think I'm not a real person; someone of no consequence. Did you truly imagine I'd be content to be some kind of concubine? Some little plaything you come to when your duties as a husband grow too boring? Never, Alastor. Do you hear me? Never."

"But you love me! You said you did . . ."

"The word love has never crossed my lips," Marpessa said. "You are thinking of another of your conquests, I've no doubt."

"There *are* no other conquests, Marpessa! Why are you being like this? Why are you so cruel?"

"Cruel? Me, cruel?" The injustice of this made Marpessa burst into tears. How could he speak of cruelty, he who had just taken her happiness and shattered it into fragments?

"I don't know whether I can live without you," Alastor said.

Marpessa wiped her tears away and whispered, "Of course you'll live without me! Another woman . . . this bride of yours, if you're lucky, will soon make you forget me. I'm just a body to you, Alastor, and when you're married, you'll think of me. The memory of our loving will be pleasant, just as though you were recalling a fine feast you once ate. Farewell. I am going back now. Don't follow me. Don't seek me out. My body will forget you one day."

"But you said you had something to tell me," Alastor said.

"I no longer want to tell you anything," Marpessa said, "and certainly not that."

"What was it? I'll suffer if I never know."

Marpessa smiled. "Really? Will you? How happy

252

that makes me! I find I want you to suffer a little. Isn't that strange? I'll keep my secret safe, then, and you'll never discover what it was."

Iason was awake and outside the stables preparing water for the horses. Glancing up toward the temple, he noticed someone running. Where could they be coming from at this time, before the sky was even light? And who was it? It didn't seem like a man to him . . . There was something about the gait. At last he could see clearly. Marpessa. It was Marpessa. He shrank against the wall so that she shouldn't see him. What was she running away from? Was she in danger? Should he ask if he could help her? He looked toward the temple again. No one was following her. Had she been there, offering up a sacrifice perhaps? Xanthe had often told him that Marpessa saw the Gods walking about. But no one went there in the middle of the night, surely? Should he say something? To Xanthe? Or should he ask Marpessa herself? He scarcely knew her, and found her very hard to talk to. Maybe it was none of his business. Iason decided to keep silent for the moment. He turned and went in to the horses. A small ginger kitten wound itself in and out of his legs as he walked, and he picked it up and said to it, "I'll stick to talking to you, little thing. There's nothing difficult about that."

THE GOSSIPS

DEIPHOBUS'S PALACE

Theano was doing her best to make Helen's new quarters look something like what she was used to, without much success.

"How'm I supposed to make this room beautiful when she's said nothing must be taken from the chests? No hangings, no cushions, no ornaments, nothing. It's impossible."

"She never said she wanted things to be beautiful," Halie said. "Clean'll do. That's what I'm interested in. Have you ever seen so much dust? You can see that Deiphobus spends his time elsewhere—taverns and whorehouses, I shouldn't wonder."

"But why," Danae asked, "is everyone going about with such gloomy looks? Has anything happened I don't know about?"

"You must've heard . . ." Theano had found a decorated bowl and was spitting on a cloth and rubbing the bowl's sides to see if it was worthy, once it was clean, of course, to be put on display in the rooms of a princess who was used to nothing but the best.

"Heard what?" Danae was devoted to Theano, but her friend *did* enjoy spinning things out.

"That little statue they call the Luck of Troy, the

one that's kept safe by the maidens in Pallas Athene's temple . . ."

"I know what the Luck is . . . Go on."

"It's gone. Someone's stolen it."

Danae's hands flew to her face and covered it, and she stood there for some time, rocking backward and forward. At last she looked at Theano and Halie again.

"Why ever didn't you tell me? What's the matter with you both?" she said. "Do you have any idea how important this is?"

"Well, of course," said Halie. "Of course we do. Devoted to the Goddess, I am. Always have been. I sacrifice to her at every full moon, or I used to when there was something left to give her."

"You don't understand," said Danae. "There's no one in the city who'd do a thing like that. So . . ."

"So what?" Theano said. "Tell us what you mean."

"So it means that someone else did it. A Greek, for instance."

Halie and Theano both laughed. "You're cracked, you are!" they cried. "How could any Greek come into our city, when it's all locked and barred?"

"That's what you think," said Danae. "There are ways in and out. Through the drains, for instance. Thought everyone knew that."

"Even so," said Theano. "Even if someone *did* come through the drains . . . Ugh . . . How could they get right up there, to the temple, and then into it, and then all the way back with the statue? It's impossible."

"You've forgotten how cunning Odysseus is. 'Specially with a bit of inside help."

"What's that supposed to mean?" Halie said. "You know an awful lot all of a sudden."

"I remember things, that's all. Like the fact that Odysseus wanted to marry Helen, before he had to make do with her cousin Penelope."

"So?"

"So maybe they're still . . . well, *lovey-dovey.* I'm not saying more than that."

Theano took a broom made of twigs from a corner of the room and handed it to Danae.

"Here, ducky, sweep the floor. Leave stories to the storytellers." She shook her head and raised her eyebrows at Halie as if to say, *Whatever next! Lady Helen helping the Greeks! Out of the question.* Completely out of the question. Still, someone *had* crept in and stolen the Luck of Troy. That was worrying, and no mistake.

ANDROMACHE'S GARDEN

"He's lovely, isn't he?" Polyxena looked tenderly at Astyanax, who was busy making a porridge out of earth and water in a cracked bowl. He was stirring his concoction with his fingers, and Xanthe was watching him carefully to make sure that he didn't put them into his mouth. She turned to her friend.

"He's the most beautiful child in the world, and I love him better than anyone—except Marpessa—and you, of course . . ."

"Of course!"

"But he is very tiring. You can't take your eyes off him for a moment. He's always running away and hiding, or putting things he shouldn't into his mouth, or wanting to stay up all night when I want to sleep, or wanting to sleep when I feel like going for a walk, or wanting something to eat when there's nothing in the kitchen. Sometimes I find my eyes closing when I'm standing up."

"But you're good at it. You're a natural mother. Unlike me. I'd go mad and fling myself from the walls if I had to look after a baby. The Singer's bad enough, but at least I can say to him, Stop. Let me rest for a while. I hope you have lots of children of your own, and then I can be their honorary aunt and come to your house and lie on cushions and give out sweets and cakes and toys."

"I would need a father for these children," Xanthe said, distracting Astyanax's attention from an interesting-looking insect he was poking with a twig.

Polyxena sighed. There was never going to be a better time, and only yesterday Iason had asked her to speak to Xanthe again, and again she had promised. She said, "It's funny you should mention that. There's something I should tell you. Are you listening?"

Xanthe smiled. "I might have known you didn't just come here to admire the baby."

"No. I didn't. I promised someone I would talk to you. Ask you something."

Could it be Alastor? Xanthe thought, even in the instant when she knew such a thing was impossible. "Who is it?" she said wearily. "Go on, tell me."

"Can't you guess?"

"No, I can't. I really can't."

"It's Iason. He asked me to ask you whether you would consider him. Whether you'd allow him to come to the Lady Andromache and seek permission to become betrothed. He says he can't marry you until times are more settled, but as he said, the war can't go on forever."

Iason. The friend of her childhood. Someone she had known for so long that she no longer thought about whether she liked him or not. Part of her life for as long as she could remember. What did she feel for him? She said, "I've never thought of him like that."

"But he's handsome enough, isn't he?" Polyxena said. "Not the divine Alastor, I admit, but no worse

258

than any other young man, surely? And I've forgotten to say the most important thing. He loves you. He really does. He would treat you well, and respect you, and he would be faithful."

"I've heard what you think of men. You think they're incapable of being faithful."

"If any one of them is, it's Iason. He's kind. You should see the way he treats the horses. And not just them. All the creatures who seem to live in those stables."

"I'm not a horse," said Xanthe. "You can't tell anything from that."

"Maybe not," said Polyxena, "but I wouldn't marry someone who whipped his horses or kicked his dogs, would you?"

Xanthe shook her head. Iason. She picked up Astyanax, and said, "It's time for him to eat, Polyxena. Thank you for bringing me Iason's message."

"Is there anything you can say in reply? I'll pass the stables and speak to him, if you want to say anything . . ." Please, dear Gods on Olympus, let her say it. Let her tell him she could never love him. Let her say she cannot possibly marry him, ever.

"Tell him I'll think about it," Xanthe said. "That's all I can say now. I'll think."

"If you cleared your heart of Alastor," Polyxena said, "everything would be much easier." How strange it is, she thought, that my oldest friend cannot see what I am feeling. I am good at pretending, after all this time.

"You're very grown up and full of advice all of a sudden. Maybe you should set yourself up as a marriage broker."

"I'd love to, but my time is filled with the Singer. Farewell, Xanthe, and let me kiss this chubby creature."

She put her lips to Astyanax's pink cheek and made her way out of the garden and toward the stables.

THE STABLES

Iason always rose early. Horses began their snorting and neighing long before people woke up, and he was always ready to wake up when they did. There was hay to be put out and water to be changed, and as soon as he started to move around in the stables, the stray dogs and cats woke up as well, and gathered around his feet to see whether there was any food for them as well as for the horses. Since Hector's death, they'd taken up residence among the bales of straw.

"Lord Hector would never have allowed you to stay here," Iason told them. "He'd have sent you packing. All the food's meant to be for the horses, but I'll find you some scraps later, I promise."

Since Paris's death, a kind of stillness seemed to have fallen on the warriors, both Greek and Trojan, and Iason was grateful for it. Everyone said it was only temporary, and that the end was in sight. Soon, some people said, there would be a battle that would make all the other battles look like children's games. But someone was always saying something of the kind, ever since Iason could remember. Meanwhile, days had gone by, and all his stallions and mares had stayed in their stalls, and he had spent most of his time grooming them, shining their coats up as best he could. They were painfully thin, naturally, but that didn't mean they had to look uncared for. The cats and dogs were even skinnier. You could see every rib and every bump on their spines through the fur, and Iason felt so sorry for them that he let them stay, and found whatever food he could for them. At least they had escaped the cooking pots. In certain parts of the city, they said, anything that walked or flew or even crawled ended up being cooked by someone. Pet doves in dovecotes, and songbirds in cages . . . All of them ended up on some dish or other.

He walked out to the stable yard and sat on the small bench that Hector had put there. There was nothing to do now but wait. The ginger kitten followed him out and jumped up onto his lap.

"It's you, is it? My little ginger friend. Polyxena says that she will tell Xanthe soon, and I suppose I'll have to be content with that for now. Then, whatever her answer is, she'll know my feelings. That's good, isn't it, cat?"

The kitten purred loudly, happy to be spoken to, happy to have found a warm place to curl up and someone who stroked him kindly.

DEIPHOBUS'S PALACE

Marpessa couldn't sleep. She rose from her bed and made her way to the courtyard. This place was nothing like the pleasant garden Helen had made in the palace she shared with Paris. There was a bench here, and that was all. No trees and no vines; no bushes full of flowers. She sat down on the hard stone of the bench. At least it was cool now. During the day, no one would think of resting here, in the full heat of the sun. The night was almost over. The sky was tinged with pink; the air was cooler, and what was left of the moon, pale Artemis, thin and white now, with all her silver power faded, hung over the dark shadow of the mountain. I cannot carry his child, Marpessa thought. I must find a way to rid my body of it . . . his son. His daughter. She thought of the child, imagining it something like Astyanax. If she gave birth to it, if she claimed that Alastor was the father, he might acknowledge it. He would take his offspring (that's how *he* would think of it) into his household, perhaps, but without her. She would have to give up her own baby, flesh of her flesh . . . maybe never see it again. Phrontis would forbid her seeing it, and that would be that. As for the new bride, what would she have to say? Perhaps she could bring the child up herself, and demand payment. There were enough such households down in the city, but Marpessa shrank from the prospect. *That's Alastor's bastard*, people would say . . . unthinkable. A torture. And part of her, a part that she didn't want to listen to but that insisted on being heard, said in the wicked whisper of a snake, *It will be a kind of punishment for him . . . for the way he has treated you. Kill his child. It's what he deserves. Kill it. Soon. Rid your womb of every particle of his being. Cleanse yourself.*

PHRONTIS'S HOUSE

The whole household was asleep. Alastor was making sure that all the windows and doors were secure against intruders. His mother was fussy about such matters. *Bad times, my son,* she said to him constantly, *mean that bad people are wandering about in the night, and they won't mind a bit helping themselves to other people's property.* Life was easier if he obeyed his mother. He stood in the courtyard, and that was when he saw him: the same black-clad soldier he'd seen so often before.

"You!" Alastor breathed. "What are you doing here? And who are you? I see you everywhere, and you will not stop to speak to me."

"I've been somewhat occupied," the man said in a voice like knives being scraped across stone. "I gave you my name once, but you've forgotten it, I see. Ares, God of War."

Alastor thought: I must be dreaming. Marpessa sees the Gods, not I. Not someone practical and sensible like me. This is some madman, crazed by too much fighting. He noticed the sword hanging by the warrior's side and the shadow under his helmet where his eyes should have been. Why were they always hidden? The voice went on.

"It's not as easy as it looks, organizing things. Every battle has a plan, and every death, every wounding, has to be worked out. It's exhausting, I can tell you. But it's almost over . . . this war."

"Really?" For a moment, Alastor forgot that he was dealing with a lunatic and imagined that maybe he was hearing the truth from the mouth of the God of Battles himself.

"Zeus has put pressure on me. It's enough . . . That's the feeling on Olympus. It's all gone on long enough. I had to promise that the end was in sight. I had to tell him I had a plan, and now I have. A brilliant one, if I do say so myself. Worked out by Odysseus, but put into his head by me, naturally. Sometime very soon, the Trojans will wake up to find the Greek army has gone. There won't be a single tent left on that beach. You'll all think: Our enemies have sailed away, and you'll all start rejoicing. But I'll tell you something as long as you promise not to tell a soul."

"I promise," Alastor said. "Go on."

"They won't go at all. They'll simply sail a little way down the coast. They'll wait for the signal to return. And they've been busy, this last moon or two. They've cut down the straightest trees they could find and sliced them into long planks. There's been hammering and sawing and planing and putting together. Now everything's ready. They'll throw water on their campfires and slip out of the bay in their ships. And they'll leave something for you Trojans to find. I shan't say another word. You'll have to wait and see what it is."

The Black Warrior . . . Ares, the God of War,

wrapped himself in his long dark cloak and stepped out of the courtyard.

"Wait!" Alastor shouted. "Come back! Tell me more. Come back!"

Phrontis came hurrying out of the inner rooms, her night garments flapping around her ankles.

"Is something the matter, my darling son? Is someone trying to break in? We should lock up before sunset, and not wait for the night to arrive. What terrifying times we live in! Who was it? Did you get a glimpse of the robber?"

"It wasn't a robber, Mother."

"Then who was it?"

Alastor shook his head to clear it of the mist that seemed to be filling it.

"Someone . . . I don't remember exactly. He told me things, but I've forgotten them, too."

"Are you sure you haven't been tasting your dear late father's wine? You know I have some jars left in the cellar . . ."

"No, Mother, really. Go to bed now. I'm coming. Truly."

After Phrontis had made her way, muttering, into the house, Alastor closed his eyes. The Black Warrior. He said he was Ares, but that couldn't possibly be true, could it? And what was it he was saying? Alastor found that he had forgotten every word, although for a little while he had a dim memory of a voice like knives being scraped across stone. Then that, too, faded away.

MOTHER POISON'S HOVEL

Marpessa looked up and down the street to make sure that no one was following her. The servants on their way to market or anyone who had business near the walls might catch a glimpse of her here, where she had never set foot before, and tell Helen. I can't tell her. I can't tell anyone. Marpessa thought of her sister. What would Xanthe say if she knew? Would she ever forgive me, first of all for lying with Alastor and then for ridding myself of his child? A wave of sickness came over her, and she leaned against a wall till it passed. Her whole body felt swollen and raw, and her limbs were heavy. Not as heavy as her heart, but stiff and clumsy. Was this because she was growing a baby deep inside her? Was this what all women felt? She touched the coins she had taken from her box of treasures, now carefully wrapped in a piece of cloth, and wondered whether they would be enough. What if Mother Poison wanted more?

The street . . . Marpessa wrinkled her nose. She had never been to this part of the city before, almost as far away from the citadel as it was possible to walk, and had only found out how to get here by listening carefully to the women talking. Meat bones and rotting leaves and other decaying and unrecognizable things lay about outside the open doors of the houses. Who lived here? What sort of people could bear the stench? Marpessa held her wrapped-up coins to her nose, hoping to catch a whiff of Helen's fragrant rose oil from the cloth.

"Come in, child." A voice like cracked leather spoke out of the darkness. "I can feel you there, hovering like a phantom. Come in, if you seek my help."

Marpessa took a deep breath and crossed the threshold. She peered around her, trying to find Mother Poison. Where was she?

"Your eyes," the voice continued, "will soon grow used to the dimness. The sun outside has dazzled them. I am here."

"Yes," said Marpessa. "I can see you now."

Mother Poison was sitting on a low chair beside a table. She was wrinkled and small and covered from head to toe in black shreds: rags, tatters—there wasn't a single piece of whole cloth anywhere about her body. Her teeth were broken and yellowy brown, and there were wide spaces between one tooth and another. Her fingernails were black. Well, Marpessa thought to herself, she can't help that. She isn't rich. She has no bath. There are no pitchers full of water anywhere that I can see. She's old and alone, with no one to go to the spring for her. Her appearance isn't important.

On the wall behind Mother Poison's chair, strips of ox hide and lambskin hung from hooks. Dead birds nailed to wooden planks on another wall stared at Marpessa out of lifeless eyes, and in the corner a heap of small creatures—rabbits, snakes, bats, mice—also dead, gave off a stench so terrible that she thought she would faint.

"Sit, child," said Mother Poison. "You'll get used to the smell, too. Just as you grew used to the darkness. These are my . . . materials. I have to use anything that comes to hand in these difficult times. Frogs are scarce. Birds are hard to get hold of, but I have an arrangement with someone who shoots them for me on the mountain. Some herbs are also almost impossible to find, but I manage. Who is it you wish to kill?"

Marpessa burst into tears.

"I don't . . . I wouldn't . . . Please. I don't want to kill anyone . . . But yes, in a way I do. I'm worse than the worst of murderers. I want to kill my child."

"How old? You don't look more than a child yourself."

"Here," Marpessa held her hand to her stomach. "It's not yet born . . ."

Mother Poison made a sucking noise through her teeth.

"It's easier to kill the ones that are already here. There are many ways of doing that. Are you quite sure you wouldn't prefer to wait, and hold a pillow over the infant's mouth? That's simplest. There's plenty who do that, you know, and no questions asked. It's a burden these days, looking after a child. Not enough food, and who knows when a Greek knife will spring out of the air and into your child's heart, eh? Better spare it that fate. Am I right?"

No, Marpessa wanted to scream. You aren't right. Once the child is born it's a person.

"You comfort yourself," Mother Poison said, as

though she could see into Marpessa's head. "You say: It's not a person yet. They all say that, all the young girls . . . That's why so many come to me for abortions."

"Can you help me? Is there . . . something I can drink?"

Mother Poison rummaged under the table and brought out a box. She opened it and took out a small clay bottle, stoppered and decorated with a pattern of black snakes.

"You'll have pains like you've never had before," she said. "You'll feel as though your belly is being torn open with a hot blade. You'll bleed. And burning fever will come to you and sit on your pillow. Are you ready for what you must suffer?"

Marpessa nodded. "I'd rather suffer pain in my body than in my heart."

Mother Poison laughed, and the sound raised the hairs on Marpessa's arms.

"You speak from ignorance. Now go. The sooner you take the potion, the sooner your pain will begin. Three gold coins. That's my price."

Marpessa opened her bundle, and took out the payment.

"Put it in my hand," said Mother Poison.

Marpessa tried to drop the coins into the filthy palm without touching it, but the crone was too quick. As one hand closed clawlike over the gold, the other grasped Marpessa's wrist and squeezed it tight.

"Bad times are nearly upon us," she whispered. "They're there, just beyond the edges of the water. Terrible times. Better for your child not to be born. Much better. Be brave."

"Yes," said Marpessa. "I give you my thanks."

"Mother," said Mother Poison. "Call me Mother."

"I thank you, Mother. Farewell."

Marpessa stumbled out of the room. She had almost forgotten what fresh air was. The sun was low in the sky, sliding toward the ocean. Bad times were coming . . . That's what Mother Poison had said. What did that mean? When were the times good? How could things be worse than they were now, full of fighting and starvation?

By the time she arrived back at Deiphobus's palace, night had fallen. Marpessa went at once to the tiny bare room where she now slept and put the bottle Mother Poison had given her under the small cushion that served her for a pillow. Much later, as she lay waiting for sleep to come to her, she remembered about the pain—what were the words? *As though your belly is being torn open with a hot blade.* She trembled. When at last her eyes closed, her sleep was full of dreams. She saw a young woman, gray-eyed and draped in a glittering bronze tunic, standing at the foot of her bed, and even in her sleep she knew this was Pallas Athene, looking just the same as she had on the Plain. A white owl with its wings folded sat on the Goddess's shoulder, and it stared balefully at Marpessa out of amber eyes.

"Wait," Pallas Athene murmured. "Wait before you swallow that draft. For a little while at least."

"Speak to me," said Marpessa in the dream, rising from her bed. "Tell me what will happen." But the Goddess had vanished. Marpessa found herself awake again and standing with her face to the wall.

"Goddess . . . ," she whispered. "Are you still here?"

There was no answer, but the room was filled with a soft, fluttering noise, and as Marpessa turned she caught a glimpse of wide white wings and amber eyes disappearing into the darkness. She went to the pillow, found the vial of poison, wrapped it again in a piece of cloth, and put it with her other treasures in the box that she kept hidden under her bed.

THE SINGER'S HOUSE
AND ON THE WALLS

The Singer peered into the darkness and blinked. No, it couldn't be. Something was not right. Perhaps this was the moment he had always dreaded, and his eyesight had grown so weak that he could no longer make out something as bright as leaping flames. He looked again out of the doorway and down the hill from his house toward the place where he knew the Greeks kept fires lit all night long. Nothing but black and more black from one end of the beach to the other. Impossible.

"Grandfather, what are you doing?" Polyxena appeared at his shoulder quite suddenly, and she sounded sleepy and cross. "It isn't even daylight yet. How long have you been standing here? It's cold. Take a cloak at least."

"Come here, Polyxena. I'm so glad you've come. I think I'm losing my mind. Look out of the door, and over to the Greek camp."

Polyxena groaned. Not even an apology. An order instead. Truly the Singer was growing impossible. Still, she went to see what it was that had so excited him, and saw nothing.

"What do you see? Tell me." The Singer sounded breathless.

"Nothing."

"Are you sure?"

"Quite sure. Nothing at all. Nothing but darkness. Grandfather, it's still nighttime. We should be sleeping."

"No, no," said the Singer. "We're going to the walls. Quick. Fetch my walking stick and put on a cloak. We must go at once."

"I'm not going anywhere till you tell me what's happening." Polyxena sat down on a stool and smiled at the Singer.

"Not one single Greek watch fire is burning on the shore."

"What does that mean?" Polyxena began to feel a stirring of excitement. Could it be? She held her breath while the old man fiddled with the fastening of his cloak.

"Unless they are all the worse for wine and have let their fires go out—and I doubt that, I very much doubt that—the Greeks have gone."

Polyxena felt as though her heart was beating in her throat. For almost her whole life there had been Greek armies on the beach. They were as much part of life as fruit appearing on trees, and now, maybe, everything was going to change. Could this be, could it possibly be the end of the siege?

"Let's go and see," she said. "Come, lean on me."

Together the Singer and his granddaughter made their way out of the citadel and down through the silent streets of the city. Behind them, as they walked, the sky was lightening gradually. From the stables, as they passed them, came the soft whinnying of the horses. In Deiphobus's palace a torch was burning. Was that Helen or Marpessa, or someone else? Probably only one of the servants, Polyxena thought, preparing some food and drink for the morning. By the time she and the Singer reached the walls, the sky over the city was palest pink. They climbed up the massive stone steps to the top and looked around.

"Call themselves sentries," the Singer muttered. "Disgraceful!" He sucked his teeth in disgust. Two soldiers were asleep, sitting on the ground with their backs against a boulder, and there were flasks beside them, which had once, clearly, been full of wine. "I abhor drunkenness. The entire Greek army could be waiting to attack."

"But it isn't. Look."

The Singer and Polyxena stared down at the Plain. From the walls to the shore there was no sign of anything human. No Greek ships floating at anchor in the bay; there was not a single fire burning. An army of men shouts and cries and curses, and the sounds it makes are carried in the air and come to the ears of their enemies whatever the time of day or night. Now the Plain rang with silence. Even the winds, which loved to rush toward the walls of Troy and fling themselves against the stones, were still. And down there, near the beach, there was something. Something enormous, and dark, and unmoving.

"What is it?" Polyxena whispered. "Can you see it?"

"Not very well . . . Can't you?"

"I think it's . . . No, it can't be, it's much too big. It looks like a horse."

"A horse? Are you sure?"

The sun had risen and was chasing away the few shadows that lingered among the stones. Polyxena could see more clearly now. The thing was a statue of some kind. It was hard to see exactly what it looked like, but it was definitely a horse, and there were flowers and garlands all over it, hanging from its neck and wound around its legs. There was the mane, and the rump. . . . How could she not have seen at once that it was a horse?

"Yes," she said at last. "But it's huge. Hard to tell how tall, but it must be at least as high as three men, because I can see it quite clearly now that it's properly light, and it's standing on some kind of table, or platform. There are garlands around its neck."

"And not a single Greek to be seen anywhere. Am I right?"

"Not one. They've gone. Grandfather, can it be true? Have they gone? Is it over?"

The Singer smiled. "It does appear to be." He began to shout, and the sentries woke up suddenly and rubbed their eyes. "They've gone. This is an offering, this horse. An offering to Athene. They have to do that. They stole her statue from the temple, and now they're afraid. They need fair winds to take them home. They have to appease her . . . Oh, happy day! Polyxena, run. Run as fast as you can and rouse the city. Go to Priam's Palace and tell him everything. I will wait here. Go, go."

Polyxena ran. A few people were awake, walking about the streets, and she called out to them, "They've gone! The Greeks have sailed away. It's over." And as she ran, she didn't look behind her to see how the citizens stared after her with their mouths open. By the time she arrived at Priam's Palace, she could scarcely breathe.

"Take me to the king," she told the servants. "The war is over. Priam must come down to the walls to see what the Greeks have left us."

ON THE PLAIN

Mist like a white veil came down from the mountains, drifted around the Offering and wound its way in and out of the flower garlands that lay against its shining neck. The horse's head was set at a graceful angle to its body, and its flanks were round, the pale golden color of newly cut wood. Also, it was fragrant, with the fragrance of the trees that it once was. Its legs were strong and hard, and if this horse were given the breath of life, it would gallop over the Plain and over the hills, as far as the winds could blow and as fast as an eagle flying in the blue air. No one knew the secret of the horse and what it held in its dark, hollow belly. Silence surrounded it. From the city came the sound of shouting, and the great Skaian Gate opened with a groan.

Xanthe had never in her life seen such a sight. Every single person in the whole city must be here, she thought, out on the Plain, where we haven't been able to stand for nearly ten years. The horse stood four-square on its platform and towered over the heads of the crowd. Had there ever been such an enormous statue in the whole world? Perhaps (and this was the gossip that was being whispered by all those gazing at it) a God or a Goddess had helped to make it, for surely mortals on their own could never have fashioned such a thing? Old men were weeping, young girls were throwing flowers at its feet. Priam and the royal party, with Polyxena and the Singer in their midst, were near enough to the horse to be able to touch it. Andromache stood and stared at it silently, but at her side Astyanax was jumping up and down.

"Horsie!" he said. "Big, big horsie. 'Tyanax ride . . . 'Tyanax ride . . ."

"You can't," Xanthe whispered, because Andromache was lost in thought, scarcely aware of her little son. "It's a special horse. We mustn't touch it. Look at all the flowers it's wearing."

Xanthe looked up at it and wondered why the Greeks had left them such a creature as a gift, when she noticed Iason standing beside her.

"Iason!" she said. "It's been a long time since we've spoken . . . Isn't this a wonder? Have you ever seen anything like it? What is it? Who has left it here? And why?"

"I don't know," Iason said. He craned his neck to gaze up at the horse. "Look how huge it is. Its body is as wide as . . . what? Six barrels tied together? It's beautiful." And so are you, he wanted to add and didn't. You are more beautiful than anyone, and I want to tell you so. Iason made a coughing noise. "Have you an answer for me yet, Xanthe?"

"I'm sorry. I have been thinking, truly. But I haven't really decided. I'm honored at your question. You know that. I think very well of you, Iason. You're my oldest friend."

Will that do? Xanthe wondered. Will he be satisfied with that? What should I say? Why do I hesitate to think about it properly? And even though she knew Polyxena's opinion exactly, Xanthe wished she'd discussed it with her at greater length. It was too late to worry about that now.

"I thank you for those words. The thing is . . ." Iason scratched a line in the sandy ground and stared at it. "I wanted to ask about Alastor."

"Why? What about Alastor? I haven't seen him for a long time."

"Do you still love him?"

"I never said that." Xanthe blushed. "I never said I loved him. I just . . ."

"You did, though. You did love him. Can you deny it?"

"If I'd known that this was about Alastor, I wouldn't have let you talk to me at all. He's going to be married. I never think of him." Hermes, God of tricksters, forgive me for lying, Xanthe thought.

"Then I want . . . Don't say anything now, but think and give me an answer later . . . when things grow more quiet." Iason took Xanthe's hand and held it. For a moment she considered shaking him off, and then her heart filled with tenderness for him. Poor Iason . . . Why should I hurt him? And on such a happy day, when the war is over, and we are all going to be settled and peaceful forever?

He continued, "I haven't got much to offer you, but what I have is yours. I want to ask you myself, face-to-face, not through Polyxena. Will you allow me to be your husband? If you let me, I'll speak to the Lady Andromache and seek permission to be betrothed.

You wouldn't have to leave Astyanax. It would be some time before we could be married, but when we do . . . we could be so happy. I . . ." He turned away, and his words were carried off by the wind.

"What was that?" Xanthe asked. "What did you say at the end?"

"I said I loved you. You heard it, I'm sure, and you're just tormenting me by making me say it again. But I don't care. I was shy before, but I'm brave now, and I'll shout it out here, if you like, in front of all these people and . . . in front of this horse."

Iason grinned, and then opened his mouth wide.

"Don't." Xanthe was laughing. "You don't have to, truly. I *did* hear you. And I thank you. I can't say that I love you, but you know that you're very dear to me, don't you?"

"Perhaps you'd grow to love me," said Iason. "If we're married."

"Perhaps," said Xanthe. "I'll consider your offer, Iason, and I thank you for it."

Suddenly something of the glory had gone from the day. I could marry him, and live a life like everyone else's, Xanthe thought. There won't be a love that burns and transforms, like Paris and Helen's. There'll be friendship and shared memories, and later we'll come together in the flesh of our children, but will I ever feel for Iason as I did . . . do . . . for Alastor? Breathless, and damp, and trembling. Do I want to? Perhaps a settled life is best, after all. A quiet life.

"I thank *you*, Xanthe," said Iason, and he turned and made his way back toward the Skaian Gate.

"Shh," said Theano to Halie, "listen to what the king has to say on the subject before airing your own opinions."

"He's not saying anything," said Halie. "I don't see why we can't talk while we wait for him to pronounce."

"He's thinking. You can see he is."

"Well," said Halie. "I don't know what there is to think about. It might be enormous, and it might have just appeared as if by some enchantment under our walls, and we may not exactly know who left it here and why, but when all's said and done, it's just a horse. I don't see why we have to spend the entire morning admiring the thing. I've got work to do, even if no one else has. Danae has the right idea. First things first. Someone has to prepare the midday food."

"But everyone is here!" Theano cried. "How could you bear to miss it?"

"But we've seen it now. Can't we go back?"

"No . . . King Priam is about to speak. Listen . . ."

The old man had walked all around the statue, pulling on his beard and craning his neck to see how high it was. Hecuba and the princes and Cassandra and Polyxena stood in a group, in silence, and all of them were smiling, except for Cassandra, who was staring at the earth and looking over her shoulder at the walls.

"There's someone else who wants to be back in the city," said Halie. "Princess Cassandra."

"She took leave of her senses years ago, and well

you know it," said Theano. "Since when is her ex-
ample one to follow?"

Halie said nothing, but she was thinking that
much of what Cassandra had been afraid of, over the
years, had come to pass. It was simply more con-
venient for people to forget that, she thought, but she
wasn't going to mention it on this day, which was
turning into some kind of festival. Silence had fallen
on the Plain. King Priam was about to speak.

"Citizens of Troy," he cried, and a sudden gust of
wind blew his voice away so that only those who
stood near him could hear. "This gift is an Offering to
the Goddess Pallas Athene. I have come to this con-
clusion: The Greeks, who have abandoned their camp,
as you can see, have put it here as a kind of apology—
to the city and to the Goddess. We must pull it into
our gates. I will arrange for the strongest young men
to bring it in . . . Ropes can be tied to the wheeled platform. And I declare the rest of the day and the night
that follows it a time of rejoicing for everyone. Give
thanks to all the Gods that our city has been spared
and that we have lived to see this triumph. Would that
my sons Hector and Paris were still here to enjoy this
sight. Would that all those who have fallen on this
Plain and watered it with their blood were here to
celebrate with us . . ."

His voice faded to nothing as Hecuba whispered in
his ear.

"She's telling him to stop," Theano said to Halie.
"And quite right, too. It's getting hot, and we should
all be going home."

"We are," said Halie. "The queen has given the
signal, and here comes a wagon to take them back to

the citadel. The rest of us will have to walk, I suppose."

"Have you thought about the feast?" Theano asked
as she covered her head with a scarf against the sun.
"Someone's going to be cooking all through the hot-
test hours, and I'm sure I don't have to tell you who
that'll be. I could have done without this gift from the
Greeks myself."

Halie made no reply. She was staring at someone.
An old man. I've seen him before somewhere, she
thought. He was making his way through the crowd
and toward the beach, and it was his beard that she
recognized: a silvery blue color, as though glinting fish
scales had become caught up in the hair. It fell almost
to his waist. He seemed to be wet. His hair was
streaming over his shoulders, and a powerful smell of
fish came to Halie's nose as he passed her. Some fisherman she had seen once, but where? She turned to
ask Theano whether she'd noticed him, but in the
turning of her head, all memory of the man left her
and she began to think about nothing but the Offering.

Helen stood alone, considering. There was something
unsettling about this creature that everyone was admiring. The men who made it (and it *was* men in spite
of all the superstitious mumblings about Gods and
sacrifices) had made it enormous for no reason that
she could think of. If an Offering to the Goddess Pallas
Athene was called for, surely something a little more
modest would have done just as well? The polished
sides of this monster gleamed in the sunlight, and
even though it was horse shaped, there was nothing

of a horse's benevolence about it. Maybe it was the eyes. They were empty sockets, and too high up for anyone to peer into, but Helen had the feeling that if she were to look, she would see nothing but darkness.

Alastor stood with his mother and looked down at the beach. Everyone else was *oohing* and *aahing* about the statue and wondering what to do about it, but his mother was still preoccupied with the wedding.

"And I think we should invite the Singer," she was saying. "I'm sure he'll be honored. And he loves his food. Perhaps he might even compose a wedding song, if I ask him. We used to be quite fond of one another, years ago, you know."

"Yes, Mother," said Alastor, wishing she would go and talk to someone else, and then he saw them: the Singer and his granddaughter. A chance to divert his mother's attention. "He's over there. You should go and ask him now."

"Do you really think so?" Alastor could hardly believe it. His mother was blushing like a young girl.

"Yes, yes," he said. "He looks as though he'd love to talk to someone."

Phrontis hurried to where the Singer was standing, and Alastor began to scan the crowd to see whether he could catch a glimpse of Marpessa. He was grateful that Agamede had chosen to stay indoors. She came from the mountains and was unused to the heat. And because she was a foreigner, the possible end of the war didn't mean as much to her. The days that had gone by since he had seen Marpessa had been a torment to him, and he had come to a difficult decision.

He was not going to marry poor Agamede. It would not be fair to her, when he loved someone else. He dreamed of Marpessa. Her face was in front of his eyes all through the day, and his whole being longed for her. He hadn't been brave enough to tell his mother of his intentions, and whenever he'd thought of doing so, his courage failed him. Seeing her walking farther and farther away from him made him feel suddenly brave. I will tell her tomorrow, he thought. Let her be happy during the feast time tonight, and then I'll be strong and speak to her. And to Agamede. And, most important of all, to Marpessa.

Marpessa watched Alastor accompany his mother through the Skaian Gate. He'd looked straight at her and smiled, and she knew that if he'd been alone, he would have come and spoken to her, in front of everyone. Most of the crowds had gone now, and those people who still remained were milling around the creature's platform. Some children had climbed onto it and were clinging to its legs. Marpessa walked slowly to the seashore. She remembered a day, before the black ships came over the water and anchored in the bay, when Charitomene had taken her and Xanthe to splash in the waves and sit on the sand. She had forgotten how soothing the sound of the ocean was, and she dipped her feet in the cool water and kicked a fine spray up into the air. Then the wind began to blow her hair back from her face. She looked around her. There was an old man with a long bluish beard hanging down over his chest standing beside her.

"You know who I am, do you not?"

Marpessa nodded. She had seen him before, in the fish market and walking along the walls sometimes.

"Lord Poseidon . . ."

The God nodded. "And there's a bloody fool up there near the Offering who doesn't know what's good for him. Laocoön. Can you hear him? Can you hear what he's saying?"

Marpessa listened, and the voice of a man screaming came to her. "Beware! Citizens of Troy, beware! Don't let this monster into your city. Burn it now. Bring your axes and hack it to pieces. It's a trick . . . a Greek trick. Why should they leave us a gift? Have you taken leave of your senses? *Think!* Before it's too late."

Poseidon's face reddened. "Can't be allowed. This is the plan . . . How he does he dare to speak against the Offering? Something . . . I must do something at once."

Marpessa watched as the God frowned at the water and made a movement with his hands. Clouds came drifting into the sky and gathered like puffs of bruise-colored smoke along the horizon. The sea, which had been flat and calm, seemed all at once to be boiling, and huge, white-crested breakers rolled toward the land and crashed onto the shore with a sound like hissing.

"Do you see how furious I am?" Poseidon shouted. "Flee, if you value your life, young woman. But watch and see what Poseidon's rage will do!"

Marpessa started to run backward, away from the angry waves, and stumbled and fell heavily onto her back. I must get up, she thought. I must get home to the city. Something black and terrible is happening.

Above her head, the sky was like beaten silver: gray and shimmering like the surface of an upturned shield. She wondered briefly whether the fall would leave a mark on her skin, and she pushed to the back of her mind the dull pain she felt in her lower back. There was Laocoön, a little way away from where she was standing. He had run down to the thundering waves on the shoreline and was still screaming as loudly as he could. Two young men stood beside him. Perhaps they were his sons; they were pulling on his arms, trying to stop him from rushing into the waves. A small crowd of people had gathered to see what was going on, and one of them cried, "It's Laocoön . . . He's lost his mind. What's he shouting about?"

"He's calling the Offering a monster. Take no notice."

They turned away from the beach and the screaming Laocoön and started running back to gather around the statue and watch the ropes being attached to the platform. But Marpessa couldn't stop watching the water. Poseidon was there striding into the waves and moving his hands above his head. Something stirred in the sea. Something—she couldn't see exactly what it was—rose up from the black and foaming waves, and coiled and wound itself into spirals that suddenly spilled onto the sand of the beach. She froze in terror. A sea serpent, she thought. One of the Sea God's creatures. There were stories told about them: how they lived deep, deep, in underwater caves, and were silver and green, and patterned with strange shapes unseen in other living things. This serpent moved through the breakers so fast that Marpessa's eyes could scarcely keep up with it. Others had noticed it now, too, and screams of horror went up from all sides.

"Poseidon's serpent!" someone said, and another cried: "Run!"

Those nearest to the shore scrambled over the sand in the direction of the city as quickly as their legs could carry them. "It's attacking!"

Laocoön ran with the rest. The serpent turned fiery, scarlet eyes on him and recognized prey. Ignoring everyone else, it slid across the sand and wound its slimy coils around the unfortunate man, and it twisted and twisted until every breath was squeezed out of his body. Marpessa stared at Laocoön's two sons. Two smaller serpents had coiled out of the water and were slithering toward them, but they seemed turned to stone. In the blinking of an eye, the creatures wound themselves around legs and arms and necks and then tightened their hold, until, together with their father, the young men were tossed onto the shore like fruit rinds when the fruit has been pressed for juice and sucked and thrown away. A great howling, a terrible wailing rose from the throats of all those who were watching, but Marpessa was silent, shivering with terror as the slippery horrors crawled back to the sea, dived under the surface, and disappeared. After they had gone, the clouds thinned and vanished. The sky grew pink, like the inside of a shell, and a dreadful calm settled on the ocean. She looked around for the God, but he had vanished as completely as his slimy creatures.

"It's Poseidon's punishment," a man shouted. "Laocoön dared to speak against the Offering left for Pallas Athene, and look what's become of him. Quick!

Let's take it into the gates quickly, before anything worse happens."

The Skaian Gate stood open. Ropes were tied to the creature's legs, and six men took hold of each one and began to pull. With a noise like a distant storm growing in the mountains, the Offering rolled slowly over the Plain and into Troy. Marpessa followed the crowd slowly, looking at the men sweating and straining, muscles standing out on their arms and eyes squinting against the light of the setting sun. Briefly she thought: Why is it so heavy? Can it be that the creature is solid? Was there a tree in the world as wide across the trunk as the statue was across the stomach? It had passed into the city now, and the Skaian Gate stood open. She turned to look behind her at the shore, where the three bodies lay with their faces hidden. Waves came and washed the bodies, and seabirds had started to wheel above them, searching for food. No one would dare to approach the corpses, fearing that the serpents might return. Someone should prepare them for Hades, Marpessa thought, but no one will. The bodies would be pulled out to sea, and fishes would feast on them. Maybe Poseidon would gather all the smooth white bones and scatter them over some other beach. A familiar sickness overcame her then, and she forgot Laocoön and his poor sons altogether and thought of nothing but herself.

The Offering reached the citadel and stood now in the lengthening shadows, still decked with wreaths of flowers. The sentries at the Skaian Gate decided to join the celebration, along with every other citizen.

"No more enemies on the Plain, lads," said their captain. "So no more duty until I tell you different."

"What about the Gate?" said one of the men.

"Shut it," said the captain. He was a tidy man, and liked the look of everything closed up safely for the night, whatever the state of hostilities might be.

"Bloody unnecessary, I call it," said the sentry, but he and his comrade pushed the heavy gates closed and slid the thick wooden bar across them, as they had done for more nights than they could count.

DEIPHOBUS'S PALACE

Xanthe followed the servant who had been appointed to take her to Marpessa's bedchamber. This young woman didn't seem to want to say a word, and slunk through the corridors like a hunted creature.

"In here," she said, standing aside in a way that should have been polite but was sullen instead.

"Thank you," Xanthe said, and the girl disappeared without a backward glance.

Her sister's room was nothing more than a cell. There were no hangings on the walls, and the covers on the bed were not what Marpessa had been used to in Helen's palace.

"Well," said Xanthe. "I don't blame you for lying facedown on the bed in a chamber like this, but turn and greet your big sister. I've come to visit you, on this wonderful day. Isn't it a wonderful day? Imagine. No more war. No more Blood Room. No more fighting. Wonderful!"

Marpessa rolled over onto her back, but she spoke without smiling.

"I'm glad to see you," she said, "but it's not a wonderful day. Three men died down there on the beach, and I saw it. I saw it all."

"Everyone's talking about it," said Xanthe. "They

say it's a punishment from Poseidon. Those men dared to talk against the Offering."

"Is that what they're calling it?" Marpessa wiped away tears that had sprung up in her eyes. Tears came to her frequently now, and she wondered whether it was because she had a reason to cry, or because her body was changing every day, to prepare for the child. Alastor's child. The old women always said that you lost your mind when your body was carrying a baby, but she'd never believed them until now. The pain in her back still troubled her, and Xanthe wasn't making things any better, either. My life, Marpessa thought, would be much easier if I didn't ever have to see her. She makes me burn with shame. I look at her and see only my own dishonesty.

The tears, which she had thought were under control, welled up in her eyes again and spilled over onto her cheeks, rolling down and making her neck wet. She sat up quickly and said, "I'm sorry . . . I don't know what's come over me. Perhaps seeing all that has upset me."

Marpessa turned her face away, and her tears turned to sobs. Xanthe sat beside her sister and took her hand.

"Oh, Marpessa, it's not just the serpents and those men," she said. "It's something else. I know you. You're my sister. Is it this place? Are you missing your old home?" She glanced around. "It's not very comfortable, that's true, but surely once Lady Helen has hung her woven pictures from the walls . . ."

"I wouldn't cry because my room wasn't comfortable. You know me better than that!"

"I do," said Xanthe. "And I'm glad to see you can

still be angry. Now, wipe your eyes and listen to me. We're all invited to the feast. At King Priam's Palace. There will be songs and music, and someone has been sent out of the city to see what meat there still is on the farms near the mountain. People have taken jars of wine out of their hiding places . . . We'll dance and drink and celebrate, and another kind of life will begin."

"I have to tell you something," Marpessa said, picking at a loose thread in her blanket. "I have to speak. I've been carrying a secret for a long time. I didn't want to tell you. I know it'll hurt you, and you'll be angry with me, but I have to. I can't bear it any longer. In my dreams, you're always there and turning your face away from me and not speaking to me."

"I'd never," said Xanthe, "not speak to you. You know that."

"Will you listen?"

"Of course I'll listen. And when you've told me, and we're laughing about how silly you've been, I'll tell you a secret of my own."

Marpessa stood up. She spoke in a whisper, so that Xanthe had to lean forward to hear.

"Alastor," Marpessa said. "I took Alastor into my bedchamber and into my bed, on the day that Lord Hector was killed. He was heartbroken, and I consoled him."

Xanthe sat silent for a long moment, staring at the floor.

"I did not hear your words properly," she said, and she could feel the blood going cold in her veins in spite of the heat of the day.

"Don't make me say it again. Alastor and I are lovers."

Xanthe gave an animal wail. "Lovers? When you knew . . . when I told you over and over again how I felt? How could you? How could you do such a thing to me, to your sister? If you really felt like killing me, then why didn't you do the honest thing and just take a dagger and push it into me? I'm going . . . I can't bear to look at you any longer . . ."

"No, Xanthe, wait . . . I didn't mean . . . And in any case, it was Aphrodite's fault. She told me. She said she was punishing you. She said you didn't believe in her, so she was going to hurt you to make you see."

"Typical!" Xanthe was on her feet. "That's typical of you, Marpessa! You've always hidden behind the Gods. It's not their fault. *You're* the one who says you see them all the time, but I don't believe you. I've never *truly* believed you, if you must know. You just make these things up. I'm never going to trust you again. Never, ever. I'm going. I don't care if I never see you again. You're no sister of mine . . ."

"No, wait, Xanthe, let me explain . . ."

"I don't want to hear your stupid excuses. *The Goddess . . . I couldn't help it . . . He's so beautiful.* You're exactly the same as everyone else, and like a fool I thought because you were my sister and loved *me* you would stop and think before you did something you knew would hurt me."

Marpessa jumped to her feet, and her voice rose to a scream. "I *did* think! I *did* know . . . exactly what you thought. And I did it anyway. I don't care what you think. You're boring and stupid, and you can't see what's going on even if it's in front of your face. Alastor just doesn't love you. Understand? It's very simple. If he'd wanted you as a lover, you'd have been the first to jump into bed. But he didn't. He wanted *me*. Me. He loves *me*. I'm the one telling him to hold back, telling him he has to go and marry that stupid Agamede that Phrontis has lined up for him. And don't you go giving me that smarmy stuff about loving sisters. You don't know a thing. You don't notice a single thing about me. I'm pregnant. Pregnant."

Xanthe sank to her knees and covered her face with her hands. His child. Alastor's child. He'll have to acknowledge it, she thought, and then Marpessa will be part of his household . . . his concubine . . . and I'll go on being nothing to him. Less than nothing.

She stood up.

"I have to get Astyanax ready for the feast. What you've told me will turn the food I eat to ashes in my mouth."

"Go!" Marpessa screamed at Xanthe. "Don't come back. Don't ever come back to where I am! Take your fine feelings and go and sit with Andromache and her child, and leave your own blood sister to rid herself of this child all alone."

Xanthe turned in the doorway and looked at Marpessa. Did she really mean it? She almost went to Marpessa; almost weakened, as she had weakened in every single quarrel they'd ever had. Then an image came to her of Alastor, breathing a kiss into her sister's hair, their white bodies entwined like two green vines, and she felt sick.

"Do whatever you want," she said. "I don't care what you do. I have other business."

Xanthe made her way out of the palace and up the

hill. She gazed down to where the Offering was standing, with a crowd of people still milling around it. Standing near the head of the creature was a figure she recognized: the tall soldier dressed in black; the one who'd been in the Blood Room and walking in the streets of the city near Phrontis's house. Who was he? Why was he there? Xanthe turned her head away, and at once forgot all about him. A blood red sun was hurtling toward the sea with long strands of cloud like living flames streaming out behind it. She could hardly see it for the tears filling her eyes.

THE STABLES

Iason sat outside the stables watching the last of the light draining out of the sky.

"Spectacular, isn't it?" said a voice almost next to his ear, and he jumped.

"Who d'you think you are? Creeping up on me like that!" Iason peered at the man standing beside him. "I don't know you, do I?"

The stranger was dressed in robes that looked as though they had been woven from pure gold. Iason found it difficult to look him straight in the face, but his eyes were blue: clear blue and burning. He was probably a visiting prince from beyond the mountains.

"Close," said the man. "I am a God, and not a visiting prince, but prince is near enough in human terms. And of course you know me. Phoebus Apollo. Everyone knows me. Some prefer my sister's rather quieter form of beauty . . . Don't look so stunned. I'm talking about Artemis, the Goddess of the Moon. She has her followers, but she never, ever puts on a spectacle quite like that, does she?"

"Like what?" Iason said, and thought, This man read my thoughts. Could he really be a God? Or was there some drug in the water I drank when I came back to the stables?

"Like a sunset. I plunge my chariot into the waves every single day, and it's something to see, isn't it? Also, it's the only time men can face me directly. Usually they squeeze their eyes together when they look at me or hold their hands over their faces to shade them from my radiance. Can't really blame them. Nothing's quite the same when I'm not around, is it? All that darkness . . . not only boring but also dangerous. People get up to every sort of mischief at night. Take tonight. Priam has ordered a feast, and by the time Artemis shows her face, everyone in the city will be drunk, or asleep, or asleep because they're drunk. They'll be happy. The Greek ships have gone: That's what the Trojans think, but I can see them still. They're waiting at anchor in the next bay. When all my light has gone, they'll set sail again, their oars muffled, and with no lights showing. They're on their way, and the warriors lining their decks are looking silently toward Troy."

Iason said, "Why should I believe a word you say? You might be a dream I'm having." He peered into the darkening shadows. There was no sign of the man in the golden robes. Iason laughed. "See? I was right all along. I must have closed my eyes for a moment and dreamed you and all you were saying."

He tried to remember what that was, but his head was suddenly filled with confusion, and he shook it, exactly as Aithon shook *his* head to rid it of flies. I'm getting, he thought, as bad as Marpessa.

THE GOSSIPS

THE KITCHENS

"Someone," said Theano, "always has to clear up. We do it after ordinary meals, so why're you grumbling now?"

"It's a special night," said Halie. "Everyone else has gone home to their houses, and imagine this: For the first time in years they'll lie down without a weight in their hearts about what's going to happen tomorrow. The men won't have to fight, and the women can make plans to wash clothes and sweep their rooms without wondering whether it's worth doing, if their husbands are about to be slaughtered."

"And I tell you what," said Danae. "Nine moons from tonight, the midwives will have their hands full!" She laughed, and began to stack the platters that had been used at the feast onto a shelf.

"The Singer's still there in the Great Hall," said Halie. "He and Priam are talking and talking, and drinking more than is good for them. Nothing but a couple of old windbags. But did you see Andromache? For once her face looked as if she hadn't been weeping all night. And she'd put on the same robe she wore for her wedding. Did you notice?"

"Lovely, she looked," said Danae, who had always

been fond of Lord Hector's wife. "And little Astyanax was as good as gold, all through that long meal."

"Lady Helen looked better than anyone. She always does. Her dress was like the Goddess Iris's rainbow, and did you smell her hair? Roses and honey and spice. She's wasted on that Deiphobus, and even though she tries to hide it, you can see she's unhappy."

"When did you get near enough to smell her hair? I didn't really notice what people were wearing. I was too busy eating," said Theano. "Roast boar. What a taste! I'd forgotten how wonderful real food was. I'd got used to scrapings and making do, like everyone else."

"The Goddess," said Halie, "is smiling on us at last. And not before time. That Offering . . . that's what's done it. Bit of luck, them deciding to bring it into the city."

"Not according to some," said Danae.

"If it's Princess Cassandra you mean," said Halie, "there's no pleasing her. She's had a long face for the whole of this war. She was born like that. It's her fate never to be happy, but I don't see why she can't keep her mouth shut and not depress the rest of us."

"She can't help it," said Theano. "And Lady Hecuba told me a very long time ago that some oracle or other had told her this: The princess would never be believed, even when she was telling the truth."

Danae and Halie made *tsk*ing noises, and Theano realized that they were tired of talking about Princess Cassandra. Was she the only one who worried in case the poor demented creature turned out to be right?

CITY AND CITADEL

The Offering stood alone in front of Pallas Athene's temple, and shadows surrounded it. Silence lay like a cloak over the city. In the belly of the creature, whose head was so high that it seemed almost to be lost in the thin clouds masking the face of the moon, a rumbling began. Something was moving. Slowly, quietly, a plank on the underside of the statue came away from the body, and then another. One man fell out and crouched on the ground. Then someone else emerged from the Offering's belly. More than a dozen men crept across the open space, one after the other, to the nearest building, and flattened themselves against it. The pale moonlight shone on their daggers and the sharp edges of their spears. Without a word, two of them ran toward the city walls, and when they reached the Skaian Gate, they slid the wooden bar across so that it could open, and they pulled the doors wide apart. And there on the Plain, which had so lately been quite empty, was ranged an entire Greek army, carrying lit torches in their hands and with swords hanging from their belts.

"Come quietly," said the one who had opened the gate. "They're all asleep. They've been drinking since

303

sunset. We won't meet any resistance. Wait until all of us in the advance squad are back at the citadel, and then burn everything. Kill every able-bodied man and don't waste time on the women. Bring any who take your fancy to the ships, and we'll deal with them later. There won't be much left in the way of booty, but grab any you can find. Move."

Agamemnon, commander of all the Greeks, watched his army scattering through the streets of Troy like cockroaches overrunning a house, scuttling into corners and hiding in the crevices of the stones. He made his way up the hill, toward Pallas Athene's temple, and as he went, the tall black figure of Ares, the God of War, walked in his footsteps. Many saw him and not one of them realized who it was they were looking at. He moved through the city like a shadow among many shadows. He was everywhere, standing behind every man who carried a weapon in his hand.

Even though he'd drunk more wine than ever in his life before, Iason woke up in the middle of the night. Or maybe it was nearer morning than he knew. He was unused to being happy, he decided, and that had made him restless. Or was there a noise? As soon as he was properly awake, he felt happy all over again. He hadn't been dreaming. At the feast, Xanthe really *had* said that she would marry him. It was true that while she said it she'd looked both sad and furious, and not at all like someone speaking to the person she was going to spend the rest of her life with. Iason had pressed her. *Are you sure, Xanthe? Will you be happy?*

he'd asked, and she'd walked away from him abruptly. Her eyes were red-rimmed, as though she'd been crying for a long time. Still, she had promised to go to Andromache tomorrow—today—and ask for a dowry. Perhaps her evident misery was nothing to do with him. He didn't mind. He knew that once they were together their lives would be full of nothing but happiness. He rose from his bed, in the corner of the stable, and as soon as he was upright, he heard them. The horses were restless, stamping about in their stalls and whinnying with fear. Was it rats? Or perhaps some wild animal had come down from the mountain and somehow made its way past the door.

"Shh, my beauties, what's the matter?" he said, stroking every horse as he passed. They were rearing up now, and he could see the whites of their eyes, even though the only light came from the moon.

Iason stepped outside and understood at once. Down by the walls, something was on fire. A dull red light shone up into the sky, and he could smell burning. No wonder the horses were terrified. He listened. Someone was screaming. He couldn't make out most of it, but one word came to his ears through the still night like an arrow: Greeks!

How could that be? They'd sailed, sailed away. Later he would say that some God guided him in what he did next. Without stopping to think, Iason went back into the stable and opened the doors of the stalls. He grabbed a length of twine and pushed it over his shoulder. Then he picked up a knife and stuck it into his belt. He took Hector's beloved Aithon by the lead rope and pulled him outside. All the other horses would follow him; he knew that.

"Quick, Aithon. Quick, my lovely, we must hide."

The horses all trotted after him, and he took them around to the back of the stables and down the slope that led to the ruins close to the edge of the city, on the side nearest the mountain. It had been a noble house once. Poseidon had come a long time ago and shaken the foundations, and turned the building upside down. Iason remembered how, as a small boy, he'd hidden in the huge chamber that had suddenly opened underground. He prayed that it was still there, and it was: dusty, dark, and full of loose stones and plants that thrived in rubbish, but still a place where the horses would be safe for the moment. And some of the dogs and cats. The ginger one who was so attached to him must have run behind them all the way. Iason smiled and then turned to his task of settling the horses down.

"You'll be safe here," he said to them. He cut pieces from the twine to put around each horse's neck, and he anchored them as best as he could with heavy stones. They'd be able to pull themselves free, but Iason hoped that they might stay hidden out of fear of the fires. He prayed that they would. "I don't know what's happening," he murmured to them as he worked, "but I must go and find Xanthe. And warn them up at the Palace."

Iason left the underground chamber and clambered up to where he could see the city spread out in front of him. A chill settled on his heart. The sky above Troy was scarlet and gold, and from far away he heard it still: screams rising from a thousand throats, and underneath the screaming, the unmistakable sound of weeping. Iason ran, and cursed the boar who had robbed him of his speed. He could scarcely see for the tears filling his eyes.

More than the choking heat, more than the blinding flames that rise up into the night sky, more than the endlessly leaping colors that change shape with every moment, more than all of these is the transforming power of fire. Fire takes solid wooden beams and reduces them to charcoal. It licks at everything with a scarlet tongue and leaves it black. It spreads like the folds of a golden robe over human bodies and what is left is gray and chalky: ash, blown up and up by every breath of wind only to fall like dust on the ground. When it is burning most fiercely, it seems that it might go on forever and devour everything in its path. It does not cower and withdraw in front of princes. Palace and hovel alike are good fuel and nothing more. It is unstoppable. And when it has moved on, what remains is desolation.

Andromache lay on her marriage bed and sighed. Tonight, for the first time since Hector's death, she had felt something like a lightening of the heart. Not happiness. Never that, but still, a sort of hope, like movement returning to a limb that hasn't been used for a long time. She smiled at the memory of how good Astyanax had been at the feast, playing with his little horse, Blackie, and making him gallop along the floor in front of the throne. Priam had gathered his grandson onto his lap, and everyone said that the smiles he gave the child were the sweetest they'd seen for many moons.

"Want Xanthe!" he'd said when they were carrying him to his bed. "Xanthe sleep!"

Who could resist him, tonight of all nights? She'd given permission for Xanthe to take him into her bed-chamber. There was a little couch there on which he slept sometimes.

Happy dreams to them both, Andromache thought. And happy dreams to me, too. She closed her eyes.

Xanthe hoped very much that Iason would never learn the truth: that she had agreed to marry him in order to spite Marpessa. Just to show her that she could do something all by herself that would mean she had a life of her own, separate from her sister's. I don't care about Alastor, and I don't care about you, she said to Marpessa in her head. You can get rid of his baby if you want to. I'm going to have a husband, and she is not, Xanthe thought. She'll have to walk about the city and see Alastor with his bride, and I hope it makes her miserable. I must forget all about him. I will. I will try to persuade myself that loving him was like a pleasant dream. I can remember it from time to time, but I must be a good wife to Iason. I will.

She looked at the couch where Astyanax was sleeping, and her heart swelled with love for the baby. His cheek was resting on the hard wood of his toy horse Blackie. Xanthe smiled. Astyanax loved her. She loved him. There was nothing complicated and ugly about that. Only a child could sleep like that, and when he woke up, there would be a deep red mark on his face.

Never mind, she thought. You sleep well, little prince. And dream sweet dreams.

"Marpessa, what's the matter?"

"Nothing, my Lady." Marpessa tried to smile. She was sitting on her bed, bent almost double. All through the feast, she had felt the pain growing and growing, until now she could feel it twisting inside her like . . . like serpents—the ones she had seen on the shore, black and slimy. That was what it felt like: as though they were biting her in the back and in the stomach with their venomous teeth. But there was nothing to be done. Perhaps she had eaten too much. Her belly was used to small quantities.

"May I come in?" Helen stood at the door of Marpessa's tiny bedchamber. "Deiphobus is still with his father at the Palace. I know that something *is* wrong. You shouldn't lie to me, child. Are you in pain? Is it your time for bleeding?"

Marpessa shook her head.

"No, it isn't that. But it's true that my stomach is hurting. I think it must be Theano's honey cakes." She smiled weakly.

"I'll go and fetch you something. I have all sorts of potions in my chamber."

"Thank you, Lady," said Marpessa, and Helen vanished into the corridor. Marpessa lay down and thought of the vial under her pillow. If I swallow the mixture now, she said to herself, when I'm already in agony, then maybe I won't notice another pain. Then, for a moment, a vision of the child she was carrying came into her head. How beautiful it would be! A son from Alastor . . . How could she think of destroying him?

Marpessa closed her eyes. Her head was swimming and she could sense herself growing hotter and hotter. Xanthe. If I hadn't shouted at her, if we hadn't quarreled, she would be here now with me, helping me. Did I really say it? Did I really tell her never to come back to where I am? Oh, if only someone could go and tell her no, no, I'm sorry. I never meant it. Please come and look after me. Where are you? Where? Tears fell from her eyes and soaked into the pillow she was lying on. Her skin was burning, and every bit of her hurt. Was this fever? Behind her closed eyelids, she saw the Gods drifting about, with their faces turned away from her. Why wouldn't Aphrodite look at her? Save her from this torture? They were punishing her. If she hadn't gone to Mother Poison . . . if she hadn't wanted to be rid of the baby, none of this would be happening. A fierce pain tore through her body from her breastbone to her thighs, and Marpessa cried aloud. Suddenly she felt a wetness flooding out from between her legs. She sat up at once and saw a stream of blood. Thick, sticky blood so dark that it was almost black on the bed linen, and on her clothes, flowed and flowed out of her, and she looked at it and fainted away from the horror.

When Helen returned with the potion and saw the blood, she recognized it at once. This was not the normal flow that came with every moon, but a miscarriage. Oh, my poor little Marpessa, she thought, and memories of her own childbed, when Hermione had been born, came back to her. Which was the God who decided that mortals had to be born like this? And whose child was it? How did silent Marpessa, shy Marpessa, who never left the palace as far as she knew . . . How did she get pregnant? A cold dread filled Helen's heart. Could it be Paris's? No, never. Marpessa would never let him . . . and yet so many others did. Was it his? She shook her head. What am I thinking of? Marpessa must be cleaned and tended. The Gods have seen fit to take her baby from her, and maybe they knew best. Perhaps it had been deformed in some way. The sweet smell of blood filled the air. Tomorrow, she thought, I'll burn everything that's been stained. Tears came to her eyes, and she blinked them away. This wasn't the time to be weak. Marpessa needed her.

"Come, little one," she said, "and I'll bathe you and dry you and give you a soothing medicine to ease the pain. And then you can sleep in my bed with me."

"Deiphobus . . . ," Marpessa murmured.

"He's too drunk to bother us tonight," Helen answered, "and if he does appear, I'll get rid of him. Close your eyes and stop fretting. I'll take care of you."

She bent down and put one arm under Marpessa's knees and the other under her shoulders.

"Hold on to my neck," she said. "It's fortunate that you're so light."

Marpessa closed her eyes and let Helen's fragrance calm her. Roses and smoke mixed together, she thought, and I'm a baby again. She opened her eyes, and all she could see was the scarlet stone that hung around Helen's throat, filled with a red light as though a fire burned at its heart.

*It doesn't take long. The buildings nearest the Skaian
Gate are on fire, crackling and blazing, and everyone
inside them is lying dead. They'd all been drunk, so
there wasn't much skill involved. We just went in,
cut a few throats, and then torched the place, whoever's it was. Some've got away, scurrying for the
gates, and others are racing for the temples and the
citadel, but you've got to expect that. What's it matter, after all? The whole of Troy's going to cotton on
soon enough and wake up. Some of them might even
fight back. Odysseus warned us of that. I don't care.
As long as I get my fair share of the really important
ones. Priam. He's king, so he ought to go first. It'll be
a pleasure. Pyrrhus, slayer of the King of all Troy,
they'll call me. That'd be something.*

Where was he? Polyxena wandered through the house
looking for the Singer, before she remembered that
he'd stayed with King Priam. She'd tried her best to
get him to come home, but he wouldn't hear of it.

"Priam and I are going to carouse. That's the word
for it, and it's a long time since we've done anything
remotely like carousing. Aren't I right, Sire?"

"Quite right, my old friend," Priam said, so that
was that.

Polyxena wondered whether there was anything at
all left to eat, and smiled when she remembered that
food wouldn't be a problem from now on. The farmers
and the fishermen would start working, and soon
there would be all sorts of good things on every table.
The Singer would be happy at last, and she wouldn't
have to deal with all his moaning. How glorious peace

was! And how happy everyone had been last night! Except for Xanthe, who looked as though she had been crying. When this is all over, Polyxena thought, I'll go and find her, and see what the matter is. Iason had asked her to marry him, that much she *did* know. Anyone with eyes in their head could see that Iason would make a much better husband than Alastor, who'd be a temptation for almost every woman who laid eyes on him. There was such a thing as being too beautiful for your own good. You had only to think of Paris.

Someone was shouting. What was going on? Polyxena stepped into the courtyard. The whole sky was alight. Everywhere she looked, there were flames and shrieking, and then she heard it: the alarm being sounded from farther up the hill. The guards there must have seen the fire, or the noise might have alerted them. It made a rushing sound, like a fast-flowing river, but it glowed like an enormous furnace. She was too far away to see flames, but there was no darkness left in the sky, and the moon was hidden by thick clouds of smoke. What could possibly have happened to set the entire city alight? Who, who would do such a thing? She ran back into the house as a gang of screaming men suddenly tore past outside.

"Priam's mine, Agamemnon, remember that!" someone shouted, and pure terror filled Polyxena's body, and she stood stiff and cold with her back pressed against the wall, thinking. Agamemnon. The commander of the Greek armies. They hadn't sailed away after all. She listened for voices, but they'd gone, those men. Polyxena went quickly to the back of the house, and without even stopping to put on her sandals, she raced up the hill by another path. I'll get there first, she thought. You think you're so clever, Agamemnon, but you're only a Greek, and so you don't know the shortcuts. I must warn them at the Palace. I must get the Singer out. I must get there before . . . Polyxena closed her mind against the thought of what would happen if she arrived later than those wild beasts she had heard roaring outside the house.

Rich pickings in this house. One young girl of marriageable age just managed to get away before we could nab her, but she wasn't the tastiest morsel I'd ever seen, so who cares. Then there was a woman with a tongue like an ox whip, who kept screaming. How dare you? I'm Phrontis . . . Everyone knows me . . . Your commander will hear of this . . . I haven't lived this long for some Greek pipsqueak to invade my house like this . . . And then she shouted for someone called Alastor, but guess what? She was out of luck. No sign of this Alastor, whoever he was, anywhere. Anyway, her yelling was getting on my nerves, so I shut her up, know what I mean? Didn't take much effort, really. A bit like skewering an old chicken. But, by Ares, she didn't half bleed. Made a right mess of the floor coverings. I sent some of the lads to look about, and they came back with all sorts of stuff: gold vessels and plates, and quite a haul of women's things—necklaces and bracelets and such. Find a bag, I said, before you do anything else, to carry this lot in, otherwise we'll be dropping it all over the place. Was it worth going to look for this Alastor? I didn't think so, especially since someone came across a huge jar of wine, which didn't taste half bad. What's the hurry, that's what I said. So we pulled the old woman's body into a corner and got down to some serious drinking.

Forgive me, Gods, Alastor said to himself as he made his way from one sheltering wall to another. Forgive me for leaving her. The Greeks won't kill my mother. They'd never dare. She'll talk to them, and they'll know at once that she's someone to be reckoned with, and she'll be taken to Agamemnon, or someone in authority. No one, not even a Greek soldier, would murder a defenseless old woman. Agamede. . . . Alastor saw her running out of the house before the soldiers came, and perhaps he ought to have stopped her, but by the time this thought occurred to him, she had disappeared, and now he had to find some way of fighting. This was an emergency, and he was a soldier, first and foremost. Lord Hector would be proud of me, he said to himself, but his heart was thudding in his breast as though he were nothing but a girl. What about Marpessa? Where was she? He had to find her and carry her to safety till all this was over. Suddenly he felt himself grabbed around the neck, and his arm was twisted behind him. The pain made him swear. He tried to reach the dagger he'd stuck in his belt, but his attacker was too quick.

"Thought you'd stick this into me, did you, Greek bastard? Well, here it comes—straight between your damned ribs. Courtesy of Boros, dog."

"Boros! Wait! I'm not a Greek—don't you recognize me? Alastor. My name's Alastor. You saved my life on the Plain, have you forgotten? You brought me to the Blood Room! Stop! Let me go."

Boros stood back at once and looked at Alastor.

"By all the Gods, I *didn't* recognize you. You shouldn't go creeping around like one of those Greek scumsuckers. You'll get yourself killed."

"What's happening, Boros? I thought they'd gone. I thought it was all over."

"What they wanted you to think, right? Tricky lot, they are. They left that cursed Offering, and we did it. We let 'em in. There was soldiers in it."

"In it?"

"In the belly of that Offering. Hollow, it turned out to be, and they all jumped out and let their buddies in, and now look at 'em. Can't you hear what's going on? They're in the Palace. King's Palace, I mean. Don't give two figs for Priam and his lot. Throats cut by now, the whole lot of them."

"We must help, Boros. We must fight. And Marpessa. I've got to find her."

Boros considered this.

"Na, no time for heroics now. 'S all over for us. I'm getting out. You will, too, if you've got any sense left. We could get out of the citadel, then hide in the mountains, right? You coming, lad?"

"No, Boros," said Alastor. "I must stay. But the Gods go with you. And I thank you for rescuing me from the Plain."

Boros sniffed and wiped his nose with his hand. "Wouldn't have bothered if I'd known it'd end like this. You'd've died a hero on the field of battle instead of at the hands of a Greek in some burned-out door-way, which is what's going to happen to you."

"You don't know that," said Alastor. "I can't leave Marpessa to the mercy of these animals."

"Right, I'm off then," said Boros. "Have your knife back, though it won't do you much good. Farewell."

He slipped from one shadow to another until Alastor could no longer see where he was.

The fire was not enough. The swords and the spears and the shrieking and the blood and the broken bodies were not enough. Anger and revenge and hatred and bitterness and darkness were not enough. The earth itself—that hard brown crust the Gods had given men to walk on—suddenly began to ripple as though it were no more than a carpet laid in a small room that a maidservant comes in and picks up and shakes, to rid it of dust. And then it was still again, but even in the few moments of the moving, stone buildings and wooden roof struts, walls, and ceilings, and the high lintels of every dwelling danced and swayed and settled into new patterns, as if they had never been truly solid at all, but nothing more than flimsy defenses against the cold and the rain. There were some who lost their lives in the upheaval, crushed under boulders or buried in the rubble of their own houses, but with the Greek army running through Troy and laying about them with weapons and torches, many did not even notice the brief swelling and buckling of the ground beneath their feet, or if they did, they put it down to all the wine they'd drunk the night before.

There was no one left alive in the Palace. Polyxena walked through the corridors and tried to find her way into the Great Hall, stepping over bodies and making sure she didn't slip on the tiled floor, which ran with blood. She thought that maybe she, too, was dead. This place, where stone columns lay across doorways and level floors now looked like mountain ranges, was nowhere she recognized. A great emptiness filled her, and she found that she was rigid with pain and fear. She tried to scream, but no sound came from her lips. One leg after another along the floor: That was what she had to do. Concentrate on that, and don't look down. She kept her eyes on the highest beams, to be sure that nothing more was about to plummet down on her head, but that meant that she stumbled. Once, she fell and found herself face-to-face with someone whose mouth had spewed a fountain of blood, and whose eyes were fixed and open, and looked like peeled grapes. She stood up again, shaking all over, and found that the front of her gown was damp and streaked with scarlet. The Singer. She had to find him. Such a silence hung over everything that Polyxena knew she was too late.

As soon as she entered the Great Hall, she saw them: King Priam and the Singer, lying below the throne. Their throats had been cut, and they lay almost in one another's arms. The floor around their bodies had buckled and moved, and there were pieces of painted tile and fragments of decorated stoneware scattered over their bodies.

"Grandfather!" Polyxena screamed, and ran to

where he was lying. "O Zeus, what have they done to you!"

How long it was that she sat cradling the Singer, she didn't know, but she shed all the tears she had been holding back; they ran down her face and neck and streaked the bloodstains that covered her face. Then she stood up and took her grandfather's cloak and moved it so that it hid the gaping wound in his neck.

"Lie quietly," she said, "and I will return and bury you with all ceremony, if they'll let me. And I'll tell the stories. I'll sing the songs."

She burst into tears all over again and wished more than she had ever wished for anything that she could hear her grandfather's voice again. Saying anything. Anything at all.

Polyxena stared at the Great Hall. Even before Poseidon had shaken the earth, the Greeks had burned everything and stripped the gold from the beams. They'd torn the hangings from the walls, and now the chamber that was once the pride of Troy resembled a slaughterhouse. Bodies were piled in the corners, and then Polyxena noticed that not one of them was female. She shivered. What had they done with the women? Where was the queen? And Cassandra?

"Theano!" she called out. "Where are you? Halie? Danae?"

Her own voice echoed from the bare walls. Suddenly a vision of something so horrifying came into her mind that she sank to her knees and cried out in terror. She knew all at once exactly who it was the Greek commanders must be looking for. For a moment, she wondered whether she should go to the stables and find Iason. There wasn't time. She would have to go by herself and try to warn Xanthe. Polyxena forced herself to stand up and began to pick her way as well as she could through the dark corridors until she reached the courtyard. Then she began to run.

"Polyxena! Polyxena!" Theano stumbled into the Great Hall, followed by Halie and Danae.

"It wasn't her," Halie said. "You were hearing things."

"There's nothing wrong with my ears . . . I heard her quite clearly. She was shouting for us. Didn't you hear her, Danae?"

Danae paid no attention to her friends. Her robe was torn and dirty, and the front of it was streaked with her own blood. One wrist was bound up with a cloth, now stained and dirty, and, as Theano put it, was "about as much use for binding up a wound as a donkey is at javelin throwing."

"She's not herself," Halie whispered to Theano.

"*I'm* not myself. *You're* not yourself. And look over there . . . I suppose you'd agree that the king isn't himself, either. That's no excuse for going completely to pieces. Danae took one look at the Greeks coming up the hill, and that was that. We haven't had a word of sense out of her ever since."

"Something fell on her head," said Halie. "You're unkind, you are. She's not as young as she used to be."

"But you're just as stupid as you ever were, I'm glad to say. Take more than Poseidon losing his temper to shake a bit of gumption into you! We're in danger. Don't you understand that? They'll be back for us. Just look around. What do you see?"

Halie burst into tears. "I'm sorry, Theano, truly, but just look at them! Those poor old men. All that blood. No one to see to their funeral rites. And the Palace. See what they've done to it." She sat down abruptly on the filthy ground and covered her head with her skirt and sobbed.

Theano sat down beside her and said, a little more gently, "There's plenty to cry about, and no mistake. But it won't do any good. We've got to look after ourselves. What I meant when I asked you what you saw was: The queen, Princess Cassandra, all the women: D'you see them lying there with their throats cut?"

Halie shook her head.

"They've been captured," said Theano. "Taken down to the Greek camp. The Gods know what those animals will do to them. We must hide. They mustn't find us."

No sooner were these words out of her mouth than a gang of four young men came running into the room.

"Kill 'em," said one, glancing at the two old women sitting on the ground, and at the other, who seemed to be embracing a doorpost. "Kill that one first," he shouted, pointing at poor Danae.

Theano struggled to her feet and strode right up to the Greek soldier who had given the order and looked up at him.

"Don't you dare lay a finger on her, young man!" She almost spat at him. "Didn't your father and mother teach you any manners toward your elders? Shame on you! You'll die a pig's death, and Hades himself will roast you over the fires he keeps for really evil men."

"Shut up! Shut that mouth of yours, old hag. I've got better things to do than listen to your squawk-ings."

"Then I curse you and your children and your children's children, and may roots grow in your belly and squeeze your innards till they bleed."

The young man turned to the others.

"Don't kill 'em. I've changed my mind. Take 'em down to where the others are."

"But they're old," said another soldier. "What use are they to anyone?"

"Don't argue. Take them. Put a gag on that one."

Theano allowed herself to be bound with her hands behind her back and led away. The second young soldier tied a disgusting piece of cloth around her mouth so that she couldn't speak, but that was of no importance. They were going to survive. Halie's eyes were so wide open that Theano thought they might pop out of her head, and Danae was still walking around in some kind of bad dream. As they were led out of the Palace, Theano aimed a kick at the young man who was pushing them through the corridors.

"Oww!" he shouted, and Theano felt as triumphant as the bravest of leaders.

By rights, thought Menelaus, I should drag her out of that palace by her hair and slice her head off her shoulders. Look at Troy. Its destruction is complete, and even though it isn't Agamemnon's beautiful My-cenae—nothing but a prosperous little town, when all's said and done—it's a dreadful thing to see all this waste and devastation. I've never been one who enjoyed wrecking, and this upsets me. All these men, men I've known for more moons than I can count, have turned into animals. They won't listen to reason, and it's only Agamemnon's orders that stand between some of these women and assaults of the most brutal kind. Bring them to the ships, *he told the soldiers, and they've obeyed. So there the females are, being led down to the Skaian Gate with their arms bound behind their backs. Old ones, young ones, pretty ones, ugly ones: Anything that's wearing women's clothes is good enough for them. Our men have killed a few. Most were burned alive in their houses, like that crone down by the walls, who refused to leave her cave when instructed. The whole place was hung about with the bodies of dead creatures, and she looked Odysseus straight in the eye as he put the torch to a pile of dried leaves and plants, and she laughed and said something like,* So you think you're going home, do you? *And then she shook her head and sucked her teeth and muttered about how many moons it would be before he saw his wife and child again. Odysseus isn't one to listen to the ravings of an ancient hag, so he set the place alight, and we left. The stench of all that muck burning made our nostrils sting. Quite apart from the particular horror of burning flesh, which is enough to turn a man's stomach. What did she have in her hovel? Odysseus was quiet and somber, though, on his way up to the citadel, and didn't seem quite himself. Still, something like this attack is like a river and we all get carried along by it. What will I do when I see*

323

*Helen! What will I say! She always knew how to re-
duce me to silence. Will all the years make any difference!*

"Xan-ee! Up! Up, Xan-ee!"

Xanthe opened her eyes and saw Astyanax sitting
next to her, on her bed, hitting her shoulder gently
with the head of his carved horse.

"It's the middle of the night, my darling." She
sighed. "You can't get up yet. You have to wait for
Phoebus Apollo's chariot. Remember? And why have
you woken up? You must go back to bed. Come on,
I'll carry you."

Astyanax shook his head violently.

"Xan-ee's bed!" he cried. "Want Xan-ee's bed!"

Tears stood in his eyes. Xanthe said, "Very well,
then, just this once. But you must be good and quiet
and go straight back to sleep, otherwise I'll put you in
your own bed."

"Don't like, don't like," said the child, and he put
his hands over his ears. "Noise! Bad noise!"

Xanthe listened. That was why Astyanax had
woken up. Who was it, shouting? And there were
other noises she could hear, now that she was properly
awake. Someone was screaming—not just one person,
but a lot of people, and there seemed to be a crackling,
as if a huge fire was burning in the courtyard. She sat
up in bed and put her arms around the baby. A dim,
reddish light filled the room. Astyanax's couch wasn't
in its place, but right up against the opposite wall.
Outside the door, the corridor seemed not to be flat

and straight any longer, but piled up with broken tiles and bits of wall. Xanthe closed her eyes. The earth had moved. She'd seen it before. It happened sometimes when Poseidon was angry and shook his fists under the ground. The serpents came from him, too. The ones that had come up out of the water and killed Laocoön.

"Don't worry, lovey," Xanthe whispered, trying to keep her voice calm, but Astyanax must have sensed her fear, because he began to cry and ask for Andromache.

"Want Mama!" he shrieked, and Xanthe cuddled him and said, "Shh! We'll go and find her, I promise."

Then they burst into the room: three men armed in bronze and with their nosepieces hiding most of their faces. One of them held Andromache around the waist. She was tightly bound and gagged, but still Xanthe could see that her eyes were trying to express everything she was feeling. She was writhing from side to side, kicking out with her feet and her elbows, and a dreadful sound came from her stifled mouth and was swallowed up by the gag.

Xanthe said, "Lady, don't . . . Don't struggle. It won't help. I'll look after him. Be brave. Please, please, don't look at me like that; I can't bear it."

Astyanax, seeing his mother's agony, began to scream as only he knew how. Xanthe's head filled with something like a mist. What should she do? One thing she knew above all others: The baby must be protected. She tightened her arms around him and muttered soothing words into his ear, but still he wriggled in her arms, trying to reach Andromache.

"That's him," said one of the men. "Seize him. Doesn't matter about the girl. Kill her or leave her, but get the child."

"No-o-o . . . ," Xanthe shrieked, and the sound she made tore her throat. Everything that she looked at seemed to ripple with a kind of heat, and she heard nothing but the beating of her heart and Astyanax's crying. Suddenly nothing mattered anymore. She shouted, "Stop! You think you're heroes, don't you? Well, you're not. You're nothing but animals. No, not even animals turn on their babies to kill them. You're monsters. Ogres, and the Gods in Olympus are sickened and turning their faces away from you. Kill me. Kill anyone. Take us. Me and the Lady Andromache, but let this baby live."

Then her voice, her strong, angry voice failed her, and she sank back against the wall, still clinging to Astyanax, sobbing as though she would never stop.

"Enough!" roared one of the men. "I'm sick to death of whining women and screeching children."

He leaned over, and with a hand half-covered in armor, he hit Astyanax on the side of the head, and the baby was silent.

"Murderer! Dog!" Xanthe spat at him. "Baby killer. I hope you're proud of yourself. I hope you rot! I hope you die in agony and lie unburied forever. I hope your children are born without eyes . . ."

"Shut up!" said the soldier. "You don't know what you're talking about, do you? We're not baby killers, and this isn't a baby. It's Hector's son. D'you seriously think any Greek is going to let this child grow up to avenge his father? Forget it. But he's not dead yet. And he can't die here. I'll tell you something for nothing.

You're going to wish I'd stabbed him in the heart. I can promise you that." He signaled to his companions, and they stepped forward to take the baby out of Xanthe's arms.

"She's hanging on, boss," said one of them. "What'll we do?"

"What're you pussyfooting around for? I'll do it."

The boss, as his comrades called him, pulled Xanthe's arms away from Astyanax's body by force. He picked her up and carried her to where Andromache was standing.

"Tie her up like this one, and gag her, too. I've had just about as much screaming as I can take."

Xanthe watched as he picked Astyanax up and threw him over his shoulder as though he were a doll stitched out of rags and stuffed with straw. Blackie, the carved horse, fell out of the child's hands and onto the bed. Andromache fainted, and one of the soldiers said, "Let's leave these two here and torch the place."

Xanthe closed her eyes. It's going to be over soon. I won't have to hear or see or feel anything else ever again. Let them do it, please let them do it, she said over and over again in her head. I don't want to live. How will I walk about in the world after this? Where's the fire? Please, please, light the fire, and let us die.

"Don't be a bloody fool. That's Andromache. Agamemnon wants her alive, and this one's young and quite pretty, if you like that sort of thing."

"We'll have to carry the older one."

"Then get on with it. Pick her up. And you . . ." He prodded Xanthe in the side. "Get moving. We haven't got all night."

Xanthe looked down at the buckled floor of the

palace, then at the earth of the courtyard, then at the stones of the street. From somewhere a little in front of her, she could hear Astyanax crying again. He must have recovered from his beating.

"Xan-ee! Want Xan-ee! Want Mama!" he wailed, and the sounds he made came toward her on the night wind, and she thought that her heart would burst out of her body. The crying didn't last long. The monster who was carrying him must have struck him again. Xanthe thought: I'm broken. She felt like a clay jar that someone had thrown against a wall: shattered into sharp-edged fragments. She tried, she tried with all the strength that was left in her, to put pieces of herself together again in her head. Sister. I have a sister. Marpessa. I loved someone once. He was beautiful. I knew Hector while he lived. Polyxena, where are you? I'm a girl. These thoughts wove in and out of her head like ghosts, like drifting phantoms, and then they were gone, and she was left with a pain that grew and swelled and took up the whole of who she was. She couldn't even lift her head to see where they were going, but the slope of the land told her that they were being taken to the walls.

That was a narrow squeak. I never saw him, no one would've seen him. He just barreled out of nowhere at me, and what was I supposed to do? No quarter, that's what Agamemnon said, and now there he is, taking up more space on the ground than any man has a right to. Great fat greasy bastard coming out of the darkness at me, and yelling and starting to pull at the guard in charge of holding one of the women.

Xanthe, *he kept calling,* Xanthe, it's me, Boros. *As if she gave a shit. Didn't even turn her head in his direction. She's staring at the kid, and I wouldn't want this known about among the lads, but I reckon they're being a bit, well, over the top as far as the boy's concerned.* Son of Hector, *said the captain.* Bound to come back and slaughter someone. Just preventive measures, that's all. *But there's ways and ways, that's what I say, and they could've just cut his throat, quick and easy, like preparing a young heifer for the sacrifice. Instead of which they're going to do something spectacular, and I don't feel good about being a part of that. Not good at all. That's one reason I overreacted with this Boros creature. I just took my dagger and struck out at him, and as Ares is my judge, I only wanted him to go away, but it was an unlucky thrust, and before I know where I am there he is, doubled up on the earth, dead as yesterday's haunch of ox. I haven't got time to worry about him, though. Nothing but a fat bastard. Yelling like that. Distracting, that was.*

"You can't," said Polyxena. "You just can't, Iason." She was weeping, and her face was streaked with dust, and her hands were as bloody as a butcher's. "I went to warn her. I ran as fast as I could, but I was too late."

"What do you mean . . . too late?"

"They've been captured. Xanthe and Andromache . . . and the baby." Polyxena sank to the ground and put her head between her hands and rocked from side to side.

"Where will they take them? What will they do?

Help me, Polyxena. I must see her. I must get her back."

"They'll kill you. Haven't you noticed? Look around you. They're all dead. Everyone. Old men, kings, they're sparing no one. They're going to raze the city to the ground, can't you see?"

Iason shook his head. He had come across Polyxena huddled in a dark corner between two smashed walls, and finding a friendly face at such a time raised his spirits so that for a few moments, before she began to speak, everything seemed possible. They could run and find Xanthe and rescue her from wherever she was, and then everything would be all right. The killing would be over. He and Xanthe would be married and start again. Build their own house. Tend their own vines, so that out of the blood-soaked earth, new things would grow. The horses would be theirs, and they would be happy. But then Polyxena spoke, and all his daydreams looked silly. Maybe a rock had fallen on his head without him realizing, because imagining happiness was madness.

Polyxena went on. "They're going to murder Astyanax. Priam isn't a threat, nor are any of the other princes, but they're terrified of the baby. He'll grow up and come looking for them all. That's how they think. I was on my way to warn Xanthe, and I saw them. One of the men had the child over his shoulder like a side of meat. At first I thought he was dead already, but then he started squirming and screaming. They're going to murder him. I know it. I saw him, I heard him, Iason. I can't bear it. Please, let's run away. Let's go and hide, Iason. D'you know anywhere we can go?"

Iason nodded.

"I took the horses and hid them away. There's a place . . ." He stopped, all at once remembering the shaking earth. What if the horses had been buried alive? "We must be quick, Polyxena. Come. As quickly as you can. They'll be terrified . . ."

He began to run over the rubble-strewn ground, with Polyxena at his side.

Helen said nothing to Marpessa, but she knew that time was short. This was the end. Soon they would come for her. The roaring of flames came to her ears, and the screams of the dying, but she concentrated on what she had to do and ignored everything that was happening outside. At last Marpessa lay on the bed, with her eyes half closed.

"Now," said Helen, "you look like the princess, and I like your servant." She sat next to her, smoothing the young girl's hair with one hand. There had been no time to change into a clean gown, and the one she was wearing was scarlet with Marpessa's blood. Helen had carried her and bathed her and dressed her in a purple robe stitched with gold, which was the first thing that came to her hand. Then she had mixed some spices together and put them into a goblet filled with wine, and made sure that Marpessa drank it.

"I feel as though I'm floating," Marpessa said, smiling weakly up at Helen. "All my pain is gone."

"That's the wine. You'll sleep now, and when you wake you'll be weak, but the pain will grow less and less, and soon you can forget all about it."

Two tears slid from the corners of Marpessa's eyes and ran down the sides of her neck, onto the pillow.

"I'm sorry," she breathed. "But everything is . . . Everything is gone. He . . ."

"Shh," said Helen. "Don't think about him. If he's the one the Gods have chosen for you, then you will find one another. And if not, then not." She laughed suddenly. "I should know. Look at all this . . . I suppose in one way, it's my fault, and yet what could I have done? Up there on Olympus, that's where it's decided."

Marpessa said nothing. Behind Helen the Goddess Aphrodite was standing, gazing down at the bed.

"Marpessa," she whispered, and her voice was like a distant bell. "Forgive me. I've been distracted in my mind since Paris died. Forgive me for the pain, but I had to do it, or you would have swallowed poison to rid your body of the child, and the pain of that would have been far worse, believe me. This is for the best. Helen will take care of you, and you will take care of your sister."

The Goddess slipped into the wall and vanished, and Marpessa struggled up from the bed.

"Xanthe . . . ," she said. "Where's Xanthe? What'll become of her?"

"You must rest," said Helen. "Xanthe will be taken to the ships."

"What ships? What's happening?"

"They've come back," said Helen. "My husband, and Odysseus, and Agamemnon, and the rest of them. I'm going home. And you're coming with me. And we'll find Xanthe, never fear."

At that moment, someone—a man—called Helen's name.

"Helen, wife of Menelaus. Show yourself. We are here to help you."

"See?" said Helen. "That's Odysseus."

Marpessa saw him before Helen did, because Helen's back was turned toward the door as he came into the room. He had broad shoulders and gray eyes in a handsome face.

Helen stood up and turned and gave him her hand.

"It's nearly over, Lady," said Odysseus. "You must come with me. Your husband is waiting to take you home."

"I'm ready," Helen said, and sighed. "What do you think, Odysseus? I think he's never going to let me hear the end of it." She pointed at Marpessa. "You're going to have to carry her, I'm afraid. She's not well."

"Where are your belongings?" Odysseus asked.

"There," said Helen, indicating a chest carved from sandalwood that stood against the wall and filled the room with its fragrance. "That's all I want. A few of the jewels I brought with me to this city when I came."

"What about the rest? Paris must have heaped you with gold."

Marpessa remembered how they had wrapped every necklace and bracelet and hair ornament and hidden it away.

"Leave it. Let it stay where I've put it. Someone'll find it, and I wish them joy of the whole lot. I don't want any of it any longer."

Odysseus gave an order, and a soldier came into the chamber and picked up Helen's chest. Then, without a word, Odysseus gathered Marpessa up in his arms, and they made their way out of Deiphobus's palace.

Alastor crouched in the darkness and wiped his eyes. He was weeping because of all the smoke that hung in the air and drifted through the burned-out dwellings, and not only because of that. There's nothing unmanly, he thought to himself, about mourning the dead, and everywhere he looked there they were: bodies charred from the flames, or torn apart by sharp metal, or broken like dolls by falling stones. They were men for the most part, or boys. It seemed that the Greeks were taking as many women captive as they could. Well, it made sense. A whole lot of slaves and serving women there for the taking without any kind of payment. He looked about him. Some dim light was beginning to come through the doorway, and with a sudden lurch of the heart he saw where he was: in the Blood Room.

It was almost unrecognizable, but there was the shelf where Charitomene kept the healing herbs, and there was where he had lain himself, in what felt to him now like another life altogether.

"Marpessa," he whispered into the darkness. "What has become of you? Why didn't . . ."

A groan came from somewhere very near him and startled him so much that he jumped up and hit his head on a fallen beam.

"Who is it? Where are you? Show yourself, whoever you are." He did his best to sound fearless, but his voice shook. Another groan answered him, and he ventured further into the room. Then he saw someone lying on the ground, pinned down by a section of wall that covered the person almost from head to foot.

"Wait!" he called. "I'll help you. You're trapped. I'm coming."

He leaned down to pull the stones from the body, and recognized Charitomene.

"Please . . . Please, Charitomene. Don't die. It's me, Alastor. D'you remember me? Wait for me to move this. Please. Please live. Please."

He pulled and pulled until his eyes stood out and the veins on his arms bulged. All the time, he murmured to Charitomene, but from the silence that was coming from under the heavy stone, he knew it was too late. The old woman was dead.

When at last he had freed poor Charitomene from her crushing burden, she seemed as small and frail as a bird, and it was hard to recall how she used to be, when this Blood Room was her domain. Alastor sat down beside her and took her hand.

"Charitomene, I must save myself. D'you understand? I must look for Marpessa, but I don't dare set foot outside this room as I am. They're murdering everyone, every man, however young or old. It's only as a woman that I have any chance at all. Forgive me for leaving your body like this, but it's my only hope. I'll make a sacrifice if I survive, Charitomene, and ask the Gods to look kindly on you, and transport you straight to the realms of the blessed. But for now, I need your cloak and scarf. I'm sorry."

Quickly he removed the old woman's cloak and pulled it tightly around him. Then he tied the head scarf as well as he could, in the way that he had seen his mother tie hers. Why hadn't he paid better attention? *The skin of a girl, and eyelashes wasted on a youth.* Phrontis's words came back to him, and tears filled his eyes. She had been his mother, for all her faults, and he hadn't even stopped to see what had become of her, or to help her. Forgive me, Mother, he said to himself. I must find Marpessa.

Alastor stepped out of the Blood Room and began make his way daintily down toward the walls, pretending to be a girl. Please, dear Gods, let some Greek think that I'm pretty and take me down to the ships. Please. And let me find Marpessa there.

When I get back to my island, I'm going to hang up my shield and sword, and I vow by all the Gods on Olympus that I'll never take them up again, no, not even to save my own neck. I've seen plenty, these last few years: men sliced open like logs being split; severed limbs; eyes removed from their sockets . . . I reckoned there wasn't a thing in the world that I'd not seen. But this. This is more than a stomach can stand. I'm not a young man now, and I hope I live to be an old man, blessed with sons and grandsons, but as long as I do live, this will be painted on the insides of my eyelids when I lie down, and I'll know no rest until I die.

We took them down to the walls. There were two men detailed to hold the wife of Prince Hector, Andromache. She was bound and gagged, of course, but still, just in case, they had two of us walking next to her. Then there was the girl, the nursemaid. Never did catch her name. I had hold of her, and I can tell you, if it weren't for the fact that she was walking, I'd have sworn she was a corpse. Her arm was clammy and cold, like the arm of a dead body, and she put one foot in front of the other as if she were made of stone. She was gagged, too, but she never took her eyes off the kid. The baby. Telling this story is hard, I promise you. Well. We all went down to the walls. It was getting light by this time. Not properly light, you understand, just the first peeping out of pink from behind the mountain that tells you maybe daylight is on its way when you think the night'll go on forever. And you're always glad when the night's over, aren't you? Be honest. There's something about darkness that gets to you, know what I mean? But on this occasion, I wish the night had gone on forever. I wish it had hidden something of what we saw.

The captain explained it beforehand, so we all knew where we were and what was going to happen, and we all saw his point. Of course he couldn't afford to leave Hector's son alive. I see that. But there's ways and ways. Kid wasn't any more than a baby. He could've been smothered with a pillow. He could've been stabbed in the heart with one swift blow. He could've been given a poison to make him sleep sweetly forever. But he wasn't. The captain took him off his shoulder. He was making a hell of a lot of noise for a little kid. There's no good way to tell this. The captain went and stood on the highest bit of the wall, where everyone could see: all the prisoners lined up on the Plain waiting to be taken down to the ships, and all of us soldiers. He held the child up above his head and then tossed him. That's the only word. He tossed Hector's son down from right up there as hard as he could, and the poor little baby was smashed against the stones, which were even sharper and more jagged down there under the walls since the earthquake. That's what I'll see. That's what I can't stop seeing: that small body, like a doll, flying through the air with its arms and legs flapping and waving about, and the shrieks rising from the Plain and the walls, and sounds coming from the mother and the girl I'm holding that I'll hear in every dream I ever have until I die. Then the girl fell against me, senseless, and I had to pick her up and carry her the rest of the way, but I hardly noticed, to tell you the truth.

The little body, flying through the air. Flying and flying and its arms and legs flapping and waving. A baby smashed to a pulp against the stones. How to forget? A baby.

ON THE PLAIN

"Everyone's here," said Theano. "But how long d'you think they're going to keep us waiting? You'd think they'd be quite glad to get away from here, wouldn't you? After all this time."

The Plain, from the walls of the city right down to the beach, was crowded with women standing about in small, silent groups. Many were weeping. Some had fainted and were lying on the ground or leaning on their companions. Small bands of Greek soldiers moved between them, herding them together like sheep.

"Heartless, that's what you are, Theano," said Halie.

"But just look at us all. Look at Hecuba, who used to be a queen and who's reduced to this now. But have you heard about Cassandra? They're saying that Agamemnon himself has taken a fancy to her. He'll change his mind before the moon's full again. And over there, with Menelaus—it must be him . . . skinny sort of man with reddish hair, just as I remember him from before the war—Helen and Marpessa, and what d'you think's become of poor Xanthe?"

"How can you twitter on like this, woman?" Halie

turned on her friend. "Didn't you see what we all saw? Didn't it mean anything to you?"

"You're a fool, Halie." Theano was scornful. "I mean to survive. That's all that matters to me now. I don't care anymore. I don't care about men, or women, or even babies . . . I'm not thinking about any of that. I'm thinking about me and nothing but me, and I'm going to put the blood behind me, and the screaming and the wailing and the sorrow, and I'm going to wipe the inside of my head clean of everything that's happened since this cursed war began, and I'm going to get onto that Greek ship and go wherever it takes me, and I'll serve anyone who gives me a crust of bread to eat, and I'm going to forget I ever belonged to Troy or that I saw Hector and Hector's son and how they died, and I'm going to survive." Theano finished speaking and sank to the ground and wept and wept as though she never intended to stop.

"I'm sorry," said Halie quietly. "Don't cry, Theano. Please. We all need you. Danae needs you."

Theano stood up and wiped her eyes on her scarf. Her voice still shook as she spoke, but Halie was relieved to see, from her friend's words, that she was her old self again.

"What Danae needs," Theano said, "if she doesn't pull herself together, is a knife between the ribs. She's no more use to anyone as she is than a plucked chicken."

"We're not all as strong as you are, Theano."

Theano sniffed, as if to agree with Halie, and said, "Maybe not, but that's no excuse for collapsing altogether."

She went to where Danae was sitting on the ground staring silently in front of her and said, "Come on, Danae, dear. Pull yourself together. We're going on a sea journey."

"This one," Helen said, indicating Marpessa, who was sitting on the sandalwood chest. "And this one's sister, when I find her. She will be with Andromache, poor thing."

"Lady," said Menelaus. "You may have anything your heart desires."

Helen smiled. Menelaus hadn't changed. Far from striking her head from her shoulders, he'd fallen to his knees in front of her and kissed the hem of her skirt. No fool, she thought to herself, like an old fool. The years hadn't been kind to Menelaus. His red hair had turned a dirty, sandy sort of color, and much of it had fallen out, leaving the top of his head quite bald. Helen thought fleetingly of Paris's golden hair, and how it used to fall onto her own shoulders when they made love, and then she shook her head. This wasn't the time for such memories. If she didn't speak now, she'd find things had been arranged without her. Suddenly, from out of nowhere, a girl pushed her way past Menelaus and fell at Helen's feet.

"Lady Helen, I implore you. I beseech you. Take me with you. I'll do anything."

A hand clawed at her skirt, and she drew back a little.

"Stand up when you speak to me. Who are you? What's your name?"

"Agamede," said Alastor, thinking, Forgive me, Agamede, but I must see Marpessa. Oh, Marpessa, if I can only be near you once again . . .

"You're very pretty," said Helen. "But I have Marpessa to attend me, and her sister. Why should I listen to you?"

"May I whisper something in your ear?"

Helen nodded. There was something about this girl, about her ocean-colored eyes under long lashes . . . What harm could there be in listening to what she wanted to say?

Alastor put his mouth to Helen's ear. The most beautiful woman in the whole world, he thought as he whispered, "I am Alastor, and I have left my home and the bride my mother picked for me, because I love Marpessa. If the Greeks find out I'm not a girl they'll kill me, so say nothing."

Helen smiled. So this was the one. She could hardly blame Marpessa. Did he know about the child? Better to say nothing, and let Marpessa decide the fate of this beautiful young man.

"You may come with us, Agamede. As you are a . . . friend . . . of my Marpessa. Do you think she will be happy to see you?"

"If the Gods will it, Lady," said Alastor, and cast his eyes down to the ground modestly. Again Helen smiled. In another kind of life, at another time, such goings-on would have amused her, but now there were other things to worry about. Where was Andromache? There was the matter of Xanthe to be arranged. She turned to Menelaus, who was busy giving orders about the loading of the booty, including her sandalwood chest.

"Take me to where Andromache is being held. There is something I have to ask her."

Menelaus said, "Come, I'll go with you. It's easy to get lost among so many people. I'll be glad when it's all over and we've set sail."

Helen said nothing, but strode ahead of him, and the women gathered on the Plain opened a path for her as she walked.

Andromache saw her coming from a long way away, and waited, trembling, to see what words would come from her mouth. Helen. When Hector died, Andromache thought, I didn't know there could be a greater pain, but now I know why the Gods made him suffer like that, and made me suffer for him. It was a rehearsal. How else could I still be walking and in one piece? After what they did to him . . . my baby. She blinked. Where were the tears? Why didn't they come to cleanse and heal her heart? There was a howling in her head that came sometimes to her mouth, so that when she opened it, nothing but noises came out, as though she were an animal crying for its young. Once, long ago, when she was a little girl, she'd come across a bitch in her father's courtyard, and the poor creature was making a sound that the young Andromache had never heard before: a keening, almost human cry that made the hairs stand up on the back of her neck.

"Why is the doggie crying?" she asked her father.

"Because her puppies have been taken away."

"Why have they?"

"Can't have too many puppies running around the place. We drowned them in the river."

Now Andromache remembered how she had dreamed of the dead puppies for many nights. And she remembered the sorrowful bitch. That's me, now. Those are my noises, she thought. No words, because there are no words for what I feel. Only sounds. And now here comes Helen, and will I howl at her, too?

Helen came up to her and without a word put her arms around Andromache and held her tight.

"No words, Andromache. No words, please. There's nothing to say."

This was so exactly what Andromache had been thinking that she cried out in agony, and at last, like rocks that have been burning at the heart of a mountain and finally explode and flow like molten gold, tears rose up in her heart and spilled out of her and ran unchecked down her cheeks.

The two women stood for a long time clinging to each other, and when at last Helen drew back, she said, "Andromache, will you let Xanthe come with me? Marpessa wants her. Her only family, after all. Will you spare her?"

Andromache looked at where Xanthe was standing with her head turned toward the walls, staring at the city with unseeing eyes. An image came into her head of the girl, and there *he* was in her arms . . . Astyanax. She began to tremble all over.

"Yes," she said. "Take her." I don't want her, she thought. I can't look at her. I love her. I can't bear even to think of her. Take her away. Never let me lay eyes on her again. I don't want her. She's always with him. She plays so nicely with him. She sings to him every night. Take her away. I love her.

344

"Thank you, Andromache. May the Gods be kind to you."

"And to you, Helen." My sister, my helper.

Helen made her way to where Xanthe stood.

"Xanthe?"

There was no answer from the girl, so Helen touched her on the arm and took her hand away at once. Xanthe's skin was cold, as though she were dead, even though the sun was climbing now, and the day was growing hotter and hotter.

"I've come to take you to Marpessa," said Helen soothingly. "Your sister," she added. It was clear to her that this poor girl was so hurt that it would be a long time before she could speak.

"Can you walk?" she asked, but Xanthe didn't move.

"Menelaus," said Helen. "She can't walk. Will you carry her?"

Menelaus nodded and without a word picked Xanthe up and carried her toward where Marpessa was waiting.

Helen turned to say farewell to Andromache, but she had moved away, like a ghost drifting about the Plain. And there was Hecuba sitting on the ground, rocking backward and forward in her grief. Helen ran and crouched down beside her.

"Mother . . . ," she said. "Farewell. May the Gods look kindly on you."

"Your fault, whore," said Hecuba. "I've always thought so. Your fault, and I hope the Gods look unkindly on *you*."

"Your grief is speaking, and you are silent," said Helen. "Farewell."

Hecuba looked at Helen for a long time, and then struggled to her feet.

"My son loved you," she said at last. "My Paris loved you. I bid you farewell and good fortune. I have lost most of my reason, as you can see. Forgive me."

"We must forgive one another," said Helen, and she put her arms around Hecuba.

going somewhere in the sun and where is blackie now that theres no bed and dont look at me like that charitomene it isnt my fault that marpessa doesnt listen they never listen little ones theyre too busy with their toys and this ones a special favorite isnt it blackie you really love blackie and if youre good ill take you to the stables and iason will let you sit on a proper horse till youre big you mustnt touch its sharp and iwish icould say something but my mouth is full of earth and someones carrying me marpessa look at me come to me help me where is she my sister marpessa where come to me and where is my room and my bed and where is the sun to make me warm again cold cold cold and the poor little thing cold and broken and his arms and legs flapping a small doll he looked like not much bigger than a doll something but my mouth is full of earth and someones carrying me marpessa look at me baby my little baby go to sleep and ill sing songs go to sleep cold cold cold

OUTSIDE THE
UNDERGROUND CHAMBER

Polyxena sat on the ground and looked at her hands. The palms were bleeding, and there was dirt under what remained of her fingernails. They'd arrived at the underground chamber just in time. It had been blocked by a fall of huge boulders, and they'd spent what was left of the night scrabbling about with their bare hands, and digging in the earth with their nails. Polyxena wondered at first whether Iason would say that a girl was too weak to work like a common laborer, but he hadn't said a word, and as they dug and scratched and tore at the stone, they could hear the terrified noises that the horses were making. Polyxena noticed that Iason talked to them all the time he was working: soft, silly words like you use to soothe babies. Crooning. Snatches of nonsense. Now he stood at the entrance to the underground chamber, still out of breath. His hands were in an even worse state than hers, but he was happy because Aithon and the others had been saved. Polyxena felt sorry for him, though, because she knew he still hoped for all sorts of things that were impossible. He still wanted to go and find Xanthe, and it was up to her to tell him the truth. Such things were always up to her. Polyxena sighed.

"I should go and look for her," Iason said. "I shouldn't just leave her there with all the others, waiting on the Plain for the Greek chieftains to lay claim to them. I should rescue her."

"You can't, Iason." Polyxena tried to speak gently, but she had to warn him. "Did you hear that cry . . . the one cry in the night that sounded like the noise we heard when Hector was killed. Do you remember that?"

Iason nodded.

"That was the Greeks killing Astyanax."

"Killing the baby? Why? How? How do you know?"

"I know it. That's enough. And Iason . . ." Polyxena looked at her hands, and at the ground, and last of all at Iason's face. She went on, "They must have killed Xanthe, too, because she would die a thousand times before she let anyone touch a hair of his head. She'd never, never, have let them take the child, so . . ."

Her voice faded away. Iason stood silent. Then he said, "You're right, of course. But I didn't know there could be pain like this." Iason fell silent, wondering if he could describe to Polyxena how raw and hurt he was.

"I know," she said. "It's as though someone has stripped off a layer of skin."

Iason nodded.

Suddenly, tears that she had been holding back spilled out of Polyxena's eyes, and she sank to the ground and covered her head with the ruins of her skirt. She wept for the Singer, and for Xanthe, and for baby Astyanax; for all the dead, and for the shattered stones of her city. Iason knelt beside her and stroked her shoulder gently.

"I'm sorry." Her words came out muffled. "I'm not going to be a burden to you, Iason. I promise. I'll help you. We'll do what has to be done together. Those of us who are left."

She struggled to her feet. Iason took hold of her hands.

"We must go into the city and find the dead and bury them. And take care of the horses. You've lost a friend, and I've lost . . ." Iason didn't know what to call Xanthe.

Polyxena said, "Someone you loved, Iason. Everything's gone. We have to start again, and I've waited years to say this, but you must hear it now. My feelings for you are . . . very tender. I've always admired you."

"Admired me? What was there to admire?"

Polyxena smiled.

"Your modesty, for one thing. Your kindness. Your brown eyes. And you're blushing."

"No one's ever spoken like this to me before. I don't know what to say, Polyxena. I've always thought of you as my good friend. I've never been tongue-tied with you. I didn't know."

"I made sure no one knew. Not even Xanthe. Blabbermouth Polyxena . . . Who'd have thought I could keep such a secret for so long? Do you like me, Iason?"

"You know I do. We've known each other since childhood."

"It's enough. If we work together, maybe your feelings will grow deeper." *Maybe you'll forget Xanthe and learn to love me,* was what she was longing to say, but it was not the time.

349

"I've nothing but good feelings for you," Iason said quietly. You're not Xanthe, he thought, but you're good, and strong, and my heart is bruised, and you'd never hurt me. And we want the same things. For the horses. For the city. For each other. It's enough.

He took her in his arms, and she buried her face in his shoulder. Then she stood back and said, "We should begin."

He looked around and wiped his filthy face with even filthier hands.

"And when we've seen what there is to see, we must begin to put everything to rights. Come, Polyxena."

They started to walk into the ruined city. The sun was low in the sky, and black smoke still rose from fires in almost every house. The stench of blood and charred human flesh came to Polyxena's nose, even through the cloth of the scarf that she was using to cover her face. It made her feel sick. Others, other survivors, dazed and covered in black soot and dirt, wandered through the streets like ghosts, but in every doorway there was a body, or more than one, hideously broken and flung across the threshold. Blood had soaked into the ground everywhere they walked.

"Don't come into the Palace," said Iason. "I'll bring the Singer and King Priam out of there with the help of some of these men. Stay here and wait for me. Rest. Just for a while. You'll need your strength to bury your grandfather."

"Yes," said Polyxena. "I'll wait."

After Iason had gone, she sat down heavily on a

stone seat. She felt both as though she would never sleep again and so weary that her head was filled with a kind of dizziness and everything she looked at shimmered and swam. Silence lay over everything, and then she heard it. Someone was singing somewhere. Singing a sweet, sad song. Who was it? Polyxena looked up, and then she saw her. A young woman was sitting beside a tree that Poseidon's earthquake had half torn out of the earth. She was weeping and singing. How did she come to be wearing a tunic that was so white? It shone against the blackened stones, unmarked by blood or smoke. Why was she carrying a quiverful of arrows and holding a huge bow? Polyxena was near enough now to see the young woman's face, and the tears that ran down the pale, pale cheek were like drops of liquid silver.

"Who are you?" she asked, and then wondered whether such a question was impolite or unkind. Surely when someone was crying, comfort came first and questions later? Polyxena approached, meaning to bend and put an arm around the woman's shoulders, when suddenly she turned and spoke: "I am Artemis, the Goddess of the Moon and of the Hunt."

Polyxena nearly laughed out loud, thinking that the events of the night had uprooted the woman's reason as surely as the earthquake had pulled up the trees all around. Then she fell silent and listened to her—to the Goddess—singing.

> *"Cover my face. Bring me a veil of smoke*
> *from fires blossoming among the stones*
> *and hide my eyes. They cut King Priam's throat*
> *and every Trojan street was slick with blood.*

The blackened corpses on the shaken earth
lie twisted, broken, torn. Lifeless as dolls.
And smoke as thick as nightmares rises up
and stains the sky above the Trojan walls.
The birds of prey gather on every gate.
The Offering has fallen on its side.
Its belly gapes, hollow and empty now.
The Trojan women wail and wring their hands
and look toward what used to be their home
and know that they will sail, and not return.
The silver tears drop from my silver eyes.
Cover my face. I cannot look on this."

A weight of sadness closed Polyxena's eyes. When she opened them, the young woman was nowhere to be seen. The tree she had been leaning on bent crooked branches to the ground, but the singer had gone. Her tunic had been too white. What mortal could have kept her garments so clean? And those silver tears . . . Had she seen Artemis, or was it nothing but a vision, a dream brought on by tiredness? The sweet voice was still in her ears. She sat quite still, waiting for Iason to come back. In the pale sky, the moon had risen, so thin that it was almost invisible. She closed her eyes.

"Polyxena?"

"Yes, I'm awake. I'm not really sleeping. Have you found them? The Singer and the king?"

"I have. We've taken them up to where the temples were. There's nothing really left there now, but we must perform the rites as best we can." He sat down beside her. "There are others here. One of them is a young woman called Agamede. She was betrothed to Alastor."

"I know her."

"She was left for dead after running from Phrontis's house. She had the sense to lie still until all the Greeks had gone down to the Plain."

"And Phrontis? Was she taken?"

Iason shook his head. "Killed."

"Poor thing," said Polyxena. "I didn't like her, but I'd never have wished her dead."

"There are very many of them . . . the dead. It will take a long time to see them all properly buried. All the rites performed." He sighed. "And there are the animals to care for, too. Will you help me, Polyxena? Will we work together?"

"Yes," she said. So little was left. Xanthe had gone, and the Singer was dead, and yet somewhere in her heart, hope was growing. She was alive. She pictured that small hope like a green tendril from a vine or climbing plant. She and Iason together. That was something good. And while she worked she could forget for a while the things her eyes had seen. Someone had to find food and cook it. Soon she and Iason would take two of the horses and ride out of the city and into the mountains, and to the greener lands beyond the walls, to search for grain and fruit and anything that could be planted.

Can you hear me, Singer? she said to herself. *Can you hear my silent thoughts? I'll tell the stories now. I'll tell them what happened. I promise you, nothing will be forgotten.*

Polyxena stood up. Someone had been singing a

song by that tree a while ago, she was sure of it, but when she tried to think about who it might have been and what it was the person had sung about, there was nothing in her head but a mist.

"What're you thinking about?" Iason asked.

"Nothing. Truly."

He took her hand, and they made their way together to where the bodies had been laid out.

SAILING AWAY

Marpessa stood on the deck of Menelaus's ship and saw the city growing smaller and smaller. Wherever she looked, there were other ships, and the sea was smooth and blue. It had taken some time to make sure that all the omens were favorable, but now it seemed that Poseidon was happy. He would send fair winds. She sighed. "Don't sigh, child," said a voice, and Marpessa turned to see Aphrodite standing beside her. "I've brought him back. Your Alastor. He left his bride, disguised himself as a girl, and risked his life. It will be some time before it's safe for him to approach you, but he's here, on this ship. Haven't you seen him? Hasn't he shown himself?"

"I knew him at once, but I said nothing. I'm still weak, and in pain when I walk, and I've been looking after Xanthe. My heart is sore and bruised, too, Goddess, when I think of my sister. The last words we said to one another were so bitter, and they wounded her. And me, too. Now, she is broken. And there's no one but me to put her together. She won't speak, nor eat, nor move. It's as though she's been turned to stone. Sometimes I think it would have been better if she had died."

Aphrodite shook her head. "No," she said. "It will

be long, but she will come out of the darkness. You'll take care of her and tend her, and she will heal in the end, although you can't hope for her to be entirely as she used to be. But you ought to speak to Alastor."

"Later," said Marpessa, wondering how she would tell Alastor of her feelings. And would she speak to him of the child, or keep silent? Down there on the Plain, she had looked for Phrontis and also for Alastor's betrothed and had not seen either of them, and now they were sailing far away. Perhaps she would be happy one day. To the Goddess she said, "When we are settled in our new country, then I will consider the matter of Alastor."

"I have put love for you into his heart." Aphrodite smiled. "Be brave. And as for that . . ." She looked toward Troy, now vanishing into the distance. "I didn't really mean for so much destruction."

Marpessa said nothing, but thought: It's a little late for remorse. She watched as the Goddess floated over the water, her turquoise robes billowing around her like sea mist.

"Xanthe? Can you hear me? Xanthe, I'm so sorry. Speak to me. Xanthe, please," Marpessa whispered into her sister's ear. Xanthe was lying close to her, with her head on a bundle of clothes. They had found a quiet place on the wooden deck crowded with weeping women. Troy was nothing but a dark shape on the farthest horizon, and soon all sight of it would be lost.

"Please. Please say something. Say you know me. Say you forgive me. All through it—everything—the words I said to you were like hard stones in my heart, and all I could think of was, Oh, Gods, don't let me die without seeing my sister. My only sister. And speaking gently to her. I think about it all the time . . . the words I said to you! I wish I could have them back, Xanthe. I wish the words could be unsaid. I didn't mean anything. I said such horrible things. They go around and around in my head all the time, buzzing like bees. Can you hear me, Xanthe? Do you know what I'm saying? Please know this, wherever you are. Know I love you. Know I'd be so happy forever if only you'd speak to me. Xanthe. Please speak. Say my name. Say you know who I am. Marpessa. Say *Marpessa.*"

Xanthe lay as still as a corpse, and Marpessa started to cry.

"Don't cry," said a voice that sounded in her ears like music. She looked up and into the clear gray depths of Pallas Athene's eyes. The Goddess was dressed in the same bronze garments that she always wore.

"You helped them . . . the Greeks," Marpessa said. "Why should I listen to you? You could have turned Achilles' spear away, and you chose not to."

Pallas Athene said only, "Even a great hero cannot avoid his fate."

"What about my sister? What's her fate? Am I going to have to watch her eaten up with misery?"

Pallas Athene was silent. She folded her arms across her breast, and a mist enveloped her, and when it dissolved she was gone. In her place, a huge white owl stood perched on one of the wooden chests nearby. Marpessa watched as it turned the light of its amber eyes on Xanthe. She stirred, and moved, and her own eyes opened. Something like the ghost of a smile came to her mouth.

"Bird," Xanthe whispered, and Marpessa said, "Yes, yes, can you see it? It's an owl . . . Pallas Athene's owl. Speak to me, Xanthe. Do you know who I am?"

"Marpessa. My sister. You're Marpessa."

Marpessa gave a cry of joy. "Yes, yes, I am, and I'll look after you now. I will. I'll always look after you. Oh, Xanthe, I'm so sorry. So sorry for everything."

Xanthe shook her head from side to side as if to say, Never mind. She put out a hand and stroked her sister's skirt. Then she whispered, almost too quietly for Marpessa to hear, "The owl, Pessa. Flying away . . . the owl."

The bird launched itself over the water in a shiver of white wings and made its way through the gathering darkness toward Troy.

Adèle Geras is the celebrated author of many novels and stories, including *The Tower Room, Watching the Roses,* and *Pictures of the Night,* all from Harcourt. She has lived all over the world, including in Jerusalem, North Borneo, and Gambia, and her books are very popular with readers in Great Britain.

Adèle Geras lives with her husband in Manchester, England.